H. R. F. Keating was the crime books reviewer for *The Times* for fifteen years. He has served as Chairman of the Crime Writers' Asssociation and the Society of Authors, and in 1987 was elected President of the Detection Club. He is a Fellow of the Royal Society of Literature.

He has written numerous novels as well as non-fiction, but is most famous for the Inspector Ghote series, the first of which, *The Perfect Murder*, was made into a film by Merchant Ivory and won a CWA Gold Dagger Award, as did *The Murder of the Maharajah*. In 1996 H. R. F. Keating was awarded the CWA Cartier Diamond Dagger for outstanding services to crime literature.

He is married to the actress Sheila Mitchell and lives in London.

BRIBERY, CORRUPTION ALSO

Inspector Ghote is not a happy man. His wife has inherited a beautiful house in Calcutta — and she is determined that they both move from his beloved Bombay to live a life of luxurious retirement there. But when the couple travel to view the legacy, they find it is a decaying ruin inhabited by squatters. Their lawyer advises them to sell it immediately — but Ghote detects a whiff of corruption and is determined to get to the bottom of it. But the corruption extends way up the political ladder, and soon they are putting themselves in very great danger . . .

Books by H. R. F. Keating
Published by The House of Ulverscroft:

THE MAN WHO . . . (Editor)
A REMARKABLE CASE OF BURGLARY

H. R. F. KEATING

BRIBERY, CORRUPTION ALSO

An Inspector Ghote Novel

Complete and Unabridged

ULVERSCROFT
Leicester

First published in Great Britain in 1999 by
Macmillan Publishers Limited
London

First Large Print Edition
published 1999
by arrangement with
Macmillan Publishers Limited
London

Extracts from 'City of Dreadful Night'
by Rudyard Kipling are reproduced by
kind permission of A. P. Whatt Limited
on behalf of The National Trust

British Library CIP Data

Keating, H. R. F. (Henry Reymond Fitzwalter),
1926 –
   Bribery, corruption also.—Large print ed.—
Ulverscroft large print series: mystery
1. Ghote, Ganesh (Fictitious character)—Fiction
2. Calcutta (India)—Fiction
3. Detective and mystery stories
4. Large type books
I. Title
823.9'14 [F]

ISBN 0–7089–4149–4

Published by
F. A. Thorpe (Publishing) Ltd.
Anstey, Leicestershire

Set by Words & Graphics Ltd.
Anstey, Leicestershire
Printed and bound in Great Britain by
T. J. International Ltd., Padstow, Cornwall

This book is printed on acid-free paper

In memory of Julian Symons who,
long ago, said to me,
'*Bribery, Corruption Also*? Good title.'

1

Inspector Ghote — But for how much longer, he was thinking, will I be Inspector? — looked out at the Calcutta night from the airport bus. Calcutta, already he could feel how different it was from his familiar Bombay. Different, and better? Or different and worse?

Well, whatever is happening to me here at least I would not be facing up to criminal and anti-social elements at each and every moment. Perhaps my Protima is right and her native city is truly a better place than Bombay. A city, she was saying in the plane, where the people 'are too intelligent not to know honesty is best policy, where we would be able to get the deeds and papers for this house I have inherited without paying any of dui-nambari money.' So perhaps now at last I have seen the end of number-two money.

He sighed with careful pleasure.

And certainly the night outside was different from night in Bombay. The bus had suddenly become surrounded by celebrating crowds, celebrating more wildly, more frenziedly, than when Bombay had its festivals and people danced and sang and burst crackers under everybody's feet, when idols of the gods were carried high above. But as, hooting and honking, the bus jutted and jabbed its way onwards and he peered across his wife out of the window, he was inescapably aware that celebrating Calcuttans were noisier, more exuberant, more carried away than any Bombayites.

Yes, he felt, there is something in the air here, hazy now with blueish smoke, that is somehow alien to me. Yes. Yes, it is that. Utter lack of restraint.

And am I definitely to be spending the remainder of my days in this place? And no longer Inspector. From here on just only one Mr Ghote. Ghote Babu, as they say in Bengal. Husband of the Bengali lady I was marrying those many years ago, who has now, so unexpectedly, inherited from her distant, distant cousin-uncle this big, big house she is hardly able even to remember from her childhood.

In Calcutta. In distant, different Bengal. All right, I am in fact still officer of Crime Branch, Bombay Police Headquarters. On Casual Leave only. But, if we come to live in this house that Protima is so much wishing not to be selling but to be staying in, with the tall rooms she is remembering,

2

the sweeping staircase, the courtyards with fountains playing — and not much more than one week ago she was not even knowing it would come to her — then I must send in my resignation and begin a new life as a Calcuttawalla. Not Inspector Ghote, but just only Ghote Babu.

And one well-off man. Or, tell the whole truth, husband of one well-off woman, Bengali by birth. This wife of mine who, suddenly, is thinking nothing at all of spending out and spending out. Look at the way she was obtaining air tickets to come here. All flights full-house, and at once she was whispering to me that I must, against my each and every liking, offer a bribe, that I must say to the tickets walla *I am betting you two hundred rupees that two seats together are not available*. And, yes, at once it was tap-tap-tap on computer keys and *Sorry, sir, you have lost the bet*. But how did Protima know this was the way to do it? Truth is, she is not the woman I have all along believed.

Still, after all it was not a very big bribe. And it was oiling the wheels, as they are saying. So in a way good.

But, no, it would really be better if this wife of mine was agreeing to sell the house. We could go back to Bombay and end up there having a fine life in retirement with

3

the moncy wc are getting. I could finish my service in a decent way, doing what I am knowing I am able to do. Then afterwards we could have some fine rest and relief in a nice little house somewhere in the hills outside of the city. Outside of Bombay, where we have lived happily for all the years of our marriage.

But, no. No, she is wanting to stay here. In Calcutta. In her big house. Living a fine Bengali life. A life, she is telling, that is the only civilized one in entire India. In a city — 'Yes, problems are there, but they are getting better, better' — that is much more free from crime and corruption than Bombay, acknowledged by one and all as Crime Capital of India.

Why, oh why, was she seeing in some newspaper, just when there had come that letter from this Calcutta lawyer, A. K. Dutt-Dastar — if that is his high-and-mighty name — that Calcutta is holding almost lowest place in speed-money table? Very well, nice to live somewhere you are not having to pay a bribe to get anything done in right time. But — he glimpsed through the bus window a huge poster in Bengali script, almost unreadable to him — for me there would be still something of complications. And no work to be doing. No keeping of

4

law and order, howsoever difficult to achieve same.

Peering forward, he saw the whole road far ahead was now even more crammed with people. People dancing, singing, rhythmically chanting. Noise came battering at him from every angle, loudspeakers booming and blaring distorted music, fireworks popping and exploding, and from the lanes to either side piercing blasts from gaudily uniformed bands playing their trumpets, trombones, drums at unrelenting maximum volume.

'Oh, yes, yes,' Protima exclaimed abruptly. 'Of course, it is Laxmi Poornima tonight. How could I have forgotten? All Calcutta must be celebrating. Yes, look, look. There. A beautiful pandal for Goddess Laxmi. And now, on the other side, there is another.'

Ghote made an obedient effort to see, flipping his head from side to side. But the bus at that moment lumbered a few feet further forward and he got only a single fleeting glance at one of the decorated platforms. A glimpse of the brightly painted statue of the goddess of wealth, golden crowned, gorgeous in vermilion sari, seated on a wide-petalled lotus, her white owl beside her, clasping her golden vessel. Then chaos again.

Huddled in his seat with their heavy flight

bag cutting cruelly into his thighs, he made himself think that, after all, Bengal was just another part of India. In his faraway village childhood, he remembered, in the puja alcove where his mother had weaved the smoking incense to and fro and rung and rung her little bell there had been, too, an idol of Laxmi. Smaller than the image of elephant-headed Lord Ganesh presiding there, but still present to beg blessings from.

But this Laxmi celebration here was an altogether different matter. Such extravagance, such richness, such wild abandon, all making so many more demands than the simple daily puja he recalled.

The glimpse he had had of that Calcutta Laxmi showed her as somehow more elegant, more swirlingly dazzling than his mother's little statue, complete though that also had been with the goddess's lotus seat, white owl and golden vessel. No, this was altogether too much.

He shut his eyes — after the flight across India from Bombay he was tired enough — and tried to blot out even the sound of the bawling loudspeakers, the brazen band music, the shouts and the shrieks, the firework cracks and bangs.

'This is our Calcutta season of festivals, you know,' he eventually heard Protima

6

saying in his ear. 'The ten days of Durga Puja just past. Now Laxmi Puja. And in two weeks exactly, on the next moonless night, it will be Kali Puja. Yes, now look. Look up out of the window. You can see the Poornima full moon.'

Dutifully he opened his eyes and peered. But, seated on the inside, he was not in fact able to see the moon any better than earlier when he had caught no more than a quick sight of the pandals enshrining Goddess Laxmi. But, true enough, in such patches of the road where there was less glare from the strings of coloured lights cool moonlight was flooding down. However ineffectually.

Where will I be, he wondered, when this full moon above me now has turned to its dark phase? On the moonless night of — What was it Protima said? Yes, of Kali Puja?

'Oh, how I remember Laxmi Poornima in our house in Rash Behari Avenue when I was a little girl,' she burst out again now. 'Ma always set up a big, big basket filled with rice, garlanded and covered with a beautiful cloth. And all the way from the door to our own idol of Laxmi there would be the tiny footsteps Ma had made with rice paste, for Laxmi to tread along as she came in to bring us prosperity. We would set a line of lighted lamps outside to welcome her, and then we would sit up all night to — Look, look. In that doorway you can see a basket and the people of the house sitting there just as we did. You know, they won't be gifting any baksheesh tonight. You must not waste or lose any money tonight, or Laxmi will be angry.'

Ghote looked out as directed. But once again, from his inside seat and encumbered by the heavy flight bag on his knees, he was unable to see what he had been told to take in.

'And my father,' Protima went on excitedly, 'he would always tell me how on this one night of all the year you were allowed to steal if you wanted. Whatsoever you were thieving became yours by grace of the goddess. He would tease me by saying some dacoits would come to take my best doll. But, when he saw I was scared, then he would smile and say, *It's all right, baba, because there is so much moonlight, we may easily see any thief who is coming and tell them you are needing your doll too much.*'

But Ghote, exhausted as he was by the long flight from Bombay and the sudden reversal in his life that the news of Protima's inheritance had brought, could not bring himself to share her delight.

Instead, illogically reacting to the word *dacoit*, he simply clutched all the harder at the handle of the bag on his knees, suddenly feeling himself menaced here by unknown assailants. A stranger in a strange land.

2

The bus jerked to a full halt. Above the still tumultuous din Ghote heard a voice shouting 'Fairlawn Hotel, Fairlawn Hotel.' Protima thrust a sharp elbow into his side.

'We must get down. We must get down. This is it. Fairlawn Hotel, where Dutt-Dastar Babu has booked the room for us. Fairlawn Hotel.'

Fairlawn Hotel. Large letters, green, yellow-edged, shiny and smart stretched across the gateway. Beyond, the building itself loomed and faded in the everchanging light from the fireworks above and the on-off, on-off coloured lamps of yet another Laxmi pandal. Loading himself up with their luggage, he felt a new dart of unease as he confronted the building. Plainly, despite its enveloping coat of pale green paint, it dated from Calcutta's long-ago rich past. Not at all the sort of place he and Protima chose when they went on holiday. And even further away from the decent, workaday sort of hotel he stayed in if he was away on duty.

Too posh.

Altogether too posh. Why has this lawyer,

A. K. Dutt-Dastar, put us in a place like this? The fellow knows, after all, that I am no more than inspector of police. Yet this is looking like somewhere for tourists with money-fat wallets or expense-account foreign executives, even in days gone by for the sahibs of the British Raj.

'Come,' said Protima sharply, heading for the entrance.

He followed, seething with suspicions.

Inside, more green paint. On walls, on pillars, underneath the elegantly rising stairs. And pictures and paintings. The British royal family in heavily framed photographs. Time and time again. In ones and twos, in groups. With little dogs, without little dogs.

Is this really the place for us to be?

There was a bell to ring on the green-painted marbled reception counter. Setting down his load of luggage — the back of his legs ached abominably — he gave its brass knob a gentle pat. The loud ring that resulted brought, from somewhere behind, a lady he guessed was an Anglo-Indian or possibly an Armenian, wearing a severe black skirt and a black and white blouse with an ornate pattern that seemed to echo the hotel's heavy British-days architecture.

'Yes?' she said in a ringingly assured voice. 'I am the proprietress. What are you wanting?'

Ghote swallowed, and told her that he believed Mr A. K. Dutt-Dastar had booked a room for them 'under the names of Mr and Mrs Ghote'.

He wished he could have said *Inspector Ghote and wife*. But, even if he had, he doubted whether the statue-stern lady on the other side of the counter would have been much impressed.

But at least she reached for a large blue-covered book and slapped it down in front of them.

'Ah, yes,' she said. 'Mr Dutt-Dastar, a good friend of ours. D. D., we call him. Yes, D. D. Though, of course, we have many other good friends here, film stars, famous authors. British film stars and American enjoy their stay when they come to the city to shoot. You know our hotel was shown in that great film about Calcutta, *City of Joy*? Patrick Swayze is a very good friend.'

'Yes, yes,' Protima broke in. 'I was seeing that film. Many, many shots of Calcutta. Very good, first class.'

Her eagerness evidently pleased the proprietress.

'I will call a bearer to show you your room as soon as you have signed in,' she said. 'But first let me tell you the rules of the hotel. Your room price' — she glanced at the big blue book — 'which is 750 rupees, non-airconditioned, includes all meals. They are served exactly to time. No Indian slackness here. If you are late, you are late. Dinner at eight. Breakfast, seven-thirty. English luncheon, one o'clock. Afternoon tea, quarter past four.'

Ghote, astonished at how much A. K. Dutt-Dastar had agreed they would pay — Must be very, very good friend of the management, he thought — hardly took in all the times and conditions that had been shot out at him. And, following the bearer carrying their cases, up the elegant stairs, out on to a balcony, in again, and on upwards, he felt nothing but a tiny glim of pleasure at the thought that in a few minutes he would be able to lie down on a bed.

But when at last they reached their room Protima refused to think of sleep. Eyes dancing with excited joy, she insisted that they should watch the continuing celebrations even though the window instead of looking out on to crowded and noisy Sudder Street at the front gave them only a view of a dark back-lane. But something could still be seen. So grimly he stood there beside her, fighting off draining fatigue, even a little chilled in the mild October night. Over and over again he reminded himself it had been Protima's first thought when she had read that lawyer's letter that now he himself would be able to start a comfortable retirement after his hard days struggling against Bombay's criminal elements.

But, despite the muffled noise of celebration and the occasional sight of the pink and gold trail of a rocket ascending the moon-drenched sky, he was able to make out little more than that in the lane below there was a huge shapeless mound of something or other. To judge by the smell, distinct even at their height above, it had to be garbage deposited there layer by rotting layer over many months past.

Is that heap then, he asked himself, the reality of Calcutta? He managed to resist the temptation to point it out to his sky-gazing wife. But only just.

Then, at last and at last, he felt the time had come when he could reward himself for his forbearance. Silently, leaving Protima where she was, entranced, he slipped off to the waiting bed.

★ ★ ★

They missed breakfast. Ghote knew, as he jerked into wakefulness, that he had fallen at once into a deep sleep the night before.

He had had no idea how late it had been when Protima had joined him. But now she was fast asleep still, lying flat on her back and, if not snoring, at least breathing deeply, regularly and rather noisily. He looked at his watch. Half past eight. From outside there was coming the distant irritable honking and hooting of a day's busy traffic.

He woke Protima. As soon as he had told her how late it was she declared that what they would have to do was to get themselves ready as quickly as possible. 'Then we must set off to see the house.'

'But Mr Dutt-Dastar was saying he would reach us there by car, no? Leaving hotel at eleven?'

'No, no,' Protima had answered. 'You don't understand A, B or C. I cannot wait and wait for some dry stick of a lawyer. We will leave a message for him. I must see my house just only with you. It is my present from above.'

'But you are not a child who must open whatsoever they are given at Diwali before they have even thanked the parents who have gifted it.'

'Nonsense, nonsense. Best way to show you are pleased is tear off wrappings ek dum.'

A little offended at that quick *Nonsense,*

15

nonsense, he had said not a word more.

So, quickly as they could, they washed and dressed and hurried out, finding without trouble a taxi in crowded, half-lazing, half-bustling Sudder Street. The Sikh driver when Protima showed him the address of the house was grinningly confident that he could get them there 'in one hour time, less, less. No problem.'

But problems there were. The first of them still within sight of the hotel. An elderly Sikh stepped out blithely into the roadway right in front of them. As his co-religionist at the wheel brought their vehicle to a brake-screeching stop, the Sikh gave him a playfully joyous smile and went into an elaborate happy pantomime of hurry-scurrying out of the way. The performance took him to the far side a great deal less quickly than if he had crossed at full leisure.

City of joy, Ghote thought sourly. City of ridiculous play-acting.

However, if there were going to be as many stoppages as this — a barefoot, bare-chested rickshawalla taking a smartly uniformed ten-year-old girl to school had cut in right across their path — it looked as if Protima's determination to get to the house early was going to prove a good thing. If for the wrong reason.

16

He ventured to say as much.

Protima gave a long, tinkling laugh.

Why is she wearing that sari, he asked himself in a sudden fit of irritation. It is one of her best, I am only just now noticing. And she has draped it down her back Bengali fashion, instead of having the pallu hanging down beside her, Bombay style. The way she has always put on a sari ever since our college days.

'Surely,' she said, 'you cannot be thinking Dutt-Dastar Babu will come on time. We would be there well before, whatsoever delays there may be. You are in Calcutta now. He will be certainly more than one hour late. Not your Bombay ten-twenty minutes.'

He felt his simmering anger rise even higher. The fellow to be so appallingly late. And that name of his. Dutt-Dastar. Typical Calcutta idea, that both your family lines are so important, so — What was the Bengali word Protima sometimes used? Yes, so *bhadrolok* that both must be preserved for ever. And why must she call him Dutt-Dastar Babu? What was wrong with Shri Dutt-Dastar. Or English, Mr Dutt-Dastar?

Oh, will I ever be able to live in this place?

Now they were brought to a standstill once again.

17

'What is that trouble along there?' Protima said, breaking in on his shrouded state of sullen ill-humour. 'Are you able to see?'

Coming to, he realized they had reached the broad stretch of Chowringhee running beside the huge green extent of the Maidan. The Maidan he knew about. Any Calcuttan you ever met was sure to tell you it was the largest public park in the world, a vast area cleared two centuries or more ago to provide a field of fire for the cannons of Fort William after the Battle of Plassey. Somehow, he told himself with satisfying bitterness, most Bengalis would gather up this battle as adding to the glories of their city, making it India's capital before that was shifted to New Delhi. Even though the battle had been won by the British when Governor Clive bribed the all-India notorious Mir Jafar to turn traitor.

Looking along the road now in the direction Protima had indicated, he made out a long stationary line of open trucks. So far as he could see — the air was hazy with floating dust — each was full of protesters of some sort, packed upright together beneath long white slogan-bearing banners. No doubt this was why the traffic was delaying so infuriatingly their progress towards Protima's inheritance.

But what was the protest about? Impossible to make out what the banners were saying.

He rolled the smeary window beside him further down and thrust his head out. But the haze was still too thick to be able to make out any of the writing, even if it turned out to be in English and not that different, damn Bengali script.

'Sirdarji,' he asked the driver, 'are you knowing what-all this morcha is for?'

The Sikh turned back, grinning a wide, white-toothed smile through his curling and twirling beard.

'Oh, sahib, always protestings in Calcutta. How else would we be getting some fun?'

For a moment he wanted to question that attitude. Fun? A protest meeting should not be fun. If a wrong was worth demonstrating against, it should be demonstrated against with resolution. But to get fun out of a demonstration? A very, very Calcutta attitude surely.

However, this was not the time to state his criticism aloud. Instead he asked simply, 'But do you know what this protest is?'

The driver in his turn peered into the distance, craning his turbaned head.

'Wetlands,' he said at last.

'Wetlands? Wetlands? What is that?' Ghote asked.

'Oh, duffer,' Protima snapped in. 'Don't you even know Calcutta is built on silt? Did you never hear those lines from Rudyard Kipling, *Chance-directed, chance-erected, laid and built on the silt*? Everything in the city was once wetlands. And did you never read, even in the Bombay papers, that Calcutta has been twice invaded by millions of refugees, once from East Bengal when it was part of Pakistan and then from the same place when it became Bangladesh? Did you never realize that to accommodate all those millions living and eating and sleeping on the pavements, or beside the railway lines, or at night on the tram tracks — more, many, many more than you ever were having in Delhi, Bombay or anywhere else — it would be necessary to extend the boundaries? But where could they be extended? Only on the wetlands stretching away from the Hooghly River.'

More Calcutta pride, Ghote jetted out in his head. The city is made into one gigantic refugee camp, and they take pride in the world-record misery. Then that British Kipling has only to call the city as coming up by chance only, and all these Bengalis take it as one firstclass compliment. My wife adding more now to these praises and applaudings.

But it seemed Protima's song of praise was,

at least for the moment, at an end.

'But why there should be some protest over that I cannot think,' she said, puzzled.

'Oh, memsahib,' the taxi driver broke in. 'Now I am knowing all about. It is for what they are calling U-traffic lakes.'

U-traffic, Ghote thought in a new burst of rage, rattling in fury the extraordinary word round in his head. What in God's name did *U-traffic* mean? And, surely, only in high-and-mighty Calcutta would a taxiwalla produce such a word. And this fellow is a Sikh, not even a full Bengali.

'What are you talking?' he snapped at him.

But it was Protima who answered. 'Ah, yes, now I remember hearing about this. Water from the Hooghly River, with all the foulness of the city drained into it, is pumped back into these shallow lakes, called eutrophic lakes — *eutrophic* — and there fish digest all the contamination without doing any harm whatsoever to their flesh. So we in Bengal can eat the dishes we are so much loving in perfect safety.'

'Yes, yes,' the driver joined in with enthusiasm. 'Behind the city, which as you must be knowing is running north to south beside the Hooghly, those U-traffic lakes are being fed with water that is dirtiest in whole world.'

Oh, yes, Ghote thought. If it is Calcutta water it must be the dirtiest in the world. Or the cleanest. Or the brownest. Or the greenest. The maximum of anything, whatever it is. But haven't we got plenty of dirty water in Bombay itself? Isn't our slum at Dharavi acknowledged by one and all to be the biggest in the world, except only one in Mexico. Let this fellow drink some water from a gutter in Dharavi. Then he would have a stomach ache worth having.

But myself, he added with a sudden downward swoop. For the rest of my life am I to be a fish-loving Bengali? He felt depression welling up and up in him as if he, too, was being pumped full of filthy Hooghly water.

'Yes, yes, memsahib,' the driver said, as at last he was able to get them on the move again, 'you are one hundred per cent right. That is what our U-traffic lakes are doing. But, you see, those people up there, those Corporation and State Government burra sahibs, are wanting now to fill up even more of the lakes than they were doing before. So they can build houses, houses, houses and make money, money, money. Number-two money, black money, under-table money, with just only some tax-declare white money. But not too much, yes?'

And, Ghote added to himself, thick with misery, today is no longer Laxmi Poornima. No one has licence to steal now. Yet they are doing it in full swing. Here in this city Protima was telling is so hundred per cent corruption-free.

Into his mind there came another phrase from Kipling about Calcutta, one his schoolmaster father had delighted to repeat. *City of Dreadful Night.*

Slowly they ground and jerked their way past the long lines of trucks and their jam-packed demonstrators, the men almost all in neat white shirts and the girls in bright saris. From time to time a chant broke out, and fell silent. After a little Ghote was able to make it out. *Wetlands Minister, out, out, out. Wetlands Minister, out, out, out.* At one point a whole squad of girls, students most likely, was being marched along the roadway from one truck to another, causing yet more delay to the traffic. Shepherding the bright dazzle of the young there was a single grey-haired lady in a less colourful sari, fierce, motherly, stick-upright, proud.

Another thing Calcutta is famous for, Ghote registered. Its immense demonstrations. Well-ordered, until the car and bus burnings begin.

At last they got clear of the traffic tangle

and began to move with some speed, their driver at the least gap in oncoming traffic happily ignoring any notion of keeping to his proper side of the road.

Worse driving than any in Bombay, Ghote registered sternly. No discipline. No discipline whatsoever.

Soon Protima, as if freed of complexities, began talking about the house they were on their way to see, the unexpected inheritance brought her by a dozen deaths of relatives she had scarcely heard of. Her huge Diwali present waiting for her to tear off its wrappings.

'I don't suppose it will be just exactly as it was when I visited there,' she admitted eventually. 'I must have been only seven or eight then. It would be just before Father was posted to Bombay. Long ago. But I remember a tall gateway, with two darwans who came running out to open the gates when we stopped outside. In those days the place must have been almost beyond the city. And there were little houses belonging to the darwans on either side and out of them came, it seemed to me, dozens of children. I hoped I might play with them, but we swept on and came to rest under the big porte-cochère, as they called it. But I did — I remember this now — get to play with some other children. I don't know who they were. They can't have been related to us or, I suppose, one of them would have inherited now. But we played Snatch Hanky out on a big green, green lawn, I remember that. There must have been so many malis, you know, to walk over that grass day by day in the heat of summer squirting their goatskins of water to keep up that wonderful green. In winter, of course, everything would stay green. In one visit there — it must have been some time after the monsoons — we went up the big, big sweeping round staircase on to the roof. I think I believed I was going to swarga above. And from there you could see far, far into the distance. Everything green, green. A beautiful, bright green.'

Before long she recalled something more about this last visit she had paid to the distant — no longer quite so distant — house.

'Oh, and we had lunch that time. Or perhaps it was some visit there before. A proper Bengali meal. Suddenly it comes back to me. I can see myself sitting at the big polished table. The only child there. So those children I played Snatch Hanky with, if that was the same time, must have been neighbours' children. And we ate . . . We ate . . . Yes, we began with karela with a little rice — very Bengali — and at that time I didn't much like karela, too bitter for a little girl. But my father told me, if I ate it up, at the end of the meal I could have lots and lots of misti-doi, our delicious Bengali sweet, pale brown and so chewy, and, of course, sandesh, the best of all. Every little Bengali girl has a sweet tooth, you know. Boys also. And grown men and women.'

She turned eagerly to Ghote, who had begun faintly to wonder if it was right for a father to bribe a child in that way. Was it the beginning of a whole slow slide-away from doing the right thing?

'To think,' she said, 'I have been in Calcutta more than twelve hours now and not so much as one single sandesh has passed my lips. Sirdarji, do you think there is a shop round here? Could you stop?'

'Oh, memsahib, there would not be any such here. Look how far we have come. This is a bad area. Look only.'

True enough, the road had narrowed. It was lined now with occasional tall dirty blocks with between them lines of makeshift huts, grey and dusty. At a point where it divided they saw, hanging from the branches of a pipal tree, a cluster of glittering chandeliers, evidently taken for sale from houses pulled down to make way for apartment blocks. The people on the street, or rather all over

26

it, were as numerous as they had been in crowded Sudder Street. But they did not look like buyers of fancy sweetmeats.

Ghote began to wonder what this house of his wife's would really be like. The contrast between her memories and their present surroundings could hardly be greater.

At last they came to a turning the driver had been anxiously looking out for. A large, very battered sign in English stretching right across a single-storey, slabby, monsoon-stained concrete building, *Nufurnico — Dealers in All Pillow and Foam Matters*.

'Not far now,' he said, cheerful again. 'What number you saying, memsahib?'

'My letter says thirty-four,' Protima answered, her voice beginning to show some uncertainty. 'But I don't remember us looking for any number when I came here as a child, though there were other houses not far away, big places behind walls. But — But, yes, there was a little shrine just opposite, blue-painted. Yes, and my mother said it was a Durga temple. You should be able to see the goddess. If it is still there.'

'Oh,' the driver answered, 'that will be there. Nobody is knocking down temples to put up petrol pumps.'

They drove on again in silence. Through the rolled-down windows there penetrated a strong smell of fish, pungent and hinting at rottenness. And it was dustier even than it had been beside the Maidan.

Ghote felt suddenly sharply sorry for Protima. What if things went wrong for this dream of hers? Where is it Mr A. K. Dutt-Dastar is sending us? Could it be that his letter and the phone calls after it were some sort of hoax?

And it seemed their driver's optimism about how near they were to their destination was unfounded. They drove steadily on, unable on this pot-holed, bare tarmac road to go at all fast. Seeing no sign of a big house or a Durga shrine. The minutes went by. No one said anything.

Ghote fought down the flicker of joy that had come to him with the thought that the house and all Protima's inheritance might be no more than some inexplicable confidence trick. No, that would be too much of a blow for her. All right, he himself would be delighted to know that the Calcutta life she had offered him was not going to happen. But Protima, who as soon as she had read that letter had seen the promised idleness of Calcutta as a reward for him, the idleness and the pleasures she remembered of that old, rich life: she would be hit by the vanishing of her hopes, hit as if she had been struck in full Maidan by a bolt of lightning.

'Here. It is here,' the driver suddenly exclaimed, his delight proclaiming the fears he had kept hidden. 'Look, look, memsahib. Look, sahib. There is bluepainted shrine, and on other side one high, high house wall.'

He put his foot hard down and the ancient taxi, rattling and shaking, leapt forward. And came to a brake-shrieking, juddering halt.

Yes, there was a long tall white wall, dotted for all its length with glinting pieces of embedded glass, and in it there was a pair of high iron gates with behind to either side the darwans' houses Protima had spoken of. But the gates, leaning crazily half-open, were red with rust and entwined with tendrils of scabby growth. Beyond, Ghote saw now the house itself.

It was a battered, eaten-away ruin.

3

Eaten away, crumbling, a ruinous shadow of its former self, the once beautiful house may have been. But, Ghote realized, it was by no means deserted. From where they sat in the taxi, stunned into silence, he saw beyond the rusted, leaning gates, not a flock of smiling children emerging from the gatehouses to greet the bhadrolok sahibs coming to visit. Instead, naked, scabby-looking babies crawled in the dust of what once must have been a fine lawn. Bigger urchins were busy teasing a goat tethered to one of the patchily brick-exposed pillars of the porte-cochère under which in days gone by Protima's father's car would have come to a halt. And on what had been the smooth gravel of the entrance drive cooking fires smoked sulkily, women in almost colourless saris crouching over them.

'Squattered,' their taxi driver pronounced. 'Madam, your house has been squattered.'

Protima looked round at Ghote.

'What — What are we to do?'

He wished he could produce an answer that would bring her some comfort. But

30

he could think of none. If only, he said to himself, on the way out here or in the plane as we flew from Bombay, I had said something to calm down those wild-flying hopes and plans she had.

But he had not dared say a word. Whatever he had ventured would have seemed to be rejecting the gift she had been offering him, the days and years of the rich life that had so unexpectedly been bequeathed to her. The life that, in her mind, had seemed to be the best life of all, Bengali life at its most civilized. The Calcutta life.

The life that, in his mind, foreshadowed aimless idleness cut off from all he had known, all that was familiar to him. Even if that familiarity was often black enough.

All he could do was to scrabble back in his mind through the details of the first letter that had come from A. K. Dutt-Dastar, through everything Protima had passed on to him of his telephone calls. But, no, there had been nothing anywhere to indicate that the house she had inherited was subject to any complications of the sort in front of them.

But it was. It was a house squattered. Squattered and eaten away.

'I suppose all we can do just now,' he said, 'is to wait for — '

He had been about to say *Mr Dutt-Dastar*.

But in deference to Protima's recent Bengali sentiments he changed that.

'No, we must simply wait till Dutt-Dastar Babu is coming.'

Protima looked at him.

'Yes. Yes, I am supposing that is all we can do,' she said, small voiced. 'I — I hope he would not be as late as I was believing.'

'Shall we sit in the taxi?' Ghote asked. 'We can drive to some shady patch.'

'No, no. When Mr Dutt-Dastar is coming, he will take us back in whatever car he has. I am not wanting to see more of — Of — Of that ruin until I am hearing why it is in such a state. But there is some shade under the wall further along. Why not just stroll there? We must not be all the time spending out and spending out in taxi fares.'

So she, too, has thought what I have been thinking, Ghote said to himself, hearing the tang of bitterness in her voice. That if Mr Dutt-Dastar — and it said a lot she was calling him Mister now — had left them under the impression they were to take over a fine house in a wide compound, had his equal promise of enough money to be able to keep up the house been as much of a mirage?

The taxi with its cheerful Sikh gone, racketing and bouncing, emitting a cloud of blue-black, foul-smelling exhaust, they crossed the road and walked up and down in the shade of the long, high, glass-encrusted, graffiti-defying wall of the house. They spoke little. There was little enough to talk about.

'I hope Mr Dutt-Dastar is on his way already,' Protima said at last.

'Perhaps, even with his so Bengali name,' Ghote joked lugubriously, 'he will defy prophecy and be here even ten minutes earlier than we must expect.'

Protima could produce no response. They walked back as near to the house gates as they dared, turned and walked in the other direction.

'There must be another house not much further along,' Protima tried as they repeated the up-and-down stroll for the third time. 'We cannot see it round the bend, and it would not be worth going into the sun to look, but I remember it was there.'

'It would have been where your playmates at your last visit here were coming from?'

'Yes. Yes, I suppose so. Or perhaps not.'

Silence.

Approaching the bend in the patchily tarmacked road once more, Ghote said — and immediately regretted it — 'But perhaps that other house has been sold and knocked down now.'

'No. If it had they would have built some apartments. Even over this long wall we would see the top of the building at least.'

'Yes, I suppose so. Unless apartments are forbidden to be built here.'

'Yes, I suppose so.'

Another turn.

Oh, why I cannot think of something hundred per cent cheerful to say? But what there is?

'Would you like — We could perhaps walk back the way we were coming and find some shop. No sandesh. But something to drink. Some Limca may be there.'

'No. No, I do not want anything.'

Five or six more languid, yet inwardly tense, steps.

'Thank you, though.'

Once more up to the leaning gates of the house. For a little now they stood cautiously watching two young men in garish shirts and dirty jeans who were skittering carrom pieces over the powdered surface of a battered board set up on two old oil drums. From the bright scarves knotted at their necks and what looked like knives stuck in their belts, Ghote had instantly labelled them as goondas, no different in Calcutta from the familiar hoodlums of Bombay.

Then from behind them there came a voice.

'I think I am able to hazard a guess at whom you may be.'

They whirled round, almost guiltily.

A big, bulky individual of some considerable age was standing there, leaning his weight on a silvertopped cane and looking at them with a smile of gentle benevolence on his softly jowled face. He was dressed in a pure white dhoti, ironed to fall to his ankles in exact elegant folds, and a white silk kurta, its topmost button nicely calculated to leave a precise triangle of pale brown flesh at his throat.

'Madam, it is you who is the inheritor of my dear old friend Amit Chattopadhyay's sadly dilapidated mansion. Am I correct?'

'Yes,' Protima said slowly, as if she was once more daring to believe in her heaven-descended Diwali gift. 'Yes, Mr Chattopadhyay is — was — my cousin-uncle.'

'I think I detect the family resemblance. A most pleasing one. But let me introduce myself. Amit Chattopadhyay's former neighbour, one Bhatukeshwar Bhattacharya by name. And this gentleman here beside you? He must be the Bombay jamai Amitji spoke of in the sad days when I sat by his hospital bed, the bed he hoped always to be leaving to return to his own home. A wish, alas, that was to be denied him for year upon year. Yet a wish that — determined fellow — he never abandoned, not even within hours of his end.'

Breaking like a swimmer through this torrent of talk, Protima acknowledged that she was accompanied by her Bombay jamai.

'My husband, yes. Ganesh Ghote, Inspector of the Bombay Police.'

Ghote felt then a spurt of pride at the way she had introduced him. Yes, he was Inspector Ghote, Crime Branch, Bombay Police Headquarters.

Or am I such for just only some few weeks more? And then Bengali Protima's Bombay jamai?

'But how does it come about that I find you walking up and down outside the house my friend Amit bequeathed to you? Is there no one here to take you to look over this inheritance of yours, distressing as is the condition you find it in?'

'It is kind of you to ask,' Protima replied. 'But the truth is I had no idea the house was in this state. Dutt-Dastar Babu, the lawyer who wrote to me in Bombay, had agreed to bring me here today. He had fixed on eleven o'clock at our hotel. But — But I wanted to see the old place for myself first, and I persuaded my husband to come early and left Dutt-Dastar Babu a message.'

'Ah, I understand now. A very natural thing to do. Perhaps this Dutt-Dastar fellow should have thought . . . But no matter. No matter. The thing now is to take you away from this not altogether salubrious spot. You should have seen it once, Mr Ghote. In the old days . . . But they are gone, and we must put up with the changes. So, now. My house is not far, and I am happy to say it is still in a tolerable state of repair. I was just setting out for my morning constitutional when I noticed you walking here, and drew my conclusions. Happily right, happily right. So, if you would do me the kindness to accompany me, we will see what some tea and some sweetmeats can do.'

Sandesh, Ghote wondered. Will Protima get her sandesh after all? And, if I am offered it also, will I like it?

'But, excuse me, sir,' he said. 'What if Mr Dutt-Dastar — Dutt-Dastar Babu, perhaps I should say — what if he is coming just now?'

Mr Bhattacharya consulted his watch.

'Did you say you had made an appointment for eleven o'clock at your hotel? It is scarcely twenty minutes to eleven now. I think I can promise you your Dutt-Dastar Babu will not be here for a full hour yet. More, in all probability. Much more. We in Bengal, my dear sir, have our own ideas about time. Ideas rather more . . . Shall I say, expansive? Yes, more expansive than anywhere else in India, I am happy to state. But in any case I can send my darwan in due course to keep an eye out. So you need have no worries on that score.'

But at this new sweeping and superior Bengali assertion about the uniqueness of Calcutta Ghote, to his surprise, felt hardly a twinge of resentment.

Wondering, he set out beside Mr Bhattacharya as he slowly led the way to his house, leaning heavily on his elegant cane, each single step a separate deliberate manoeuvre. And it seemed he was no more inclined to jib at any of the references to the glories of Calcutta that the aged Bengali continued to pour out.

'Oh, yes, Mr Ghote, this is a city I love, despite all the terrible things that have happened to it over the years. Yes, it has been a city of riot, of fire and brimstone, as you may say. But those, even those, are signs of the passion with which life is lived in Calcutta. It is a passion that has always found an answer to the worst of calamities.

An answer, if I may so claim it, in wit. In healing satire and, yes, not seldom in the ribald retort. Ours is a city ever new, ever bringing forth new ideas, new politics, new religious impulses. Yet it is, too, a city for ever locked in its haunting past. A city poised, yes, poised always between death and life.'

The stream of Bengali eloquence, coming as it was from such a happily enthusiastic source, began to make Ghote feel that perhaps life in the city of joy, if that was to be his future, might be not altogether the exile he had feared to the city of dreadful night.

'I don't know, my dear fellow, how well you are acquainted with Calcutta,' Mr Bhattacharya plunged voluminously on. 'But I feel obliged to tell anyone newly coming here that my city is not as bad as she has been painted. Painted? No, there must be another word for what the journalists and the travel writers have done to us. Yes. Yes, they have cartooned us. And cartooned us in no very friendly manner. You would agree, I take it, that the essence of the true cartoon — I instance the charming drawing of your Bombay's Laxman — should be to hit at an evil, yes, but hit, as it were, with a buttoned foil?'

Ghote thought an answer was required, or at least requested. But he had no strong ideas on the subject of newspaper cartoons. He was even a little unsure what a foil with a button was. So he reverted to one of the affable Bengali's questions which he felt he had been able to grasp.

'You were asking, sir, have I been to Calcutta before. It has been just only once, and some years ago also. My time here, which was on police duty, was a matter of just only come-and-go. To my regret I was not able even to see your Great Banyan. Oldest in existence, isn't it?'

For a kind, if hard to follow, mention of Bombay's best-known cartoonist, a balancing mention of Calcutta's world-renowned tree.

'Well, we must hope, Mr Ghote, that before many days have passed your charming wife will take you to our Botanical Gardens. Certainly, they are among the few remaining delights of our city that have not been affected by the disasters that have over the years rained down upon us. Not, however, that the gardens have entirely escaped. The banyan itself, you know, no longer possesses its central trunk, mother of almost two thousand sons of dangling roots, which embrace, if I may so put it, a circle of astonishing circumference. You must walk all round it, savour it to the full. And there are other remains of our past glory that you must immediately acquaint yourself with. The Victoria Memorial, British built of course, but nonetheless — '

His meander of praise was abruptly overwhelmed by a storm of hooting from a car, a bright red little Maruti, that had come to a halt a short distance away.

From its window the driver, a man of about forty, his face distinguished by a small, close-cropped moustache and densely black, wrap-around glare glasses, called across to them in a sharply high-pitched voice.

'Mrs Ghote? Are you Mrs Ghote? Your husband here, too?'

Ghote, after a moment of police officer's ineradicable suspicion, answered for both of them.

'Yes. Yes, it is correct. You are addressing Mrs Ghote, and I am her husband also.'

'A. K. Dutt-Dastar at your service.'

In an instant the lawyer, a slight, dapper figure in a pale blue shirt — smart doubtless first thing but now sweat-limp — and matching pale blue trousers, was out of the car and darting across the road.

'My dear madam, my good sir, most delighted at last to meet you. Had I known you intended to come as early, I would have arranged to be here to welcome you. As it is, I rang your hotel. Wanted to know you had arrived safely last night. All those Laxmi Puja celebrations. I found you had left by taxi, guessed where you might have gone, hastened to come out here.'

Ghote, blinking at this machine-gun burst of not very clear explanation, saw out of the corner of his eye that Mr Bhattacharya, perhaps upset because his confident claim that the lawyer would be more than an hour late had been disproved, was looking a little withdrawn. Hurriedly he introduced him.

'Mr Dutt-Dastar, this is Mr Bhattacharya, a gentleman from a house not far off who has been so kind as to take us into tow.'

The dapper, blue-shirted lawyer offered a palmsfolded greeting which Mr Bhattacharya solemnly returned.

'Should have been here in time to explain about your property, my dear Mrs Ghote,' A. K. Dutt-Dastar rapped on. 'The unfortunate developments. But I was badly held up. Some damn protest meeting or other at the Maidan. Chowringhee almost impassable.'

'Yes, yes,' Ghote said, eager to show he was up to date with Calcutta events. 'Demonstration against the filling in of the eutrophic lakes.'

To his surprise, his swiftly developed interest in Calcutta did not bring a gratified Bengali response. Instead a quick come-and-gone frown showed itself on what could be seen of the lawyer's black-bespectacled face.

A jab of irritation. How difficult it is to please these self-satisfied Bengalis.

Now Mr Bhattacharya took his leave of them, a process that evidently could not be gone through in less than five solid minutes of mingled good wishes, regrets and protestations.

'Yes,' A. K. Dutt-Dastar said after he had watched the aged house-owner move step by ponderous step out of hearing. 'Yes, Mrs Ghote, I regret to say there are complications concerning your property. Perhaps you have grasped their nature. No question of living in the place. None at all.'

'Complications I am just only finding out,' Protima replied, not without a touch of sharpness.

'Yes, yes. I quite understand you may have felt dismay. A certain dismay. I had hoped to explain everything before you came to see the house. I had considered it best. Best not to attempt to tell you the exact situation before you arrived in Calcutta.'

'So what is that situation?' Protima pounced before Ghote could ask, as he had wanted to, just why it had been better to await their arrival.

'In a nutshell, a nutshell,' A. K. Dutt-Dastar went yakking on, 'the house and the compound have been occupied, for years. Some years now, by a number of the immigrants. The immigrants by whom Calcutta has been invaded. I can use no other word — invaded. So, fundamentally the situation is difficult. Where property has been occupied for a certain length of time, it . . . It becomes almost impossible to have persons in occupancy expelled.'

'But, surely, the police . . . ?'

'Madam, there is no difficulty in bribing a Calcutta policeman.'

No, Ghote thought sadly, nor a Bombay police jawan either.

'But you were looking after the property while late Mr Chattopadhyay was in hospital, yes?' he asked.

'Yes. Yes, I was. To a certain degree, yes.'

'Then why were you not putting in security guards before all these people were entering?' Protima banged out.

'Madam, I reply again. There are bribes. A security man is just as easily to be bribed as a policeman.'

And I had somehow thought, Ghote

inwardly admitted, that after what Protima was telling, in Calcutta with all its high sentiments bribery and corruption also would be at a decent minimum. I am not able, for instance, to imagine Mr Bhattacharya, just now going out of sight round that corner, as being some bribe taker or bribe user. But it seems the city may not be so far in this from Bombay itself.

And, while Protima was plainly racking her brains to find some other way of securing for herself the changeling gift that had come to her, A. K. Dutt-Dastar, darting glances at them from behind his impenetrable wrap-around dark glasses, rattled on full pelt.

'You must know, dear madam, your relative was in hospital for some years before his sad demise. Some years. As his lawyer, he asked me to make occasional visits. A general supervision. At best I was able to come perhaps every six months. More than once I suggested to Mr Chattopadhyay he would be well advised to sell. Before the house fell into yet worse disrepair. And, yes, yes, he wished to do so. However, for a number of reasons — I will not trouble you with them — sale did not prove possible. Then also some planning restrictions came in. No longer possible to build apartment blocks. So it seemed the property was almost valueless.'

Ghote, whose mind had drifted away a little under this rattling of Bengali verbiage, was just conscious that something in it ought perhaps to have had his full attention. What should that *general supervision* have consisted of? How much had A. K. Dutt-Dastar's firm been paid to exercise it? Why had so little apparently been done? Just when had those planning restrictions come in?

No. He could not quite lay a finger on what he felt was wrong.

'But,' A. K. Dutt-Dastar flashed Protima a quick, white-toothed smile, 'I am happy to be able to tell you now, madam, that end is in sight. A purchaser is anxious to acquire the house. As it is. Most anxious. He has, as you may say, fallen in love with it. There are some small problems still remaining. But nothing, I assure you, that a certain distribution of funds will not put right.'

Ghote experienced a little uprush of delight. If instead of acquiring a big house in Calcutta Protima simply inherited a sum of money, then perhaps they could go back to Bombay. To Bombay where his work was. And, to do himself justice, where Protima had lived happily for many years, where she had friends, where young Ved, born and bred in the city and now almost at the end of his time at college there, would like to stay and would be near to them for years to come. Yes, Bombay.

Then a thud of dismay.

If this sale went through . . . Because A. K. Dutt-Dastar had slipped in those words, *a certain distribution of funds*. And that meant, no doubt about it, that a bribe was going to have to be paid. To someone, somewhere. A good, large bribe by the sound of it. And the payment of a bribe of that size did not always produce an immediate response. It did not necessarily mean that whatever process had to be speeded up was speeded up. Dangerous territory could be entered. A large sum of money illegally handed over could, in the murky world it led into, result in a request for yet another bribe. And then another, and another. With nothing in the end achieved.

He was puzzling over these implications, in a haze of depression, when something else suddenly struck him. Abruptly he realized what A. K. Dutt-Dastar had said earlier that had started a warning light flashing in his mind. The fellow had said that old Mr Amit Chattopadhyay had been wanting to sell his house. Yet Mr Bhattacharya, Protima's uncle's long-standing friend, sitting often at his hospital bedside, had distinctly declared that the old man saw himself as coming back to his own house. Saw himself as doing so almost up to his last gasp.

Something wrong.

Surely something distinctly wrong about A. K. Dutt-Dastar, Calcutta lawyer.

4

But what exactly was wrong about A. K. Dutt-Dastar? Yes, he had told Protima something that contradicted something Mr Bhattacharya had said, and there was no conceivable reason why that nice, old bhadrolok gentleman should have done anything but tell the truth. So it must be the lawyer who had lied. And, looking back, there had been tiny indications earlier that there was more to what he said than appeared on the surface. To begin with, there was his failure to tell Protima about the appalling state of her house. What real reason could there be to keep that back? And then there was, too, his choice of such a posh hotel as the Fairlawn.

Was he intending somehow to flatter us by sending us there? Was that a sort of bribe?

Then there was his haste in coming out here. That sweat-soggy shirt the proof. He must have very badly wanted to be the one who told us about the house. The way he had waited to speak about it until Mr Bhattacharya was well out of hearing. Another pointer.

And, wasn't there one other thing, too?

His almost angry frown when by chance the Wetlands protest had come into the conversation? That quick frown and his abrupt switch to pointing out the problems over the house?

But why lie about dead Mr Chattopadhyay's intentions in the first place? What it is he is keeping from us?

'But let me take you round the house and the compound,' the fellow said now, all bustling eagerness. 'Ignore, please, all those people from East Bengal. Think only of what the house once was. What therefore the buyer who is so interested must do. Pay the police no longer to turn blind eyes to these interlopers. Pay also some first-class security firm to expel them once and for all. Pay and pay for the many, many repairs needed. But his money is there. In plenty. Far more, I am afraid, Mrs Ghote, than the sum that has come to you.'

Ghote saw now a familiar look arrive on his wife's face. Not a look a casual observer would be able to read. But one well known to him. A slow build-up of immovable obstinacy.

Immovable obstinacy, here just edged with unshed tears.

So, he thought with plummeting dismay,

it seems I am destined after all to become a Calcutta man?

'Dutt-Dastar Babu,' Protima said. 'Yes, take us round the house. But I am not someone who would know what repairs are needed. Repairs, however, must be undertaken. The house has been bequeathed to myself, and I am determined to stay in it. So after you have shown us what there may be to see, we can go to your chamber and you can give some advance on the money that is to come to me. Any person I find to examine the house would want a good fee.'

'But — But, Mrs Ghote, when you have seen the house for yourself you will change your mind. You must. There are fallen walls. Fires have been lit. Rains have penetrated.'

'No.'

Ghote, who had heard that *No* more often than he had liked, knew now that A. K. Dutt-Dastar would never persuade his wife just by leading her round her squattered and eaten-away inheritance.

However, the lawyer did not know Protima as well as he did, and in a moment he was ushering them through the half-collapsed, rusted-over gates.

'Darwans' houses to either side. Very much occupied by these East Bengal refugees. Three-four families in each one.'

No comment from Protima.

They advanced up the dusty track that had once been the gravelled drive, weaving their way past the sullen little fires of dung and coal-dust, the equally sullen women tending their blackened cooking-pots, past their crawling and scrambling naked dust-covered babies.

'These people are also keeping numerous livestock. Cows, goats. Dogs and cats also. You can see.'

'Yes,' said Protima.

At a corner of the porte-cochère, its once dazzlingly white-plastered pillars thick with green monsoon slime where they were not eaten away to the interior brick, the two young goondas scooting the carrom pieces over their board paused long enough to give A. K. Dutt-Dastar contemptuous glares.

Hurriedly he began to manoeuvre Protima onwards.

'Such people must go,' she said.

They mounted the broad stone steps leading up to the wide door of the house, one leaf of which seemed to have been chopped away for firewood or hut-making. As he stepped in, Ghote could not help catching his breath at the sight of the wide, spacious entrance hall. Its marble floor was cracked and pot-holed and covered in cow dung and dead pigeons, discarded mango peels and rubbish of all sorts. A row of ribby tethered cows stood in pools of yellow urine all along one wall with two or three women extracting from them a wretched quantity of watery-looking milk. The ceiling, where evidently a massive chandelier had once hung — Is it even now one of those on that pipal tree we were seeing on our way here? — was stained with the smoke of years of fires. From the walls where fallen plaster had exposed the brickwork bougainvillaea, seeding in the cracks, tumbled downwards. Elsewhere thin growths of acacia trees reached for the light coming through the high windows, now mostly leaning lopsidedly from their frames. In one a three-parts torn away grass sunblind still drooped. But, perhaps most depressing of all, the wide spiralling staircase now led up not to the swarga above that little Protima had once imagined but to nowhere.

'Yes, yes,' A. K. Dutt-Dastar said, almost in answer to Ghote's stunned silence. 'Dilapidations of every kind. And then there is the effect of our Calcutta weather.' A brilliant, uneasy smile. 'You know, Mr Ghote, what the famous American writer, Mark Twain, was saying about our heat and humidity? That *it was enough to make a brass door-knob mushy.* Very good, yes?'

Very typical of you, Mr Dutt-Dastar, Bengali, to turn that saying into one gold-shining compliment.

'Very well,' Protima jabbed out, her tears-filled eyes fixed on the broad marble staircase leading to nowhere. 'I have seen enough. You have made your point, Dutt-Dastar Babu. But nevertheless I intend to live here. And without all these people. So let us go to your chamber, and you can give me a cheque to cover such expenses as a qualified expert would need to make a thorough examination.'

'Ah, Mrs Ghote, disbursement in advance will not be possible. Alas. I am not able to pay out any sum without prior notice. Arrangements would have to be made.'

'Then when would we come?' Ghote snapped in, aligning himself instantly on his wife's side and giving full play to his still unaccounted-for distrust of the lawyer.

A. K. Dutt-Dastar hesitated.

Ghote felt his suspicions harden yet more.

'Mr Dutt-Dastar,' he said, 'kindly fix a time.'

There must have been enough of an edge to his request. The lawyer produced his diary and began, despite the wrap-around dark glasses he still kept on, flipping through its pages. Ghote, unashamedly leaning forward in the interior gloom to peer at it, thought he did not see many entries.

'Very well,' A. K. Dutt-Dastar said at last, closing the diary with a snap. 'Shall we say this day week? At four-thirty p.m.?'

'No.'

Protima's *No* was again adamant. Ghote recalled occasions in their married years when he had heard it explode at him. But, he felt now, his wife was filled with new fire. A fire he had not quite experienced before. Was it Calcutta passion? The riot, fire and brimstone Mr Bhattacharya had spoken of?

And, if it is, would it be with me for the rest of my life here?

'We will come,' Protima went on, 'today itself. At four-thirty p.m.'

'Madam, I cannot promise to be ready so early. Not at all. Not at all.'

'Then we will come tomorrow. Four-thirty p.m. also.'

'If you like. But I can promise nothing.'

A thundercloud of sulkiness, A. K. Dutt-Dastar turned on his heel, tramped out of the devastated house, down its dusty drive and across the road back to his little red Maruti. Dust rose in a cloud behind him as he drove furiously away.

And it was then that Ghote realized, out on the edge of the city as they were, taxis

55

would be impossible to find. How were they to get back to the Fairlawn Hotel?

★ ★ ★

So, when at four-thirty the following afternoon they arrived at A. K. Dutt-Dastar's chamber in North Calcutta, they were both fuming with long-checked impatience. A weary hunt for a taxi the day before had left them exhausted. Protima had insisted, as soon as they got back to the hotel at last, that she must have a sleep. Ghote who, though fatigued enough, found it hard to sleep in the day had left her there on the bed. He felt obscurely that this was a typical Bengali habit, to lie all afternoon on some big bed with other family members, dozing, chatting a little, singing perhaps, dozing again. He did not approve.

His feeling of alienation persisted next day. He dutifully ate the Fairlawn Hotel's enormous British-style breakfast — they had been not a minute late for it — bowls of porridge and some British preserved fish called a kipper, a torture of unexpected sharp bones, toast and thick marmalade. Protima, the Bengali fishlover, declared the kipper delicious.

Am I to eat things like this for the rest of

my life, he ... him...
of gloom. ...d,
Nearby ...d,
all the ...kfast
— was ... mana...
of the ... brown ...
his mo...th to talk to...
Ame...an sha...ing his tab...
'My dear Mr Kogan —
...een. Deen. You gotta ...
Very well, my dear Deen...
morning to come and see ...
house. In ruins now. Ruins. ...
give us your advice — and there...
better able to advise on these things ...
could make it once again a really magni...
mansion, a real Calcutta palace in this ...
of Palaces.'

'Well, I don't know,' the American replied
dubiously. 'I guess Indians don't feel much
gratitude to a guy like Clive. He was the one
who conquered Bengal, right?'

'Oh, but, you know, your Bengali takes
the long view. That's the nice thing about
them. No grudges. Calcutta businesses have
contributed tremendously to our restoration
project. Tremendously.'

Bengalis, Ghote thought. Wanting to be
the best once more.

The mildly favourable feelings he had

istening to old ... Bhattacharya
und, now consid... ly faded.

* * *

...elings disappeared altoget... when, at
...a's insistence, the rest of the ...ay up to
...e of their half-made appointm...t with
... Dutt-Dastar was devoted to st...lling
...e Maidan. 'A one hundred per ...ent
...cutta thing to do,' she had said. 'Takin... it
...y, enjoying the fresh air, meeting a friend
...rhaps, hearing the news, discussing life.'
'But perhaps we could arrive early to Mr
Dutt-Dastar's chamber. I cannot be seeing
any reason why it should be difficult for
him to let you have some money out of
your inheritance.'

Even as he spoke he realized this meant
he was attempting to hurry on acquiring the
big squattered house. The house that would
mean a lifetime cut off from his own Bombay
and the work he did there. But he was not
going to let A. K. Dutt-Dastar get away with
his trickery. Whatever trickery it was.

'No, no. Nonsense. We told Dutt-Dastar
Babu we would come at four-thirty. At four-
thirty we will be there.'

So they had walked solemnly from one
end of the huge Maidan to the other.

First, from a distance taking a long look at the imposing, domed, colonnaded and minareted Victoria Memorial behind its veil of dusty haze.

'We will go inside another day. For now enjoy what it tells of the calm of Calcutta.'

'But it was built by the British, isn't it?' And dwarfed, Ghote could not help inwardly registering, by the towering square-cut mass of the commercial Tata Centre beyond.

Then they had walked slowly northwards, past informal cricket matches, past mud-smeared sadhus sitting in contemplation under trees, past vigorous games of catch-as-catch-can kabadi, past monkeywallas putting their charges through their paces. They had lingered watching the activity round one of the Maidan's three wide-stretching tanks, the Manohar Das, the people washing, the people beating the dirt out of clothes, the naked children splashing and shouting. They had taken long detours to avoid herds of browsing, flap-eared goats. They had peered in at the hedge-surrounded little bungalows belonging to various clubs, the Calcutta Kennel, the Armenian Sports. They had noted a small pandal under which were sitting three emaciated men, members of the Headmasters Association of West Bengal, fasting, their banner proclaiming, 'unto death to secure monies due but unpaid owing to corrupt activities.'

Corrupt activities, Ghote thought then. So Calcutta, according to these Calcutta headmasters, not at all free of corruption. And . . . And, when later they confronted that somehow dubious Bengali lawyer A. K. Dutt-Dastar would there be a whiff of some other corrupt activity?

Sitting eventually to eat a snack beneath the startling white walls of Fort William, with its sun-scintillating, much-polished ceremonial cannon — Protima at last sampling her sandesh: Ghote deciding he was not going to like it — prey still to his feelings of distrust, he could not prevent himself glancing again and again at his watch.

The glances had to be quick, since at the second of them Protima had burst out in reproof.

'What nonsense is this? This-all watch-hands watching. Dutt-Dastar Babu will be there when he is there. It will be four-thirty when it is four-thirty. You are in Calcutta now. Enjoy what is here for you to enjoy.'

Eventually, standing staring up at the sky-reaching Ochterlony Monument at the vast park's northern end, he had listened, reining in his impatience hard, to Protima passing on to him what she remembered her father had told her about it. 'Put up by one Sir David Ochterlony. He was having, you know, thirteen wives. Thirteen, and they would go out in the early morning, before the heat, along the bank of the Hooghly, each one on her own elephant. Thirteen elephants all in a line. There is Calcutta for you. One rich, rich past. And something else also. That Sir David Ochterlony was dying without one rupee to his name. He never took all the bribes the other British nabobs were getting fat on. He is deserving this monument. Every inch of it.'

Resenting once again all the praise poured on Calcutta, past and present, Ghote was unable to stop himself taking a full, uninhibited look at his watch.

'What I was telling?' Protima bounced in before he had properly registered the position of the hands. 'We will be there with Dutt-Dastar Babu at four-thirty on dot. Neither before or after. And he will give me what money I am needing to find out just exactly how bad it is with my house.'

Perhaps he will, Ghote thought. Hard to see how anyone could deny this so Bengali tempestuous wife I have married. And then . . . Then it will be the Calcutta life for me.

Mouth down-curved, he followed her

61

onwards, resolutely declining to take in a word of what she said when she stopped in front of the arm-upraised statue of Calcutta's hero, Netaji Subhas Bose, lost leader of the army that had been intended in the days of World War Two to chase the British out of Bengal and perhaps the whole of India.

Entering at last the Curzon Park extension of the Maidan — statue of an orating Lenin gesturing as expansively as Netaji Bose — they came upon an odd sight. In a tree-shaded corner, a green-painted iron railing enclosed an area of dusty earth milling with dozens of rats, even a hundred or more. Brown, fat and busily happy, they kept popping out of their little tunnels and squirming back in again, utterly ignoring half a dozen voracious crows swooping down among them. It was little wonder why. Pressing up against the rails a tight crowd of all sorts of everyday Calcuttans were tossing in, fast and furious, nuts, peas and potato chips that vendors surrounding them were vigorously selling.

'Oh, it is the Rat Colony,' Protima said. 'I have read about it. Those tunnels they have made are said to go right across to the other side of the road there. I don't think it was here when I was a child. Or

62

at least my parents never brought me to see it. But it is good, yes? Calcutta, the warm, welcoming even her rats.'

Yes, Ghote thought. Welcoming rats and an inspector of police from Bombay-side. But do I want any welcome, howevermuch warm?

'But why are you lingering and lingering here?' Protima demanded almost in the same breath. 'It would be disgraceful not to see Dutt-Dastar Babu just when we have said. Come.'

So, with his watch recording the time as precisely four-thirty, he stood at last beside Protima at the doorway of A. K. Dutt-Dastar's chamber on the ground floor of a crumbling building just inside a lane leading off Rabindra Sarani.

'*Sarani* is what they are calling in Bombay *marg* a big street,' Protima had explained. 'Since Independence we have re-named many, many Calcutta roads. What was Theatre Street is now Shakespeare Sarani. Shakespeare is almost a Bengali writer, you know.'

He had thought of saying that this really could not be true. But decided against. And he had noted, too, her *we have named*. Had she already let all her Bombay years fall away?

'And, best of all, when British had gone Clive Street was named as Netaji Subhas Road in honour of our great Bengali fighter against the British. Then, even better, in the days of the Vietnam War they re-named Harrington Street where the U.S. consulate was as Ho Chi Minh Sarani.'

Ghote might have enjoyed this example of sharp Bengali wit. But the door of A. K. Dutt-Dastar's chamber had been opened by a greasy-shirted, bald-headed peon, a long thin birthmark slithering snake-like from above his left ear down to his chin.

As the fellow led into the outer office — he had a bobbing, this-side-and-that limp — Ghote had to acknowledge that, whatever trickery A. K. Dutt-Dastar might be up to, he certainly did not seem to be a person who had much benefited from any doubtful activities. The paint on the room's walls was peeling in patches. Its years-old marble floor was black-lined in every crack. The ceiling was high enough, but grey with age, its plaster flaking. True, there were rows of businesslike filing cabinets against all the walls, but their shabby green paint made it clear they had been there unreplaced for many, many years.

At a plain wooden table crammed up

against a large, grey-painted, old iron safe, a crop-haired individual, erect as a rod, chin grey-stubbled, sat on a tall bentwood chair thumping with ink-covered fingers at a large out-dated office typewriter. He wore a much-washed shirt, each of its pockets jostling with rows of ballpoints and plastic-knobbed pencils.

'To see Dutt-Dastar Babu,' Protima said briskly. 'I am Mrs Ghote. Appointment for four-thirty.'

'Not available.'

The upright old clerk had hardly looked up from his typewriter. But over the clatter of its keys Ghote thought he could hear from behind the door of an inner room, A. K. Dutt-Dastar's high-pitched, rattling voice, talking evidently to a client.

Before his Bengali wife could explode into another Bengali rage, he stepped in.

'Our appointment was for four-thirty, yes,' he said. 'But if Mr Dutt-Dastar will be available soon we would wait.'

The old clerk had stopped his typing. But it was only, peering down and tut-tutting pettishly, to remove a jammed ribbon and replace it with another, evidently re-inked, almost dripping from between his fingers. Otherwise he took no more notice of them.

So now Protima did explode.

'My husband was telling we had appointment. The time for that has already passed, by almost ten minutes. You will go in now and tell Dutt-Dastar Babu we are here and we wish to see him ek dum.'

'Madam, my duty is to remain at my post.'

Ghote thought quickly. Plainly rage was hardly going to get them in to see the shifty lawyer. He guessed it was very likely his clerk had been given orders that if they appeared he was to forbid them entry. How to get round the embargo?

Only one way. Speed money.

He slipped his hand into his back pocket and took from his wallet a ten-rupee note. Without a word, he laid it on the old clerk's table.

Scarcely taking his quick-working fingers from the typewriter keyboard the clerk slid the note to the very edge of the table and left it there.

Ghote wondered whether he was expected to put another of equal value on top of the first. But a single look at the grey-stubbled face, bent intently over the typewriter's keys once more, clacking hard away, convinced him that, were he to pile note after note on top of his ten rupees till they were as high as the flaking ceiling above, he would find the barrier between themselves and A. K. Dutt-Dastar still in place.

Yes, Calcutta could produce, then, people of ferocious honesty. So, will I after all find something of pleasure to live here?

He looked at his wife.

She shrugged.

He picked up the note, replaced it in his wallet, seeing the single black-ink fingermark on it as some sort of badge of dishonour.

'Kindly tell Mr Dutt-Dastar,' he said, 'that we would return at this time tomorrow, and that, if we do not see him then, we would take whatsoever steps we see as necessary.'

But he knew they had suffered a defeat.

5

'The clerk Haripada,' Protima said as they left the crumbling old building.

'Haripada? But how are you knowing what is the name of that fellow?'

'Duffer. Of course I am not knowing. Do you mean you have never heard of the clerk Haripada?'

'I have never heard.'

What was this? Some Bengali ridiculousness by the sound of it.

'He is the hero of one world-famous poem by Tagore called 'The Flute'. Everybody should know it. Haripada is very poor. He shares his room with a flysnapping gecko, *covered by the same rent . . . the only difference: he doesn't lack food*, Rabindranath wrote. Poor Haripada's umbrella is full of holes, like, he says, my pay after they have taken the fines. He feels he is chained hand and foot. But he continues to live. He listens to the flute.'

'Well, I have never heard of this fellow.'

'But, don't you see, Dutt-Dastar Babu's clerk is just like him, an eternal Calcutta figure, poor but upright. Despising your offer of speed money.'

My offer. But offered with at least your silent agreement. And if there are honest, unbribable clerks in Calcutta, there are also bribable Bengalis. Your Dutt-Dastar Babu for one. I am sure of it.

But it was not until next morning, the Fairlawn Hotel's British breakfast finished to the last spat-out hair-thin kipper bone — the white-haired Englishman still trying to get dog-faced Deen Kogan to see Lord Clive's ruined mansion — that he found he had to bring that near-certainty of his about A. K. Dutt-Dastar into the open.

'Since we have nothing we have to do until we are seeing Dutt-Dastar Babu again,' Protima announced as they sat afterwards in the October sunshine on the hotel's stretch of lawn running down to Sudder Street, 'I am going to visit the Kali Temple. I have already left it too long. I am sure Mother Kali will answer my prayer, and Dutt-Dastar Babu will advance me enough to have the house fully examined.'

'I would not be too sure.'

'Not? What do you mean? How dare you say he would keep back money that is belonging to me? What nonsense you are speaking.'

'If it is nonsense,' he shot back, prickling

with anger at hearing that word once again from his more fiery than ever Bengali wife, 'then why it was that he did not give yesterday?'

'But he had a client inside.'

'When he knew we were coming? When he had given the order to your clerk Haripada to keep us out only?'

'But you cannot be sure of that. Dutt-Dastar Babu is a gentleman. A Calcutta gentleman. There must have been some problem yesterday. When we are going there this afternoon you would see.'

He managed not to say anything more. But he could not keep the look of disbelief off his face.

Protima noticed it. She knew him too well.

'Now I am going to Kalighat Temple,' she snapped. 'I suppose you are not willing to pray there also?'

'No.'

He had spotted a Bombay newspaper from the day before on the reception counter. He asked if he could see it. But he found, though he waded through every column, he could take little interest in any of it. Even the latest manoeuvrings of what was called Bombay's crime-politics nexus failed to arouse him. Only a front-page item,

Pay Hike for Delhi MPs, briefly held his attention. Not because of the piffling extra 3,000 rupees a month they were to get, but because an accompanying cartoon implied the sum would hardly cover interest on the bribes they had had to pay to get elected . . . in order to receive yet bigger bribes.

But what does Bombay crime or Delhi MPs' corruption matter to me now, he thought glumly. I am to be a Calcuttawalla. However sure I am that this Dutt-Dastar fellow is playing some dirty game, Protima will not see it. She will get some money from him this afternoon. She will tell me Goddess Kali has answered her prayer. Then she will find someone to say the damages to the house, the fires, the destruction, the crumbling under monsoon rains, can be put into repair. She will get all those refugees out. We will have to live there for the rest of our days. Ganesh Ghote, Bengali bhadrolok, in well-pleated dhoti, well-ironed silk kurta, all complete.

Eventually Protima arrived back, splodgy red tilak implanted by the Kalighat Temple brahmans on her forehead. It irritated him. When she went to a temple in Bombay only the smallest of quick smudges was left on her forehead. Trust Calcutta to do even this to excess.

But yet more irritating was the fact that she had got back ten minutes after the inflexible lunch gong of the Fairlawn had boomed out all over the big house. So, tails between legs, they had to go and look for somewhere else to eat. And, worse for Ghote, Protima at once announced she had noticed a small place in a lane off Sudder Street where, despite the fact that Calcutta restaurants seemed to serve food from any quarter of the world except Bengal, they could get good Bengali home cooking.

They ate in silence. Protima had chosen a Calcutta favourite, fish heads, and, when he had refused to contemplate anything of the sort, had ordered for him hilsa fish. 'That is one great Calcutta delight,' she said. 'If you are going to be staying here, you must get to love hilsa.' So he had sat watching her expertly deal with her fish heads while attempting himself to extract from his hilsa tiny bone after tiny bone. But try as he would, peer into the white flesh as he would, each time he ventured to put a piece into his mouth he found it as full of infuriating prickles as his breakfast kipper.

At least dealing with all these damn bones means I am not having to talk, he said to himself. Because if I did, I would be bound to say something altogether to the detriment of one Dutt-Dastar Babu.

And then he saw that his wife, with every sign of pleasure, was busy taking out the glazed-looking eyes from her fish. Before they went into her mouth he closed his eyes.

* * *

At A. K. Dutt-Dastar's chamber his temper did not improve. No sooner had the limping peon with the long snake-like birthmark admitted them than upright, unbribable clerk Haripada said his master was waiting. 'You may go straight in.'

Dapper A. K. Dutt-Dastar was dressed today in well-ironed pale green shirt, very much a contrast to his sweat-stained one at the squattered house. He was, however, still wearing his ultra-black wrap-around glasses, although the light coming through the dust-thick window of his room, its walls lined with leather-bound legal tomes, already needed to be supplemented by a dangling neon tube.

Behind an enormous desk sitting stiffly upright in a wide, leather-backed chair, he nevertheless looked dwarfed between the two broad leather-padded arms. On the desk, its bare surface shining with hard polishing, there rested no papers, only a well-polished brass pen-set, its two pens planted like arrows

73

either side of a glinting glass inkwell with beside it a domed brass bell, equally well-polished. The big leather-cornered blotter held a virgin sheet of almost exactly the same pale green as the lawyer's shirt.

Does he have that sheet changed each day according to what he is wearing, Ghote wondered? The damn Bengali. And his outer office, where poor clerk Haripada is sitting at that ancient typewriter, bare almost as a police cell.

However, they themselves were greeted with an excess of politeness.

'Sit, sit. You must be tired. North Calcutta is nothing less than hell itself to get about in.'

He is up to something nefarious, Ghote thought. And once more boasting about Calcutta. We have crowded streets in Bombay also.

Then politeness was over.

'Now, Mrs Ghote, let me put it to you once more. You have inherited what they are calling a white elephant. Unfortunately. Yes, a big house that was once in a fine state of repair. Now falling down. Overrun also by squatters who have no intention of being shifted. Always ready to bribe or fight their way out of whatsoever steps are taken. But you have your piece of the greatest luck

74

in the buyer I have been able to secure for you. As I was telling you, once he was seeing the house he, as you may say, fell in love with it. And he is willing to pay the very large sums necessary to put all in good order. More, much more, my dear madam, than your resources will be equal to.'

'But, Dutt-Dastar Babu, I am determined to live in the house. It is mine. I remember it from my childhood. The perfect place on earth to live. So — '

'Madam, madam, hear me out. If you attempt to live in the house you saddle yourself with trouble after trouble. If you sell now you obtain a very decent sum. Yours to do with what you wish. A flat here in the city. Some nice South Calcutta part, say Rash Behari Avenue. Or you could return to Bombay and buy some very nice house in the countryside. A hill-station like Mahableshwar. I myself enjoyed a fine weekend there once when I had business in that too businesslike city. Madam, you really have no choice.'

Ghote did not leave it to Protima to reply.

'Nevertheless, Mr Dutt-Dastar,' he said, with all the emphasis he could manage, 'my wife would like to have the house inspected with a view to ourselves occupying same, and she would be most grateful if you could hand to her whatsoever sum is necessary to put that work in hand. Forthwith.'

What have I done, he asked himself immediately. Have I now fully admitted I am willing to live the bhadrolok life here in Calcutta? I have.

But A. K. Dutt-Dastar was not, it seemed, to be so easily deflected from his aim.

'Yes, yes,' he replied, 'you need have no worries there. But other problems . . . ' He turned to address Protima directly. 'Other problems, my dear madam, there may be.'

'What other problems? You have said nothing of other problems.'

'My dear madam, it is a somewhat complex matter. Which will not at all arise if you are willing to sell, to accept my earnest advice to that effect. So I have not hitherto mentioned the matter.'

'Then now is the time to mention and mention.'

For an instant Ghote felt a jounce of pride in his fiery Bengali wife, not letting any evasion deflect her.

Until he thought of the likely years ahead as her Bombay jamai.

'Mrs Ghote, I will of course fully inform you without delay. Let me call for the file.'

He gave a sharp tap to the brass bell on his desk — in Bombay, Ghote thought

76

sourly, fellow would have decent intercom — and when the snake-birthmarked peon lumbered in told him to fetch the Mrs Protima Ghote file.

For two or three minutes they all sat in silence. Ghote would have like to have asked Protima whether she still saw Dutt-Dastar Babu as a Bengali gentleman, or whether this latest, hitherto unmentioned obstacle to her living in the house that had been bequeathed to her had not made even her a little suspicious. But he could hardly do that in front of the lawyer himself. And the man had evidently decided that nothing he could urge in words was now going to shift Protima. So he was simply waiting to show her whatever it was in the file that might finally convince her. And Protima? Ghote had no idea what was going on in her head. But, whatever it was, for once it was not spouting out in a torrent of Bengali talk.

At last the peon appeared, clutching a fraying buff-coloured file with the words *Mrs Protima Ghote — Bombay* scrawled across it in bold green ink. He slapped it down on the blotter and lurched out.

A. K. Dutt-Dastar glanced across at the two of them on the chairs drawn up to his desk. Then, with a touch of solemnity, he opened the file. For almost half a minute he stared down at the topmost sheet of the thin batch of documents it contained.

Ghote managed to produce a small belch and leant forward as if to ease some internal discomfort.

And succeeded in seeing that the page the lawyer was studying so intently had on it no more than two lines of heavy blotched typing.

Mrs Protima Ghote
Last Will and Testament of
Amit Nirad Chattopadhyay Babu

No doubt the thumping work of the clerk Haripada.

Hastily A. K. Dutt-Dastar turned over two or three further sheets.

'Ah, yes,' he said. 'Yes.'

He shot a glance across the wide desk at Ghote and, with the appearance of needing to look more intently at what he was about to read, brought a hand up and cupped it at the top of the new sheet.

'Yes,' he said after some moments. 'This is the matter I had in mind. Complex business. If not altogether vital. It notifies me of what may seem to be a prior claim to a part of the compound of the house.' He looked up, though still keeping his hand concealing the page. 'Yes, a matter that has been pending many years. That has, as you may say, gone almost into desuetude. But is still there.'

'What it is exactly?' Protima bluntly demanded.

'A claim probably emanating from a neighbouring property,' A. K. Dutt-Dastar replied. 'Simply that.'

'The property belonging to one Mr Bhattacharya?'

'Oh, no, no. Not that gentleman — you were introducing him the other morning, yes? — no, not that gentleman at all.'

'Then who it is? I may request to see them. I could persuade them that something so long neglected should not stand in the way.'

A. K. Dutt-Dastar looked shocked.

'Madam, madam. That would be fatal. Fatal. To give an opposing party some indication that their case is better than they had thought. It would never do. Never. Never. No, the only way to solve the matter is careful and delicate negotiation. An expensive procedure, I feel bound to warn you. And inevitably long drawn-out also.'

'If it must be, it must be,' Protima retorted.

Ghote had secretly hoped that this final obstacle, however delayed it had been in coming, might at last deter his wife. A decent sum as the selling price, A. K. Dutt-Dastar had said. He thought of how pleasant life could be in or near Bombay with money to spend on some good accommodation. And he would work out his full time at Crime Branch. To the last day.

But, no. Repulse seemed only to increase the lawyer's determination.

'Madam,' he battled on. 'Let me recommend this. You go to the house with some fully qualified person and take his advice. I can give you the name of a very reputable man.'

He pulled open the long middle drawer of his desk, extracted a card, pushed it forward.

'You cannot do better than this gentleman.'

Ghote saw his chance. The lawyer's cupped hand had moved as he leant forward. A paragraph on the sheet he had been reading was momentarily visible. He strained to take in the blotchily typed words.

'Very well,' A. K. Dutt-Dastar said, swinging back to his original position almost crouched over the file. 'Let the gentleman I am introducing explain to you the condition the house is in. Trust his judgement. And only then, if you are still determined to take up occupancy, we will commence proceedings in this other matter.'

Trust the judgement of a man you have recommended, Ghote thought. I would rather trust a rat from that Rat Park.

Protima had been thinking.

'Very well,' she said eventually, taking up the card the lawyer had slid across his shiny desk.

'I may tell you,' A. K. Dutt-Dastar went on, leaning back more comfortably in his big chair, 'I have already instructed my clerk to have a cheque drawn up in anticipation of your continuing to believe you would be able to take up occupancy of the house. You may apply to him.'

Protima turned and directed a glance at her husband which said, more plainly than even a loudspeaker announcement, *I told you so, a Bengali gentleman to the last.*

But Ghote hardly noticed. He was puzzling hard over the few words he had managed to read when the lawyer's cupped hand was not hiding them.

6

With right of passage unimpeded. Ghote sat in the taxi returning to the hotel. Protima beside him, with A. K. Dutt-Dastar's cheque in her purse, was looking to his mind insufferably smug and Bengali. In his head he mulled once more over those words.

Very well, that tricky fellow — proven liar also — is making out that the query hanging over the property is because of a claim to land in its compound. And, yes, that may well involve a right of way. But if that is all, why was he so very much concerned not to let me see same?

And, another thing. That page he was reading from was in heavily smudged typing. I can see the words now only. *With right of passage unimpeded*. And, surely, the typing was one and the same as the typing I was seeing on Document Page One, *Mrs Protima Ghote — Last Will and Testament of Amit Nirad Chattopadhyay Babu*. But A. K. Dutt-Dastar stated he was reading out some document notifying him of a claim on the house. So it should have come from somewhere else than his own chamber. The typing should be altogether different.

With right of passage unimpeded. Be clear about this. A. K. Dutt-Dastar has in that file a document prepared in his own chamber, somehow concerned with Protima's inherited house, and mentioning some right of passage. Unimpeded also.

But what exactly is right of passage? How much may such a right interfere with Protima's getting the house? Take away from its value, yes. But that should not stop her getting the place, having it put in order, having the squatters moved out. If she can pay for that.

But how to find out more? Consult some other lawyer? Calcutta at least full of those. But which to choose?

No, wait. Yes, do it this way.

He leant forward and spoke to their driver.

'Not Fairlawn Hotel. Go instead to Writers' Building.'

Even I, hundred per cent Bombay man that I am, know about Calcutta's famous Writers' Building. That there are no writers inside it, only talkers. Because the secretariat of the West Bengal government is naturally full-full of incessantly talking Bengalis. When did I first hear that joke cut? I even know the place was called Writers' Building because in far-off British days it housed junior British servants of the East India Company, known as writers. There they had lived, it was said, one highly riotous life. Calcutta style.

So now he turned to Protima and explained what it was he had deduced from the words he had glimpsed.

'If anywhere,' he added, 'Writers' Building must be the place where we can quickly discover what right of passage may exist through the compound of a Calcutta house. Plenty of legal wallas there, and public servants also.'

'Yes, finding some person to look over the house can wait,' she said. 'Writers' Building is not far. It is in BBD Bagh. What was once known by the name of Dalhousie Square. But we re-named it BBD. For Benoy, Badal and Dinesh, three heroes of the Independence struggle shot by the British. Calcutta has always known how to honour her martyrs.'

Ghote let this new history lesson go in one ear out the other. Another time, perhaps. Now it was *With right of passage unimpeded*.

★ ★ ★

In less than ten minutes, despite the exuberant honking and hooting traffic, they drew up in front of the great long brick-red building, with its row upon row of yellow-stone arched windows, surmounted by four tall statues, barely distinguishable in the hovering dust cloud of the city.

But his Calcutta historian was still beside him.

'Yes,' Protima said, gazing upwards, 'my father was telling me about those statues when I was eight-nine years old only. Wait. I can recite to you the names. Yes. Science, Agriculture, Commerce and . . . Yes, Justice. They are what Calcutta is about. Truly.'

Well, Justice, he thought. Will that prove to be so? Will I even take the first step to Justice inside here?

He led Protima to the nearest entrance. There was a sliding metal grille to negotiate manned by an armed guard.

'Quite right,' Protima said. 'Chief Minister Jyoti Basu may be inside, the one man in India above all forms of corruption.'

Together with the clerk Haripada, Ghote allowed himself to think. And how many others? How few others?

Inside, they stood in line until they reached a table where a clerk laboriously entered the purpose of their visit — *Requesting legal information on right of passage* — in a heavy, crammed ledger. This entitled them to a chit to take to a long row of white-uniformed security men sitting half-hidden behind a counter surmounted by an elegantly curved wrought-iron screen.

With a sigh for India's never-ending bureaucracy, Ghote pushed the chit through a small square hole in the short protective wooden strip at the bottom of the screen. The youngish round-shouldered security officer, earnest in black-framed spectacles, took no notice. He seemed to be writing furiously on a large pad. A memo to higher authority? Someone about to be arrested? For two minutes or more Ghote waited patiently — Protima beside him showing signs of not being so patient — while his chit lay unlooked-at and the rapidly writing young man scribbled on.

But at last, peering through the wrought iron, it struck Ghote that the lines of florid Bengali script he could see, some shorter, some longer, could only be one thing. Poetry.

Bureaucracy, he thought, I expected. But poetry from a security officer? Well, the fellow is a Bengali.

He gave the elegant ironwork a sharp, ringing tap.

Abandoning his poetry, the security man proved immediately helpful. Too helpful. As soon as he had grasped from the chit the nature of their inquiry he launched into a whole hymn of speculation about what *right of passage* might mean.

'Yes, yes, an excellent phrase. A right of passage. You could set it beside the expression, rite of passage. Kindly notice the difference in spelling, R-I-T-E and R-I-G-H-T. The two are in contrast. I am thinking also that contrast might very well be the subject of a poem. You may know, sir and madam, that I am by vocation a poet. This is not at all my work.'

He gestured largely round the high but dingy entrance hall.

'No, no. It is necessary to earn. Sadly, sadly. Man cannot live by poems alone. Though he ought to be able so to do. He ought. When the political party of which I am honorary secretary — small as yet, some ten-fifteen members — when we are coming to power in West Bengal our first action will be to establish life grants for each and every one of Calcutta's poets.'

He looked up at them.

'Sir and madam, we are not only a political party. We are also highly active as a poetry society. Each Sunday on the Maidan we are holding a Mukta Mela. All are welcome to read out their poems. After we have read out ours. Sir and madam, will I see you there?'

'Right of passage,' Ghote, finally exasperated, banged in. 'Where can I find some person to tell me precisely what that is meaning?'

'Ah, my dear sir, precision, exactitude. That is to be avoided. It is with inexactitude, with the finer shades, that the truth may be — '

'Where?'

'Office Superintendent, Land Ownership Section, as it is stating here.'

A thump with a rubber-stamp on the chit.

'A peon will take you.'

They followed then the khaki-uniformed peon along corridor after corridor, the walls streaked with the red spittle from numerous chewed and ejected paans. On then up dark, narrow staircases, through huge rooms, brown with the age-long accumulation of cigarettes smoked in the course of long discussions — going on still in each room they passed through — their long tables laden with pile upon pile of papers, as brown, many of them, as the rooms themselves, some tied in bundles, more sprawling helplessly in danger of tumbling unheeded to the floor. The clerks, only a handful of whom seemed to be at work, were mostly chatting animatedly to the occupant of the wooden-armed chair next to theirs, across the table to someone else. Occasionally, very occasionally, a few papers were turned over incuriously or one of the ancient typewriters was tapped at. Even sometimes someone wrote an added note to some document or other. Others unashamedly slept, heads on folded arms or lolling comfortably back, mouths wide. Through the tall windows slanted stray bars of sunlight, thick with dust motes stirred up by the long-bladed fans above.

Perhaps, Ghote reflected as they went through yet another such room, perhaps in one of those piles of bundled papers may be the answer to my question. Some definitive statement of the meaning of *right of passage*.

Well, that is what I seem to have here, he added with grim humour. The right of passage through one warren of bureaucracy. That, but no more. Never the right to an answer.

But at last they were, in fact, ushered by the peon into the tiny cabin of the Office Superintendent, Land Ownership Section.

Its occupant was sitting at a desk piled almost as high with papers as the long tables in the rooms they had passed through. A fat, round-faced man with a cigarette, almost extinguished, dangling from his full lower lip. The big knot of his dhoti, visible above the desk, perched slightly soiled on a spreading abdomen. A plaque on the desk named him as *P. V. Bagchi*.

As they settled on two of the three chairs lined up in front of the desk, he vented a barely concealed belch. A waft of the spices that had accompanied whatever last meal he had had assailed them.

'How may I help you?' he said.

Ghote told him. He was afraid he might have been too brief. But all the mounded and entangled bureaucracy he had passed through had filled him with sharp impatience.

'Yes, I suppose,' P. V. Bagchi conceded, 'I could provide an answer. A great deal of looking into files and references may, of course, be necessary. But one is here to serve the public. That is the sole reason for my existence, you should understand. To serve the citizens of Calcutta. However, that is inevitably requiring a great deal of work. A great deal, especially in a matter of this sort. Yes, work.'

He showed no sign, though, of doing anything to begin that work. Instead he thumped the bell at his side and when a peon poked his head in at the door shouted for 'Half-set tea and one double plate singaras.'

Then while they waited for that to arrive he sat without speaking, only from time to time puffing out a breath that was half a sigh, half a belch. Even when the peon

90

returned, had been told he would be paid later and had left, sullen, all P. V. Bagchi did was to sip tea noisily and masticate one by one his savoury stuffed singaras. From time to time he mumblingly repeated how much work answering their inquiry would mean, or protested again that he was there only to serve them.

At last Protima undid her purse and brought out her money-clip.

Yes, Ghote thought, I suppose she is right. Bribe is required. This idle fellow is no clerk Haripada.

From the clip one by one Protima began to snap out twenty-rupee notes. An officer of P. V. Bagchi's standing — cosily entrenched in his own room — would require a good deal more than a typist like the clerk Haripada.

P. V. Bagchi watched for a while. Ghote presumed he was counting. But in a little he was disillusioned. It seemed it had been merely a question of gathering up some necessary energy.

'Madam, if, as I think, you are producing that ever-increasing sum of money with a view to speeding my necessary inquiries and investigations, then let me inform you that there are officers of the administration here who are above sordid corruption. Yes, they may not be many. But they exist, and I humbly put myself in their ranks. Others' ability in office may be judged by the amount of the bribes they are known to take. I prefer to be considered lacking in efficiency.'

And, yes, Ghote thought with a jab of bitterness, no doubt you are lacking in efficiency. So far you have made not one move to consult any of the books or files on that shelf behind you. All right, I am knowing bribery is not good but, by God, I would prefer a man with a mattress stuffed with what Protima called in Bengali the other day *dui-nambari money* than this bloody pompous honest man.

'Mr Bagchi,' he broke out, 'are you even able to tell us what it is we are wanting to know? Are you able to say what exactly is meant by *right of passage*? If you are not we would go. Now.'

P. V. Bagchi swallowed the last mouthful of singara in one hasty gulp, choked, reached for his tea, found the cup was empty and finally managed, with an explosive belch, to straighten out his digestive system.

'My dear sir,' he said, singara spice issuing from his mouth in clouds, 'kindly give a public servant his due. Of course I am able to say.'

'What? Now? Without consulting any of legal tomes etcetera?'

'Of course, my dear sir. Do you think I have achieved the position of Office Superintendent, Land Ownership Section, without knowing what restrictions and prohibitions apply? Do you think I was bribing my way to my seat?'

'Not at all, not at all,' Ghote said hastily, fearing that the answer he wanted was about to get lost in a sea of self-justification.

'Very well then.'

P. V. Bagchi seemed disposed to accept the apology.

But not disposed to say more.

Protima joined battle now.

'Please, Mr Bagchi,' she said, bestowing on the pudding man her sweetest smile. 'Please, tell myself, someone who has never had your experience, just what is this right.'

'Madam, simple. Where right of passage is held to exist, and this is almost always with long-established properties in the city, it must imply that, although the title to any piece of land may not allow its owner or proprietor to devote a portion of same to a right of way, nevertheless when such passage may be in the public interest in certain circumstances this right may be alienated.'

Ghote had been following closely as a wheeling kite follows a sandwich in the hand of a careless open-air eater.

'What circumstances?' he asked.

'Oh, my dear sir, you are entering now upon a field of great complexity, and — '

'No. Let me ask one question. If one was in possession of a house with a large compound, say somewhere in South Calcutta, and there was possibly some reason why, say, a road might go through that compound, could right of passage then be granted?'

'But, my good sir, one would need to know full circumstances. Right of passage in this particular context is an almost obsolete concept. In many cases the right has existed so long in some particular area that it may be held to have fallen into total disuse. Very serious complications are most likely to exist. Legal proceedings would have to be undertaken. One cannot say. One cannot say.'

'But,' Ghote persisted, 'this right might be able to be granted in some properties in, say, South Calcutta now?'

'Oh, yes, yes, of course it might. However, observe, my friend, that, although I have attained a certain position in the administrative hierarchy here, I am not a barrister. I would not lay claim to such dignity. I am, I hope, a humble man. I cannot give an authoritative opinion.'

'But you can say what is likely?'

'Oh yes, my dear sir. How else would I have risen to sit in this seat if I were not able to do such?'

P. V. Bagchi began to puff himself up, frog-like.

'And it is likely future right of passage would exist still in the compound of some South Calcutta house, yes?'

'Oh, yes. But — '

But Ghote did not wait to watch the spectacle of the frog puffing still more, or collapsing. He took Protima by the arm, almost brutally, brought her to her feet and with a curt goodbye left.

'What are you doing?' she snapped as soon as P. V. Bagchi's door had closed behind them.

'Doing? I am taking you to somewhere where I can explain without us being overheard why Mr Dutt-Dastar is trying to make you sell your house.'

'But — But why? Why? What is this?'

He looked all round. In the dim high corridor with its red paan-spattered walls there was for the moment no one in sight.

'Why,' he said in an urgent whisper. 'I will tell you why in just only one word.'

'What — What is it? What is this?'

Then he spoke his one word.

'Wetlands.'

7

Passage from where to where, Ghote had asked himself when P. V. Bagchi's blatherings had begun to make sense to him. Yes, taking into account those just-seen words *with right of passage unimpeded*, it was clear that Protima's house must lie across some route to somewhere. A route that somebody very much wanted to be able to use. And one perhaps subject to some right or other. It must start at the house, he had told himself. At its very gates, once, as Protima remembers them, guarded by two darwans night and day, now rusted and unable even to be closed. But where would it end, this passage? Why should anybody want passage through the gates of the house to . . . where?

Answer: to the wetlands.

'What you were saying?' Protima whispered hoarsely in the dimness of the long corridor. 'Wetlands? What wetlands?'

'Wetlands, I am saying. Just only wetlands. You were telling before, remembering from your childhood days visiting your house and going up on to the roof. You were saying you could look far, far out into the countryside.

It was all green. So there must be some wetlands beyond the house.'

'What if?'

'We were hearing also from that taxi driver when we were going to the house about what he was calling U-traffic lakes, and — '

'What are you talking?' Protima's voice rose, reverberating in the high corridor. 'U-traffic. You full-scale idiot. It is *eutrophic*. It is eutrophic lakes that are supplying the good freshwater fish all Calcuttans so much love.'

He swallowed a small quota of resentment. Why did she never give him credit for knowing more English? Did she think only Bengalis were first-class English-speakers?

'The Sikh in that taxi was telling why there were protesters there at the Maidan,' he ground out. 'Because they are objecting to some plan to fill in more of those eutrophic lakes. And if that plan is carried out, there would be a need for a good road to those wetlands, first for taking whatsoever is needed to fill the lakes, then for access to each and every house they will build there. Yes?'

'Yes. If you must be talking this.'

'I must. I am thinking that road will start at your house itself.'

And now Protima did pay him her full attention.

'Start at the house? You are saying they want to drive a road through the compound? My compound? So that is why they are wanting my house. But they cannot have it. It is my house. I will not allow it.'

'Well, I am supposing they would be doing utmost to obtain. If you are not willing to sell, they may invoke this *right of passage*. And use whatever of corrupt methods they may find to enforce same.'

'Then what can be done? Something must be done.'

He saw her tense with concentration.

'Yes,' she burst out after a moment. 'Having the house inspected must wait. Now it is a question of finding out just exactly how they could take it from me. Tell me what must be done.'

More Bengali demandingness. For an instant he wondered if he really could endure staying in a city filled with such people. A down-plunge of misery overwhelmed him.

'Perhaps,' he said, 'we could insist to examine the document Mr Dutt-Dastar was taking so much of care not to let us see. That would be one first step.'

'Yes,' Protima answered at once. 'Yes, that

98

is what must be done. That is what you must do.'

'But why not you also? It is your house.'

'No, no, no. That is man's work. Definitely. You are an inspector of police. Bombay Crime Branch. For you it would not be too difficult.'

★ ★ ★

So at ten o'clock next morning Ghote found himself at A. K. Dutt-Dastar's chamber once more. He felt a little aggrieved. Protima had announced as they breakfasted — the only Indians there to tackle the British fare — that she was going to shop for saris.

'Saris? But — But you also could be coming to see Mr Dutt-Dastar.'

'No. Calcutta saris are the loveliest in India and I have not got a single one.'

Of course, he had thought. The loveliest, the best. Bloody Calcutta.

And myself left facing her *not too difficult* task of insisting to see that document.

But at least, he found, he was not now confronting the sort of obstruction put in his way on their first visit. The clerk Haripada was no longer, it seemed, under orders to refuse permission even to meet with his employer, despite the sharp exchanges of their last meeting. The upright, crop-haired, ballpoints-laden, inky-fingered old man abandoned his typing the moment he was asked if his master was free.

'I will see if Dutt-Dastar Babu can receive you,' he said, and walked creakily off to the inner room.

Why no intercom, Ghote thought once again with an inner fury brought on by his fears about the task that awaited him. What a mean fellow this Dutt-Dastar is. His own room well-furnished, book-lined and polished, this outer office bare and battered.

He cast a contemptuous glance at the rows and rows of time-scratched green filing cabinets all round, filled no doubt with documents dating almost back to British days, useless, crumbling, even ant-eaten.

And then he realized that the clerk Haripada by departing had given him an unexpected opportunity.

One look at the closed door of A. K. Dutt-Dastar's room, and he nipped round to the far side of the ancient table. There he took a good look at the page of typing in the ancient machine in front of him. All right, just some legalistic mumbo-jumbo, nothing to do with Protima's house. But the typeface exactly the same as the one he had contrived his one quick glance at. *With right of passage unimpeded*. Its old-fashioned letters unmistakable. The same heavy blackness, wet-looking and messy from one of the re-inked ribbons the clerk Haripada was made to use.

So, yes, yes, yes. Not the least doubt about it now. The document from which A. K. Dutt-Dastar had read those words, *with right of passage unimpeded*, had been under typewriting on this very machine. When they should not have been. When they should have been typed by some clerk belonging to whoever A. K. Dutt-Dastar had indicated, without mentioning any name, was the sender of that document. So A. K. Dutt-Dastar was up to some dirty game. Yes. No doubt about it.

But, if he is, he will never let the document, whatever it is, out of his hands. But, to get full proof of what dirty game is being played, I must somehow leave this chamber with that document itself in my hands. But how? How?

The door of A. K. Dutt-Dastar's room was pulled open.

'Dutt-Dastar Babu may see you now,' the clerk Haripada pronounced.

Ghote straightened his shoulders.

This time A. K. Dutt-Dastar, eyes still

concealed behind wrap-around glare glasses, rose smiling from his too-big chair, pushing himself up by its leather-padded arms.

'Mr Ghote,' he said. 'Am I not to have the pleasure of seeing your charming wife today?'

Who, Ghote said inwardly, was not one hundred per cent charming to you when last we met.

'She has gone for shopping, to buy saris.'

A. K. Dutt-Dastar wagged his head.

'Ah, the ladies, the ladies,' he said. 'Not but that our Calcutta saris are reputed to be the most beautiful in all India.'

Ghote needed nothing more.

'Mr Dutt-Dastar,' he said, or almost spat out. 'When we were here last you were reading to us from some document and you were then stating that one of the difficulties standing in the way of my wife occupying the house she has inherited — one of the many difficulties you were putting forward — was an objection from the owner of some nearby property. I am needing more information. May I please have the document in question? We are wishing to study same at length.'

'My dear fellow,' Mr Dutt-Dastar replied with unexpected quickness. 'I very nearly suggested yesterday that you took the document away with you. I realized from the close interest you were showing in it that you felt it was important to you. As indeed it is. It is. It will convince you — it will convince even your delightfully determined wife — that the objections to you staying in the house are truly insurmountable. Insurmountable, yes.'

Ghote felt more than a little disconcerted. He had expected battle: he was being offered peace.

'Very well,' he said. 'Then if you let me have the document I would no longer take up your time. You are no doubt busy.'

'Of course, of course. Though perhaps I might take a minute or so to explain the situation more fully. Some things, you may agree, are best dealt with man to man. However delightful the female element. Perhaps if I could demonstrate the advantages of an immediate sale to you, you may be able to convince your — Your charming wife.'

'Most kind,' Ghote replied, meaning just the opposite. 'But I do not like to conduct my wife's business for her. She is well able to undertake same herself.'

'I am sure she is. I am sure. Indeed, I have the evidence of my own eyes. And ears.'

'Then if I could have the document . . . '

Let him put it in my hands, he thought. Then, and then only, I will begin to think I have been mistaken in the man.

'At once, at once.'

The domed brass bell vigorously pinged.

The bald-headed, birthmarked peon appeared.

'Shibu, ask for the *Mrs Protima Ghote — Bombay* file and bring it immediately.'

'Jee, sahib.'

He limped out.

Not until the document from that file is in my hands, Ghote swore to himself, will I try even to find explanation for all this.

But it was not, after more time than Ghote thought reasonable, the birthmarked peon who came in. It was the clerk Haripada. And he spoke only one word.

'Misfiled.'

A. K. Dutt-Dastar sat up sharply in his too-big chair.

'What do you mean *misfiled?*' he shouted with more immediate anger than Ghote thought justified.

'Misfiled,' the clerk Haripada replied, either for emphasis or by way of answer.

'How has it become misfiled?' A. K. Dutt-Dastar raged on. 'Are you not responsible for the filing system? How many times have I stated this?'

The clerk Haripada visibly gathered himself up for a reply.

'Shibu has done it,' he said. 'I have to

leave my seat for Nature's purpose on some occasions.'

'Yes, yes. Of course. I am hardly the man to insist that you sit there never shifting from 9 a.m. till evening. I was saying that to you only yesterday. Leave your seat, leave your seat. Those were my very words.'

'Yes,' said the clerk Haripada.

'And you mean to tell me that in your absence, your necessary and excusable absence, that wretched Shibu attempted to put that file in its proper place?'

'It is no longer where it should be.'

'And you have looked elsewhere? In the drawer below, the drawer above?'

'There are many cabinets there. It could be anywhere.'

'Yes, yes. True. Certainly, too true. Anywhere. This is a calamity. A calamity.'

He turned now to Ghote.

'My dear sir, I cannot tell you how sorry I am that this has occurred. But occurred it has. We shall, of course, do our utmost to rectify the situation. But you must know that mistakes may happen, even in the best chambers.'

But Ghote knew all too well that no mistake had happened. A. K. Dutt-Dastar's *utmost* was no more than a form of words. The lawyer had guessed he himself had seen enough of that thickly typed document to have his suspicions. And he had acted cleverly. He could have simply removed the document, which must be too important to destroy, and have locked it away. But then this police detective from Bombay-side might have made a nuisance of himself, insisted on an explanation, demanded still to know what the document was.

And, yes, by God, I would have done.

So A. K. Dutt-Dastar had simply had the whole green-ink labelled *Mrs Protima Ghote — Bombay* file tucked away in the wrong place. It was an old trick, especially in the Delhi bureaucracy when some corruption matter was in train. *Lose the file*. If you needed some delay, nothing was better. If you needed to stall an investigation till you had found the right corruptible man to bribe into overlooking whatever was wrong, then there was no better way of managing the business.

But now . . . Now A. K. Dutt-Dastar could promise from one day to the next that no searches had revealed the missing file. And he may well have personally told the peon, Shibu, where to put it. Or he might have put it there himself.

And, yes, something had been a little wrong about the way the upright clerk Haripada had spoken. The way he had simply uttered that one cramped word, *Misfiled*. All right, he was one Bengali who did not find it necessary to say everything twenty times over and then add a dozen extra flourishes. But that single, muttered word had surely been altogether too terse. *Very sorry, Dutt-Dastar Babu, it seems file in question is temporarily unavailable.* That, or something like it, was what he should have said, and it would not have made too many demands on his unBengali-like reticence.

Then there had been A. K. Dutt-Dastar's responses. Too quick, if you thought about them. He had been too ready to fly into a rage, before the matter had been fully put to him. And those sly words when the clerk Haripada — again acting on orders? — had stiffly said that 'sometimes' he had to leave his seat for Nature's purpose. All that *I was saying that to you yesterday. Leave your seat.* And laughing in his sleeves at his own cunning. How he had, no doubt, actually uttered those very words when he had given the clerk Haripada orders about the file. Chalak, yes, bare-faced chalak.

But — the thought came to him like the swift fall of night — even if I am now knowing for certain a trick has been played, there is nothing I can do. I cannot go back

107

into that outer office and work through each and every one of those filing cabinets. There must be twenty-thirty of them. Each full to brim with buff-coloured files. Files, files, files. Reaching back, I was thinking only yesterday, perhaps to British days.

And among them that one green-ink file *Mrs Protima Ghote — Bombay*. Lost. Lost for ever. Or until A. K. Dutt-Dastar chooses to have it brought to light.

8

Protima stood in their room at the Fairlawn, its bed a shimmering spread of new Calcutta saris — But you may not be so rich as you are thinking, Ghote had said to himself in dismay — and glared at her husband as he told her what had happened at A. K. Dutt-Dastar's chamber.

'The file mislaid? But that is — It is monstrous. Monstrous. There is in that file each and every detail of the will I am benefiting from, and — No. No, it is worse. The file has that document in it, yes? The one that is a clear clue to nefarious dealing? So . . . So are you telling it has not been mislaid just only by error?'

'No,' Ghote said, 'it was not.'

'Then you must be thinking what I am beginning to think,' Protima said. 'Mr Dutt-Dastar is not at all a true, decent Bengali lawyer. He is some sort of utterly corrupt individual.'

Ghote forbore saying that he had had his suspicions of A. K. Dutt-Dastar from almost the moment they had met him. And that he had tried to pass on his doubts to her. It was enough for him that she had admitted, if not quite directly, that it was possible to be a Bengali and an utterly corrupt individual. Something that, ever since she had seen herself living the bhadrolok life, she seemed to believe was impossible.

But fate gave him no reward for his forbearance.

'Then, document or no document, we must expose him. You have definite indication that something is not right. Go with it to the police here. They are your Bengali colleagues. They will take up case.'

He sighed.

'Kindly think,' he said, with slogging depression. 'What is this indication you are stating I am having? It is one glimpse of a few words. In a document I am not even knowing what exactly it is. And even if some officer there is believing I saw what I was seeing, there is nothing to say definitely what crime has been committed. Or even that a crime has been committed at all till date.'

'Nonsense. That man Dutt-Dastar is totally corrupt. I know it. You even know it. You were saying it was so. You were saying some corruption is taking place over the wetlands project. Yes, the wetlands. It is that.'

'But — '

'No, no. No buts and butting. That is not

110

at all the way to go about it. With doubts and delays. That is what is wrong with this country. Everybody is knowing there is corruption. No one is daring to try to stop same.'

This was Bengali Protima once more, he thought. He felt a burden replaced. High-mindedness, it was fine. Noble. And, yes, if he had to admit it, there were perhaps more high-minded individuals in this city of Chief Minister Jyoti Basu, of Tagore and the saint Ramakrishna, of the mystic Aurobindo, than in any other city of India. Of the world even, admit that also. And it was fine, too, to back that high-mindedness with fiery zeal. Calcutta did that also.

But . . . But when the moment came to transfer high-mindedness into something to be done, then the picture was not so fine. Especially if the person who had to do whatever high-mindedness had said should be done was not some blazing-up Bengali but a simple, down-to-earth Bombaywalla.

Especially if it is myself.

'It is all very well to be saying that,' he broke out. 'To be insisting and insisting that something should be done to stop this. But what it is we have to stop? We are not knowing. We are not at all knowing.'

'You are knowing and knowing that there is a big corruption matter to do with the wetlands, the wetlands beyond my house. My house. My house which they are plotting and planning to take from me.'

Her eyes sparked with fury.

'It is just only to get you to sell,' he replied. 'To sell quickly now for what A. K. Dutt-Dastar is calling a decent sum before all the development in the wetlands is beginning.'

'To sell? Or to have taken from me? To have stolen from me? What is there of difference? I will not have the house I have in full legality inherited taken from me, the house I have dreamed all my life that I would one day stay in.'

Should I point out that she has not dreamed that? In all our days in Bombay she was never once mentioning? That she had, until just only ten-twelve days past, no idea she was going to inherit the place?

But there are times to be silent.

She rounded on him.

'No, something must be done. You must do it.'

'But what? What? What in reality? If I went to the nearest chowkey to here, wherever it is, and told some havildar there that there was a case of massive corruption that had to be investigated, what would he do? Put

112

me in the lock-up as one dangerous idiot, I am thinking.'

'But you should convince. Convince and convince.'

'With what? It comes back down to the same thing every time. We are really knowing nothing. Suspicions we have, yes. But it would take a person with the most sharp mind to see that such hints and guesses may amount to evidences. Evidences something is going on behind scenes here in your Calcutta.'

He knew at once that *your Calcutta* had been a mistake. But his anger at the situation he was being forced into had sent it jetting out.

However, the jibe brought an unexpected response.

'My Calcutta. But, yes, it is a good thing for you, husbandji, that you are in Calcutta and not in Bombay where someone would need convincing with evidence of two-three dead bodies before they were agreeing nefarious activity was taking place. But, no, you are here in Calcutta. You are surrounded by Bengalis, and Bengalis know how to think. You are wanting to know who would pay attention to these hints and guesses? Any senior Bengali police officer.'

'But nevertheless we are not knowing by

name one single one.'

'No? Very well, perhaps we are not. But that is not meaning we cannot find out such an officer. We have good Bengali friends to ask.'

'Friends? We have no friends here.'

'Nonsense.'

Damn her, that word again.

'Yes, nonsense, nonsense. We are having one very good Bengali friend, and you should be knowing it.'

He thought, whirringly rapidly, in response to the challenge. And found no answer.

'Who were we seeing our first morning in the city?' Protima asked scornfully. 'One very good friend of my cousin-uncle who was bequeathing me my house. We bhadrolok families support each other, you know. I could go to Bhattacharya Babu, even though I was meeting for the first time only, and I could ask whatsoever favour I was wanting.'

'So,' he said slowly, 'you could ask him if he was by chance knowing some senior Bengali police officer who would be ready to listen to even the glimmer suspicions I am having?'

'Of course.'

In two minutes they were out in Sudder Street and had secured a taxi.

They found Mr Bhattacharya, after they had
directed their driver some little way past the
squattered wreck of Protima's house, up on
the wide flat roof of his own house. He
was sitting looking out tranquilly over the
clutter of tumbledown hutments beyond his
compound, half-hidden in the sluggish smoke
of cooking fires.

Looking at the wetlands, Ghote thought
at once. But, as he stepped further on to
the roof, he saw that in fact hardly any
of the wetlands were visible at this point,
some quarter of a mile from Protima's
ruined inheritance. Just beyond the smoke-
shrouded hutments a sharp ridge scattered
with sprawling krishnachuda trees hid the
distant view. Only by looking well to one side
could there be seen, glittering in the sunlight,
three small lakes, swarming no doubt with
the hilsa, the boal, the khoi fish Calcuttans
devoured so eagerly.

Yes, he thought. Protima's house, our
house, is clearly the best place for a road
to the wetlands in this area. Perhaps the
only possible place.

As they approached, Mr Bhattacharya rose
from the broad seat where he had been sitting
in the attitude Ghote had over the past few

days come to think of as inseparably Bengali; right foot resting up on the seat beside him, leg bent almost double at the knee all but touching the chin, the full weight of his body bearing down on his left hip.

'Forgive me for not descending to welcome you,' he said. 'The truth is that I am an old man.'

'Sir, it would have pained us extremely to have made you go all the way down and then up again,' Ghote said, doing his best to match bhadrolok civility.

'But now you will take something to drink? My cook prepares some excellent lemonade.'

'Bhattacharya Babu,' Protima answered for them both. 'Much as we would enjoy, we are here on business, if that is not imposing on your kindness.'

'Not at all, not at all.' He gave them a roguish smile. 'What is it? Have you come, now that you have seen your house is uninhabitable, to buy me out of mine, lock, stock and barrel?'

'No, sir,' Ghote answered, deciding to cut across all further bhadrolok laughing civilities. 'I am sorry to have to tell you that, no sooner have we arrived in your beautiful city — '

Beautiful city. Damnation. I am immediately

116

falling into bhadrolok compliments myself. Must be something in the air.

He tried again.

'Sir, I am believing we have stumbled on one grave corruption scandal concerned with my wife's house.'

There. Said. And with Bombay-style directness.

'Corruption?'

The old man's softly drooping face showed immediate concern.

For a moment Ghote wished they had not come. Why should he plague a man at the serene ending of his days with such sordid and sharp business? But he had embarked on it. With Bombay-style directness. No going back.

So he began an account of everything that had made him suspect the corruption. First, the lie A. K. Dutt-Dastar had told about old Chattopadhyay Babu's willingness to sell the house.

'Oh, yes, yes,' Mr Bhattacharya interrupted, 'my old friend never had the least intention of selling, though now I come to think of it from time to time he did mention he had received offers. No doubt Dutt-Dastar's work, though I took it for no more than sick-bed ramblings. Amitji had told me so often how much he looked forward to going back to his own home.'

Ghote went on then to A. K. Dutt-Dastar's attempts to persuade Protima her house was uninhabitable, and the way he had kept the document he had been reading from concealed and the piece of luck that had brought to light those words *with right of passage unimpeded*. Finally he recounted their visit to Writers' Building and what they had learnt there from the insufferable P. V. Bagchi.

'Yes,' Mr Bhattacharya said sadly when he had finished, 'I had not met Dutt-Dastar until he arrived outside your house, but I had heard of him as Chattopadhyay Babu's lawyer. And of course, in Calcutta, Mr Ghote, everybody knows everybody. Which is to say rather that anyone belonging to one of some few hundred bhadrolok families, as we call them, has some acquaintance with everyone else in that quite extensive circle. The thousands and thousands of others in the city, Bengalis of the so-called chotolok families, the influential Marwari community, who incidentally run most of the commerce of the city, the Muslims, the thousands of Biharis who do most of the dirty jobs the city relies upon, the Parsis, the Jains, the Gujratis, some Maharashtrians from your part of the world, Mr Ghote, the Jews, the Armenians, the Chinese, the Sikhs . . . I could go on for ever. One knows they are there. One appreciates how they in their different ways make Calcutta what it is. But, and it is perhaps sad that this is so, we bhadrolok people tend to feel that Calcutta is ours and we are Calcutta.'

'And Mr Dutt-Dastar?' Ghote cautiously put in, half-resenting the spate of Bengali locquaciousness, half-respecting it.

'Oh, forgive me. Carried away. Carried away. A bhadrolok failing, I am afraid. No, about Dutt-Dastar. I have, as I was explaining, heard of him, or heard something of him, even though we had never met. A bad lot. I think it is hardly unfair to say that of him. Yes, a bad lot. Somehow the family fell into penurious circumstances. Both families, I should say. His branch of the Dutts, and his branch of the Dastars. We none of us are much good, we Bengalis, at making money. And indeed it is often all we can do to hold on to what we have inherited. You know the tale of the Nawab at the time of the arrival of the East India Company soldiers?'

'No,' Ghote said, trying to see how he could possibly get the conversation back to practical matters.

'Ah, you should. It tells one a good deal

about us. You see there was this chap, a Nawab, immensely rich, big house, bigger far than this, servants by the score, and he knew the British were coming together with their native allies. People on the other side. So he knew he had to flee. But all his servants had run off, and . . . And there was no one to tie his shoelaces.'

Ghote produced a smile.

'Yes, yes,' Protima echoed. 'My father also was telling that story.'

'Well,' Mr Bhattacharya went on, 'the Nawab somehow managed to secure his shoes and save his life, though I suppose it would make a better story had the poor unlaced fellow perished.'

'But about Mr Dutt-Dastar,' Ghote slipped in, feeling a quiver of pride at the cleverness of what he was about to say. 'Mr Dutt-Dastar has his shoelaces always well tied, isn't it?'

The old bhadrolok chuckled delightedly.

'Oh, my good chap, most neatly put. I can see, despite your Maharashtrian name, you are fast becoming a good Bengali. And, yes, Dutt-Dastar's laces are double-knotted, you may say. The fellow left Calcutta as quite a young man, and established himself in Delhi. A permit-broker, if the gossip is true. Nasty occupation. In any case he somehow acquired a certain amount of money and returned to our city — he had a law degree, of course, what educated Bengali does not — and bought this old chamber somewhere in North Calcutta. So I am not entirely surprised to hear he has his fingers where he should not. Calcutta may be above such sordid practices in principle, but there are always exceptions.'

'So, sir, what must I do?'

'Yes, my dear Ghote, what are you to do? The evidence you have that some wrongdoing has taken place, or is in train, is only of the scantiest. You can hardly go to the customary authorities.'

'Then, sir, I must let it lie?'

He hoped the old bhadrolok would say yes. Then all that could be done would be to take whatever they were offered for the house, leave Calcutta and let whatever illegalities were taking place simply happen. To go back to Bombay, to go back a good deal richer than he had ever thought they would be. To go back to duty on the very day his leave ended. To do then what good he could do.

But he knew this was not to be. He had been tentacle-gripped by the business and it would not let him go. And nor would Protima.

Before she could voice the opposition

he knew she would utter, he stepped in. Before even Mr Bhattacharya could answer that question he had been unable not to ask him.

'But, of course, sir, knowing what I know, suspecting what I am suspecting, I must do my level best to put one stop to whatever is going on.'

'Yes, Mr Ghote, I expected you to say that. But as to what is going on, well, I think my advice to you at this moment is: wait and see.'

He must then have seen the expression on impatient Protima's face.

'Ah, Mrs Ghote, do not be in too much of a hurry to equate me with the shoeless Nawab. I propose to do what I can to assist you. But I must make some inquiries first. Some inquiries of a legal nature — I, too, Mr Ghote, am qualified as a barrister though I have never practised — and then also some inquiries, shall we say, of a social nature. So I suggest that the day after tomorrow — I shall need that much time — if you would care to lunch with me at the Bengal Club I may have something to tell you.'

9

Ghote was hardly pleased at the delay Mr
Bhattacharya had imposed on his efforts to
get to the bottom of the business that was,
at the very least, preventing Protima coming
into full possession of her house. He felt
frustrated, too, at being caught up in an
investigation he was unable to pursue as he
would have done in Bombay. There, given
orders by the Additional Commissioner in
charge of Crime Branch, he would have
worked if necessary day and night. Now
he had to sit and wait till they met Mr
Bhattacharya for lunch at the Bengal Club.

Not the way to carry out any investigation.
A leisurely Bengali lunch. And at a club.
However, here in Calcutta, not an inspector
of police but an ordinary citizen, all he could
do was to wait. Or, as it turned out, to do
worse. To sightsee.

Protima had insisted.

'You are going to stay here in Calcutta.
You should know what the city has to offer.
All its riches.'

Could he say they might not be staying?
No. That would be telling her he believed she

would never get her house, that she should give in to A. K. Dutt-Dastar's insistence and agree to sell it. And that would mean submitting to the fact that they had been defeated by corruption.

And this he would not submit to.

'We should go to the Victoria Memorial,' Protima went on. 'It is not enough just only to have seen it from the Maidan. Or there are the Botanic Gardens. This is a good time of year for them. Not too hot. No one should live in Calcutta who has not seen the Great Banyan, largest in the world.'

He did want to see it. He had a lingering mild regret that he had not been able to do so on his only hurried, on-duty visit to Calcutta once before. But somehow he felt admitting that to Protima would seal for her his willingness to make the city his home.

And like an inflexible growth at the back of his mind was the thought that he still did not want to be part of this too exuberant city of joy.

'Too far to go to the Gardens now, and we would need more of time for Victoria Memorial,' Protima said. 'So full as it is of glories of Calcutta's past. But there is St John's Church.'

'A Christian church, why should I want to go there?'

'Oh, I was not meaning you should see it as a place of worship. If you were ever wanting that, I would take you to Kalighat Temple.'

'No,' he exclaimed. 'You know that — '

'Yes, yes, I am well understanding this husband of mine. I would have some truly hard work to get you inside Kalighat Temple. No, I am suggesting St John's Church for what it has to tell of the days when the city was founded by the famous East India Company.'

'All right,' he said quickly.

I have put up too many objections already. No need to be irritating her more. Let her show off this city she feels suddenly she has always belonged to. Let her give out one more history lesson, even if it is the British. Any time-pass will do. Until Mr Bhattacharya tells me what I am needing next to know.

So an hour later he found himself on the steps leading up to a Christian church. Dutifully he read a plaque, *Built in 1783 on Land Presented by Maharajah Nabo Kishen Bahadur.*

'Maharajah Nabo Kishen,' Protima said, 'was the man who entertained Clive of

India after the Battle of Plassey to a rich, rich celebration of Durga Puja. By claiming and stating Clive's victory was one and the same with Goddess Durga's victory over the demon Mahisasura he was founding the tradition of celebrating that puja which is going on still even in these times.'

The little historian.

And there was more.

'This building, which is almost precise copy of one church in London by the name of St Martin's in some fields, was built by one Lieutenant Agg, Bengal Engineers. You see, even in the far-off days Bengal was foremost in building.'

'Yes,' Ghote said, tiredly.

He was beginning to suspect that, whenever his back was turned, his wife was going through some guidebook she had got hold of. How else, when she had left Calcutta before she was ten years of age, could she know so much about the city?

They entered the building.

Quiet, yes. Gloomy also. Rows of dark wooden cane-seated chairs with arms. At the back some huge painting of Europeans in the past. In large colourful robes eating some meal.

'By the famed artist Zoffany,' Protima said. 'Under the title 'The Last Supper'.'

126

Yes. Guidebook. Definitely.

'You have brought me here just only to see that?'

'No, no. Come this way. Come. We can go into the Council Room, very historical. It was where Warren Hastings used to sit. You know, the Englishman who came after Clive as Governor.'

Ghote did know, though Clive and Hastings were not much more than history lesson names to him. But he was not going to confess the extent of his ignorance to his wife. He had already had all the lessons he wanted from her.

He followed her up a short flight of polished stairs and into the Council Room. A room surprisingly small, with in the middle an eight-sided table covered with a green baize cloth. In a corner, with a faded notice on it, there was the big chair the great Warren Hastings had sat in.

And he got another history lesson after all, though a mercifully short one.

'Yes, look at that chair,' Protima said. 'In it there sat the man who was ruling from here all of Bengal. A name famous in history. He was . . . He was . . . '

Guidebook facts not so well recalled as they might be?

'Yes, when he was going back to England,

there he was impeached.'

'Impeach? What is impeach?'

He guessed that she would be unsure. But he felt he had a right to make her wriggle a little. A right earned by all the Calcutta-this and Calcutta-that he had suffered since their arrival.

'Impeach? It is some kind of trial. They were accusing Hastings of amassing great wealth by illegal means. I think after six years he was acquitted.'

So, he thought, even then the high-and-mighty were obtaining money by corrupt method. And in the end not paying any penalty.

'Yes, yes, I remember now. Hastings was dying in retirement in UK, in some poverty and busy studying our Bengali culture.'

All right, perhaps not as corrupt as he might have been. But touched by corruption. Yes.

'I think I have seen all I am wanting,' he said, his mind flooded once again with thoughts of the dubious affair he had just touched with the tips of his fingers.

Will I ever grasp more? he asked himself. Will in the end I have to concede that I cannot pull down even one piece of what I know is there?

He had hoped that Protima would give way

to his plea of having seen all he had wanted. But he ought to have known better.

'No,' she said. 'There is more to see about Mr Warren Hastings. His house is still here just as it was in those old days, somewhere in Alipore. They tell that on nights when the moon is full you may hear his ghost. On the full-moon night we were coming here to Calcutta, Laxmi Poornima, we might have heard his coach with its four horses halting under the portico while he was going inside to search in a frantic manner for some papers he had lost. Yes, this afternoon itself we must go also.'

He sighed.

Lost papers in history days. But what about that paper of today, lost somewhere in A. K. Dutt-Dastar's battered old green filing cabinets? Lost on purpose. Never to be found?

'And outside in this churchyard there is more,' Protima said.

More. More guidebook pages she must have gone through.

He allowed himself to be led out. Nothing else for it.

Solemnly they inspected the tomb of the man said to have founded Calcutta more than three hundred years before, Job Charnock — Jobus Charnock, the inscription said.

'Jobus,' the little historian chipped in, 'was one very, very fine man. When he was seeing a widow just only about to throw herself in suttee on late husband's pyre he was rescuing her and the same night marrying. For twenty years they were living a happy life till she was dying, and then and thereafter Jobus was sacrificing one cockerel each year on her death day.'

Oh, but we also have been happily married twenty years, Ghote thought in sudden panic. Will Protima soon come to her very end? Well, yes, if she was wanting I would kill one cockerel per annum also.

'And here,' the still well alive guidebook reader went relentlessly on, 'is the memorial to the English men and women suffocated to death in what was known as the Black Hole of Calcutta. Not as many dead as it is always stating, and also this famous Black Hole was just only a guard room where some prisoners had been put for the night. You cannot be believing everything you may read, you know.'

'Yes, very true,' he agreed, hoping that falling in with her might bring to a quick end this chant of praise even to the city of the Black Hole.

It did not. After Protima had had her Bengali afternoon sleep she insisted on going to look at Hastings House, even if by daylight there would be no ghostly coach and horses to see. What he did see, however — the well-preserved white columns of the portico, the well-ordered grounds — reminded him all too sharply of the greened-over, plaster-fallen pillars in front of his wife's eaten-away house and the mysterious threat to it that he had touched with the tips of his fingers.

But at last it was over. History book, or guidebook, closed for the day.

And tomorrow, Ghote thought, at the Bengal Club will Mr Bhattacharya have something to say that will get my fingers nearer grasping the slippery truth somewhere hidden?

★ ★ ★

Mr Bhattacharya did have something to say. Eventually. A club servant whisked them from the entrance just behind the wide stretch of Chowringhee, through tall rooms, past a long bar in deeply glowing dark wood with clusters of comfortable armchairs facing it and on into the green-and-beige decorated dining room. There the aged bhadrolok was waiting for them, wearing not his customary beautifully hanging dhoti but a lightweight suit with, at his neck, a tie. Ghote admitted hastily

131

to himself that Protima had been right in insisting he, too, wore a tie, his only one. On the table at which Mr Bhattacharya stood the thick starched white cloth was arrayed with heavy silver cutlery and smoothly polished tankards.

Will I have to drink so much of beer? Ghote panicked.

But he ought to have counted on Mr Bhattacharya's bhadrolok understanding and courtesy.

'Mrs Ghote, can I order you something to drink? Most of the ladies here go for Coca-Cola nowadays, since we are permitted to make it in India. Will that suit you?'

Protima said that it would, and so Ghote, most occasional of drinkers, was able to follow suit.

And Mr Bhattacharya was yet more understanding. Once a turbaned and cummerbunded waiter had decorously served them with soup — it was a procedure that took not a little time — he leant confidentially forward.

'Now,' he began, 'I know you will be anxious to hear if I am able to bring you the help I was offering. I am sorry indeed that I had to make you wait as long as I did. But I wanted first to refresh my memory of the law affecting what you were calling *right*

132

of passage, and I wanted, too, to discuss the matter with a few chosen friends. Discussion you know, Mr Ghote, is our Bengali vice. An *adda*, as we call it, may take place wherever any two-three, six-ten of us happen to congregate, at a tea stall, in this club, in our crowded coffee houses, anywhere. And it was to an adda that I wished to put what might be the moral implications of investigating a corruption affair when you cannot be sure that it even exists. Is it right, I had asked myself, to stir up mud when there may be nothing to be found underneath? Would that cause more harm than it would do good?'

Ghote had begun to chafe as this long Bengali introduction pushed further and further away any indication of what it was that he could do. But now he felt a sudden jab of despair.

Had this bhadrolok fellow summoned them to this posh, posh club just only to make them believe once more that they should do nothing?

But evidently, however much as a guest he was doing his best not to show his feelings, Mr Bhattacharya had sensed he was unhappy.

'My dear fellow, I have digressed. It was wrong of me. But I will allow myself no

133

further licence. The fact is: I have to tell you, brutally I am afraid, that you have been grossly misinformed.'

So I am right. He is saying *forget*.

But Protima had jumped in.

'Misinformed? Misinformed? Who has dared?'

'One,' Mr Bhattacharya answered, unperturbed, 'whose name you said, if I remember rightly, was P. V. Bagchi.'

'Office Superintendent, Land Ownership Section, Writers' Building,' Ghote tapped in. 'But, please, how was such an office-holder misinforming?'

'His legal knowledge does not appear to be as reliable as one might expect,' Mr Bhattacharya replied. 'An hour spent in the library here has made me rather better acquainted with the facts. Let me tell you that there is no such thing in our law as the *right of passage* your P. V. Bagchi was leading you to believe existed.'

'But we were seeing those words — My husband was seeing.' Protima swung round to Ghote. 'Or were you making some mistake. You duffer.'

'No, no,' Mr Bhattacharya intervened. 'I assure you, my dear lady, your husband almost certainly saw those words. But, I think I am right in hazarding the guess, that the document which that deplorable fellow Dutt-Dastar was reading from, or even appearing to read from — that document he was so careful not to let you have full sight of — must have been something like a memorandum compiled by himself for the use of his principal. His principal, I must say, in what does begin to look like a scandal of some proportions. The reason that phrase *right of passage* was there, I have come to believe, was to state to this principal the importance of securing passage one way or another through, my dear Mrs Ghote, the compound of the house you have inherited from my good friend Amit Chattopadhyay. And, yes, I have used the words *a scandal of some proportions* not without weighing them.'

'Then,' Ghote said, grasping the situation, 'Mr Dutt-Dastar has been so concerned to persuade my wife to sell the house in order that some gentleman — and I am wondering will we ever discover who it is — can drive a road through and out to the wetlands where it is proposed to make a valuable new colony.'

'So it would seem.'

For once Mr Bhattacharya's Bengali verbosity had deserted him. Ghote saw it as a tribute to the seriousness of the illegal

135

activity it seemed they had touched now with more than fingertips.

And who was this principal Mr Bhattacharya had seen as lying behind what he had labelled a scandal of some proportions? No telling, of course. But it must be someone of influence. Much influence.

He felt a shiver of apprehension run up his spine.

Now their waiter approached again, holding rock-steady a large silver platter.

'Ah,' Mr Bhattacharya exclaimed. 'Now here is a custom of the Bengal Club that I fear I must explain to you. A custom established, I would venture to guess, in the full flush of the British days, and preserved by tradition ever since. Between the first course at luncheon here and the fish, which you, my dear madam, as a true Bengali must be looking forward to, we always have served, irrespective of what has gone before, irrespective of what is to come after — and let me reassure you, Mr Ghote, you will not be subjected to fish unless you have already become a Bengali addict — an omelette. I am sure you will find them delicious.'

Back to Bengali talkativeness once more, Ghote noted. It seemed even the looming scandal could not put a cap on that spouting fountain. Or was it perhaps that the elderly bhadrolok could not for long bring himself fully to face the ominous truth?

The waiter placing a small, perfectly cooked omelette on each of their fresh plates, asked Mr Bhattacharya if all was satisfactory and then bore off his huge platter to other tables.

'So, sir,' Ghote said firmly, looking at Mr Bhattacharya with some anxiety, 'what are we to do now?'

'Ah, what is to be done next is the question I contrived to bring up at the adda I became part of last night. Mind you, I never referred to specific matters. Wholly a case of *if for instance one happened to . . .* '

'And what was decided?' Ghote shot out, forking up a mouthful of omelette.

Mr Bhattacharya smiled.

'My dear fellow, it is plain you have never taken part in a Calcutta adda. A decision is the last thing ever to be arrived at. No, the point of it is the talk itself.'

'But what of use is that?'

Ghote knew the moment the words, bitterly expressed, had exploded from him that he should not have said them.

But Mr Bhattacharya did not take exception.

'Yes,' he said, 'I know what you must feel, my dear chap. I know what anyone not bred and born a Bengali must feel about our

137

genius for talk — I claim that word *genius* — and our severe lack of talent for action. Nevertheless I would suggest that quantities of talk are not after all such a bad thing. All right, one leaves an adda with one's head full of contradictory notions. You might say that no decision could arise from them. But those contradictory notions are there in one's head, and, you know, sometimes, not always but sometimes, after they have swirled about there for a little, all of them, they come to form a pattern. And in the end one does have the wherewithal to make a decision.'

Ghote found he was thinking.

After a moment or two he noticed that he had the last mouthful of omelette poised on his fork in front of him, and it was slowly slipping off. Hastily he transferred the pale yellow morsel to his mouth.

He swallowed. And spoke.

'Yes. Yes, I see that the Bengali way may have some advantages.'

Mr Bhattacharya smiled once more.

'So,' Ghote said, 'what pattern was at last forming inside your head? Or has that final outcome not yet been reached?'

'Oh, yes, my dear fellow, the pattern has formed. I have come to a conclusion.'

10

Mr Bhattacharya sat there at the Bengal Club's white-clothed, silver-laden table looking pleased with himself.

Bhadrolok, Ghote thought, all his prejudices — only just shifted by what Mr Bhattacharya had said about the advantages of the adda — coming swirling back.

'Yes indeed, my dear chap, the pattern formed. All the gossip, speculation and, yes, mere chatter of last night's talk over our little supper of hilsa roe in lemon juice, with a litre or two of Starka to accompany it, shifted and cleared in my head. And then I saw the answer to my seemingly casual inquiry about what to do in circumstances parallel to your own, my dear Ghote, Mrs Ghote. It was, yes, to go unofficially, unofficially mind, to a very senior policeman. I regret to say that perhaps an official approach might fail of its intent. If this business will in the end benefit some person high within the West Bengal Government, and, however far beyond any corruption our exemplary Chief Minister is, one must take into account the fact that such people occasionally have what they are inclined to call *good friends in the police*. High-rank officers, to put it bluntly, whom they can bribe — if not with money then with good postings and advancement — to turn a Nelson's eye to their misdoings. However, one of the people I was talking to here at the club happens to be connected by marriage, or rather in our bhadrolok way by various linked marriages, to a certain senior police officer whom he is happy enough to vouch for.'

Ghote checked an impulse to pounce. He wanted to jab out *What is the name of this senior officer? Who he is? When can I see?*

But he had come to realize that this was not the way to go about it with an old bhadrolok like Mr Bhattacharya.

'Yes,' Mr Bhattacharya went on. 'That, of all the suggestions made, whether seriously or in a somewhat bantering tone, was the one that seemed to me, by as it were the light of day, to be the answer. But, remember, it was by no means the only contestant jockeying, like one of those fellows crouching on the back of a horse at our celebrated racecourse, to come to the forefront of my mind. And some of those contestants, those riders as you may say, those suggestions, were not without merit. There was, for instance, a remark made by the editor, in fact, of one of Calcutta's premier journals. And take careful note of what he put forward. Not that his own newspaper should send some sharp-nosed reporter to hunt around what little we know of this scandal. No. His notion was — and I thought it a good one, and a credit also to its proponent — that one should discreetly draw the attention of *The Sentinel* to the business. You know *The Sentinel*, my dear fellow?'

'No,' Ghote answered, once again refraining from saying something like *If you think going to this senior police officer is a better way, then for God's sake let me have his name.*

But Protima was not going to let anything to the credit of Calcutta go unpraised.

'*The Sentinel*,' she said. 'Really you should be knowing it. It is the foremost crusading paper of India, one knocking into very much a cocked hat Bombay's old *Blitz* or anything else. More corruption exposed than anywhere else in the world.'

'Well,' Mr Bhattacharya intervened, 'perhaps that is going a little far. But it is true to say that *The Sentinel* has more than once tackled corruption issues that no other newspaper in this city of a hundred newspapers liked to touch. However, excellent though that suggestion was, it was cried down by all and sundry at the little adda I put your case to, my dear chap. If this business is as much a serious affair as you are saying, Bhattacharya Babu, they were telling me, then *The Sentinel* has not got the weight for it. It lacks the ability finally to persist. Eventually with *The Sentinel* it comes down to *Why quarrel with the crocodile when you share the pond*, as our Bengali saying has it. And there was another case made by my friends over that lemon-doused hilsa roe. A case, I must confess, that much impressed me. It went something like this: it is evident that the person you have cited, or invented, has by chance caught a whiff of what must be a truly major piece of corruption, but should he thoughtlessly pursue that, regardless of what may happen? And the answer some of my fellow participants at our adda put forward was that the fellow whose case I had put to discussion would be very well advised to say to himself that there is nothing he can do. That, in short, he should leave well alone. Or, in this instance, leave ill alone. But in the end I thought that particular proposal, though there was much to be said for it, was, well, perhaps premature.'

And now Ghote could no longer hold back the question that had been boiling and bubbling in his head.

'Sir, who is it that I must go to?'

'Ah, the man of action. I must not forget, my dear chap, that you are not simply the Bombay jamai of your Bengali wife but a detective officer, a bringer of criminals to swift justice. So, let me tell you. The man you should see, and indeed the man I have already arranged for you to see — we Bengalis are not always all talk, you know — is one Assistant Commissioner Bhowmick. He is not directly concerned with fraud and corruption, you understand. He is, in fact, I gather, one of those responsible for attempting to do something about our traffic problems — the worst in India, you know, by far the worst — and he has a fine reputation for curbing the incessant bribe-taking of the traffic police, their demands, too, for free snacks and cups of tea or paans from paan-stalls. So the heart evidently in the right place. And my informant spoke very highly of him. A cousin of his, or the cousin of a cousin, something of that sort. Do let me know eventually if I have found you the right chap.'

'Assistant Commissioner Bhowmick,' Ghote repeated. 'And at what time am I to see?'

'Ah, you think you'll be with him in half an hour, eh? You tiger. But, no. No, I'm afraid I have not been able to arrange anything before the day after tomorrow. Always best,

143

I think, not to give the impression of wanting anything too urgently. I have always found you get what you ask for much more certainly in that way. Yes, go roundabout. Roundabout. That at least is my way, the Calcutta way, you might say.'

'Yes, sir,' Ghote said. 'Good advice.'

But he hardly meant it.

* * *

Ghote declined, with firmness, to do any sightseeing during the period of nearly forty-eight hours before his appointment with Assistant Commissioner Bhowmick. He found he was filled with a not unpleasant feeling that matters were for the moment out of his hands. There was nothing for him to do until he met Assistant Commissioner Bhowmick about the dark business that had risen up on him.

No need just now to put my shoulder to the wheel, he said to himself. Sit idle and wait only till I am seeing that man.

He had expected Protima to insist on more trips round Calcutta. But to his surprise she accepted his very first attempt at rejecting both the Victoria Memorial and the Botanical Gardens.

'If you are doing nothing to be making

sure I would get my house,' she said. 'I will go once more to Kalighat Temple. Perhaps I have too long neglected Goddess Kali while I was staying in Bombay. Perhaps she is teaching me by all this trouble-bubble one sharp lesson.'

Or perhaps, Ghote thought wickedly, you have not yet read enough of the next pages in your guidebook.

But when she said she ought to go first to the bazaar at the Armenian Ghat to buy flowers for the goddess, he volunteered at least to accompany her there. If he had his anti-priestcraft principles, he was prepared for his wife's sake to go to the very edge of them.

He felt when they got to the riverside bazaar under the shadow of the giant latticework of the Howrah Bridge that his loyalty was being rewarded. The whole tumbledown wharf — there since Calcutta's long-ago commercial heyday — was a sight to see. A great mass of flowers of every variety and colour, baskets piled with ropes of jasmine and tuberoses, huge gunnysacks of dazzling yellow sunflowers and, as dazzling, orange marigolds placed in the water at the river's edge. Yellow, blue, purple and bright red hibiscus, flowers of every shape and colour, far more than he was able to name, joyously assaulted his senses. Everywhere the scents of them, heavy and almost intoxicating, invaded his nostrils. The air all round was almost yellow with the clouds of pollen, overpowering even the city's ever-present dust. His spirits took a great upward leap.

Yes, there were flower markets in Bombay and in every city in India. But this seemed, if only because of the laughter-filled shouts of the hundreds of vendors, somehow more exulting, more passionate, more life-loving than any other. It outdid them all.

I think, he found himself saying inwardly, I think perhaps I really could like to live in this place.

His delight scarcely faded as Protima went endlessly from vendor to vendor, making up her mind, unmaking it, deciding for, deciding against. But this, too, he told himself, is part and parcel of Calcutta life. I could get to go along with even this.

Perhaps.

By the time Protima had made her purchase, a crimson garland of hibiscus, the morning bazaar was drawing to its close. Basket after basket of unsold blooms were being carried down to the water's edge and tumbled out in front of a gathering of wandering cows, evidently regular visitors, for them to plunge their noses into their fragrant meal.

Putting Protima into a taxi for the Kalighat Temple, he made his way slowly and thoughtfully back to the Fairlawn Hotel.

Calcutta? Do I like it, or do I hate it? All this passion and excitement, is it for me or is it one hundred per cent too much? Protima, my Bengali wife, do I want to throw in my lot with her? Or will I, if I stay here, never be truly contented?

He had come to no decision before he found himself under the wide arch with its green, yellow-edged letters, *Fairlawn Hotel*. Sighing in puzzlement, he climbed the stairs to their room. There he could think of nothing better to do than stare for most of the rest of the day out of the window from which on their first evening in the city they had watched the last throes of the Laxmi Puja, bright rocket trails red and gold against the moonlit sky. He found a source of unaccountable interest — When I am meeting Assistant Commissioner Bhowmick how much will he help? — in the huge garbage pile he could see through the all-pervasive drifting dust in the lane below.

It was subject, he found, to constant change. Mostly this came from the ever-arriving additions to it. There seemed never to be any major subtractions, no Corporation carts arriving to shovel anything away. Instead people from the tumbledown houses and the shacks nearby constantly came with the scraps they could not finally eat, with objects that disrepair had made totally impossible to use, with the dangling bodies of dead cats. From the start there had been, too, an especially putrid reek, every now and again sharply tickling his nostrils as a puff of breeze moved along the lane. It was coming, he eventually realized, from the corpse, in the last stages of decay, of a large dog.

He wondered whether it would stay where it was on one side of the huge heap until it at last disintegrated altogether. Or would some Corporation worker eventually arrive to smother it or even remove it.

There were minor removals, however. But not conducted by any human agency. And there was a strict order among the removers. First on the scene, but first too to be scared from it, were the crows, hopping and pecking. Soon they yielded to a pair of cats, lean and mangy but alive. They in turn were succeeded by a rootling black pig. A single growling and snapping pidog chased away the pig, and finally a wandering bull came charging at the shoulder-high heap with wild swings of its heavy head and, once all opposition was chased away, turned to and tore from the mouldering pile whatever suited its appetite.

But, just as he became aware of the room-bearer quietly beginning his work behind him, even the bull was shoved aside. It seemed, typically of a Bengali he thought, not to be as fierce as its charges at the pi-dog had indicated. Now at last a man in a battered khaki uniform had appeared. Ignoring everything but the dead dog, he unwrapped a length of rope from round his waist and with it lassoed the reeking corpse and dragged it off.

The room-bearer, who had idly joined him at the window, explained what had happened. The man hauling the foul-smelling body away was, he said, a Corporation jamadar who during the night had dumped the dead dog at the side of the mound, there to stink out the whole neighbourhood. This afternoon the fellow had appeared at the hotel reception desk. And had been given his usual bribe to remove the offensive object.

Bribery not so bad, Ghote thought as he left the room to the bearer. In this way the worst odours and putridity are got rid of, and a poor man also ends up a little better off.

The hotel's proprietress, dressed today in a chiffon blouse of purest white and a blue skirt ironed to the last degree, was in the entrance hall when he got down there, giving brisk orders to the servant who each day took her white, white poodle dog for its walks.

'Ah, Mr Goat,' she said. He had corrected her pronunciation of his name — natural enough in Bengal where a Bose is just one syllable — twice before, but now he gave up. 'If you are going to be here all afternoon, let me remind you tea is served at a quarter past four, not later. We have a very nice fruit cake always. You will enjoy that. Come at once when the gong is sounded.'

Her dog-walker had left. She turned and ascended the stairs to her private apartment.

A fellow guest, a smartly bearded Sikh in blazer, blue turban and knife-edge trousers, gave Ghote a conspiratorial wink.

'Better be on parade on the dot, old man. Memsahib doesn't really care for Indians, you know. We weren't allowed in at all, any of us, until recently.'

'Thank you. But I am thinking fruit cake is not what I am liking at this time of the day.'

So that is why, he thought, there has been somewhat of stiffness when we have come down to that breakfast. It was not because Protima and I were not on time. To the minute. We were. It is because that cunning Dutt-Dastar put us into this altogether British-like place.

Well, when I tell Assistant Commissioner Bhowmick what he has been attempting to do, he will find his chalak has not at all paid off.

He secured the day before's copy of *The Times of India* Bombay edition, and took it out to the hotel's pleasant little leafy courtyard. There, mercifully alone, under the coolly disparaging gaze of a plaster copy of the Venus de Milo, he sat at one of the green plastic marble tables and read. *Ex-Prime Minister on Corruption Charge.*

He groaned softly aloud. Corruption, corruption, corruption. Suspected even in the highest places, known of beyond doubt in place after place lower in society. Would it ever be rooted out? Could it be rooted out?

He turned the page. But, once more, found all the Bombay news, even of the scandals and scams, deprived of the savour he would have relished only a week earlier.

If I am not to be any kind of a Bombayman hence-forth, he said to himself, then what is there here of interest and meaning also?

A sharp hissing sound broke in on his gloomy reverie.

It was loud enough and insistent enough to make him look all round for its source.

151

In half a minute he spotted it. At the top of one of the courtyard's walls a head had been thrust through the tangle of vegetation growing up from a row of big reddish pots below.

Plainly the insistent hissing had issued from the pair of thick lips in the face staring in at him. But there was something else also about the face.

Then, as the head was pushed even further in, he realized what it was. All down its left-hand side there ran a thin, snake-like birthmark.

The peon from A. K. Dutt-Dastar's chamber.

But could it really be him? What had the fellow's name been? Ah, yes. Shibu.

'Shibu, it is you?'

'Jee, sahib. I am wanting to see. But they saying no natives allowed. Just only servants.'

'I see. But why are you here itself? You are bringing a chit from Dutt-Dastar Babu? They should have let you leave it at the desk.'

'No chit, sahib.'

'Then what it is? Are you wanting myself?'

'Jee, sahib.'

'Well, say what you have got to say and jump down.'

'No, sahib. Talking wanted.'

152

'Talking? What talking? Tell whatsoever you have got to tell here and now.'

'No, sahib. Much of talk needed. Private. Very-very private.'

He wondered what to do. What the devil could the fellow be wanting? Something of *very-very private*. But what? What?

Curiosity won. After all, the fellow did come from the chamber of that proven liar A. K. Dutt-Dastar.

'Jump down. I will come out into Sudder Street.'

★ ★ ★

Outside, amid the lazing throng of Western backpack tourists, of wretched dealers in poor quality 'brown sugar' heroin, of vegetable vendors, of beggars, of kerbside barbers skilfully swishing their razors round the scantily soaped faces of their squatting customers, of drivers leaning out of their battered vehicles to call to every passing tourist 'Want taxi? Want taxi?', Ghote eventually spotted the peon's bald head.

He pushed his way over to him.

'Well, what it is you are wanting?'

'Sahib, it is what you are wanting.'

'What do you mean? What do you think I could be wanting?'

153

'Mislaid, sahib.'

'Mislaid? Mis — ' Light dawned. 'That file? The file Dutt-Dastar Babu was saying you had put in wrong place? You have it?'

'Jee, sahib.'

'Where? Where is it?'

He looked at the shambling, birthmarked fellow. There was nothing he was carrying. He had nowhere to conceal anything anywhere about his flapping khaki shorts and dirt-seamed khaki shirt, let alone a large buff file with the green-ink words *Mrs Protima Ghote — Bombay* scrawled across it.

'What are you telling?' he shouted over the hubbub of the street all round.

A seller of oranges was calling, 'Yaagh, yaagh. Yaagh, yaagh,' just behind him.

'Sahib, I have it. Misfile file.'

'No. I am not at all believing. Where it is? Where it is?'

'Sahib, not far. But when it is matter of very good price is best not to keep in open.'

He felt a little affronted. Didn't this fellow know he was a senior Bombay policeman? He wouldn't . . . Well, perhaps there were officers of his rank who might. And there could even be some in the Calcutta force.

'All right,' he said. 'But you may give now. I will find you some chai-pani.'

'Chai-pani. Tea water only. By Kali, I will eat file first,' Shibu's indignation rose up over the noise of the grating traffic, the shouting vendors, the jabbering Bengalis.

'No,' Ghote answered. 'You were mislaying my wife's file. You have found same now. It is your bounden duty to hand over. But I will show I am grateful to some extent.'

'Shibu not mislay. Dutt-Dastar Babu giving order. You want? Five hundred rupee.'

Shibu's answer, brief and plain.

'No. Do you think I offer bribes? Not everyone who is coming into Dutt-Dastar Babu's chamber is a giver of bribes. Learn that.'

'Five hundred rupee.'

Shibu simply stood in front of him. Leaning towards his bad leg. But not moving in any way.

And at once he realized why. The fellow had believed refusing to meet the sum demanded was simply the classic opening move in bargaining over a bribe.

And here he was himself, not moving any more than the bribe-taker.

So am I going to pay him? Will I sink each and every one of my principles? Oh, to shell out a few rupees to someone like the clerk Haripada, as I was trying to do, for speed money. No harm in that. A few rupees oil the wheels. But this? Five hundred rupees is not such a small sum.

But . . .

But that file contains perhaps full details of a major corruption scandal. It may even name the man who is behind that former permit-broker A. K. Dutt-Dastar. Getting hold of it may break a huge criminal conspiracy. And secure Protima her house.

So what to do? Stick to principles only? Tell this money-greedy fellow to take the file back and put it where A. K. Dutt-Dastar has hidden it? Or give him his five hundred rupees, small fortune for him — and I will not bargain over a bribe, no — and get evidence to take tomorrow to Assistant Commissioner Bhowmick? Evidence that he will have to act upon?

'Do you think I am carrying rupees five hundred in my pocket itself?'

'No, sahib. But I know gentleman like you can get same. Soon as you are giving, you will be having file *Mrs Protima Ghote — Bombay.*'

That settles it. He is in possession of that file, definitely. No doubt he has it tucked away somewhere quite near. Where he is able to keep his eye on it. Behind some scraps of rubbish. Under a loose paving stone. Anywhere. Anywhere safe.

'If I am going for five-ten minutes only, I will find you here itself, yes?'

'Jee, sahib. Not move. Not ek inch.'

It took him a little more than ten minutes. He had to go back into the hotel, persuade the receptionist at the flimsy marbled counter to open the safe behind him, show his identification, get hold of the purse where they had put the money Protima had cashed from the cheque A. K. Dutt-Dastar had given her and then extract, his back turned, exactly five hundred rupees from it.

And after that there had been the business of the purse being put back into the safe and watching it being signed for. With laborious care.

He ran out, managed to slow to a walk through the courtyard — if Shibu thought he was so anxious he might put up the price — and sauntered into the noisy, bustling, dust-shrouded street again.

Shibu was there.

Exactly where he had been before. But, clutched hard in both his hands, there was now a buff file with, easily to be seen, scrawled writing in green ink on it.

He confronted him.

'The file.'

'Money.'

All right, let the fellow get the money first.

He watched the calloused fingers riffle through the notes and the thick lips silently counting.

'Correct.'

Shibu thrust the file towards him.

'Here, sahib.'

He could hardly believe he had it. The deliberately mislaid file. But it was in his possession. Here. One swift look inside, while keeping a no-tricks eye on Shibu, and he knew that he was looking at the very papers A. K. Dutt-Dastar had had on his desk. Yes, there was the document in heavily smudged typing that had included those words *with right of passage unimpeded.*

Here. Now. In his hands. The evidence.

11

He hurried back in and up to their room, relieved to find when he got there that the bearer had finished his work. The flowered curtains were drawn across the window to some exactly prescribed point. The little lacy mats underneath every object were in their correct place to the nearest quarter-inch. The big bath tub on its four claw-footed legs, glimpsed through the half-open door of the bathroom, was gleamingly clean.

If it is not for that tall thermos of boiled drinking water, he said to himself, I might be in England itself.

But no time for idle thoughts.

He went over to the dressing-table, pushed aside all the neatly re-arranged array of combs, brushes, lipsticks, tilak paints for forehead mark, pot of sindur to redden hair-parting, wooden tree for bangles, sat down on the flowery-topped stool and spread fully open the file marked *Mrs Protima Ghote — Bombay*.

There at the start was the first sheet he had craned forward to see in A. K. Dutt-Dastar's chamber, *Mrs Protima Ghote — Last Will and Testament of Amit Nirad Chattopadhyay Babu*. Then a copy of the will itself, duplicate of the one they had had in Bombay. A copy next of A. K. Dutt-Dastar's first letter to Protima. Her reply. Letter on official stamped paper certifying that Protima Ghote was Protima Ghote. And then . . .

The familiar blotchily typed document.

He read at a gallop. The heading *Memorandum of Confidential Conversation Between A. K. Dutt-Dastar and Eventual Assignee*. Details about the house and its previous ownership. On . . . On . . . And then his eye hit on *wetlands*.

The very word. The confirmation of all his guesswork, of all Mr Bhattacharya's suppositions. And, yes, here again those familiar, once glimpsed words *with right of passage unimpeded* followed by a lot of word-spinning legalistic mumbo-jumbo. A. K. Dutt-Dastar making sure that he was given his due, no doubt. But it all made clear, eventually, that getting hold of the squattered house in the near future was the key. The key to building a wide road to the housing colony proposed for the newly drained area.

Skim on.

Thing is who is going to be that *Eventual Assignee* so infuriatingly not named at the head of the document? That would be the

160

person behind the whole corrupt transaction, the one who would benefit most from A. K. Dutt-Dastar's attempt to get Protima to sell cheaply, and above all quickly.

But why did he, this mystery figure, want the sale to be quick? No way of knowing.

Skim along, skim along. What a wordy fool Dutt-Dastar is.

But then the end. And not a single name.

No, not the least hint or indication of who it is who is organizing this piece of massive corruption.

Nevertheless, still things to be done. First of all, to take this document to Assistant Commissioner Bhowmick tomorrow afternoon at the appointed time and there to watch him do the needful. See the start of whatever in the end will bring down this whole tower of rottenness.

★ ★ ★

When at last Ghote penetrated the big red-brick mass of Calcutta Police Headquarters opposite the clutter of electrical fittings and musical instrument shops of Tiretta Bazaar, he allowed himself to stand and savour the authentic police-station smell and mix of grubbiness and rigid order, no different here than in Bombay. Then he told the desk havildar he had an appointment with Assistant Commissioner Bhowmick.

Five minutes later, ushered by a peon into the man's cabin, he saw a decidedly Bengali bhadrolok figure. Long, thoughtful oval face, clean-shaven, with deep-set eyes and a high, pale-brown forehead. Somehow he even imagined him, although he was in fact wearing uniform, as being dressed in the way Mr Bhattacharya was at home, in elaborately pleated pure white dhoti and fine white kurta. His expression, as he gestured Ghote to one of the chairs fronting his wide desk, was one of distant melancholy.

'Sir', Ghote said, in reaction to that sadness, 'it is most good of you, with your many responsibilities, to be seeing me.'

'No, no, Inspector. My cousin, who dropped me a note about you, made it clear that it would be my duty to hear what you have got to say. Now, I won't pretend to you that Calcutta is a city of unsmirched integrity. Indeed, from the lowest rungs upwards we have our anti-socials, like any other big city in India, like any big city in the world, from the kangalis, as we call them in Bengali, the homeless urchins, on up through our chhentais, our pickpockets, to your fully-fledged goonda, often ready to

162

kill for an altogether paltry sum. But I have always hoped, despite the many pressures there are on us — of which the city's traffic, my own particular burden, is not the worst — that we have managed to be a little more law-abiding, a little more conscious of what we owe to our fellow citizens, than in the other cities of India. All the more reason, therefore, why any sign of a major departure from those standards should be looked at with all the thoroughness one can bring to bear.'

Yes, Ghote thought to himself, a very, very Bengali fellow. I was right. Nothing able to be said except at length. And with digressions.

'Sir, then let me at once inform you of the corruption I am thinking I have, by chance, put one finger upon.'

Then he corrected himself. Sharply.

'No, sir, I have done more now than put just only one finger. Sir, I have some proof of what is occurring.'

He tugged from his back trouser pocket his wallet and took from it the double-folded sheets of A. K. Dutt-Dastar's *Memorandum of Confidential Conversation*.

Briefly as he could he ran over what had first roused his suspicions and what he had been able to do to confirm them.

'Sir', he ended, 'I have now acquired — I

am preferring not to say altogether how — this document. Sir, kindly peruse same.'

He spread out the two sheets of blotchy typing in front of the grave-faced Assistant Commissioner.

ACP Bhowmick leant forward, took out a pair of dark-framed spectacles, put them on and read.

Ghote, sitting opposite, tried to see if the serious face showed any signs of, hopefully, anger. Or of disturbance at least. Of amazement. Of disgust.

But there was not a flicker.

At last he realized that the steady progress of the Assistant Commissioner's eyes down the second blurred sheet had ceased. But he neither looked up nor spoke.

What it is he is thinking? Must be some deep Bengali intellectual ideas. Is it mulling and mulling like Mr Bhattacharya after he was hearing all the views and news at that adda he was mentioning?

Or will this Bengali, too, need even to discuss the case at another adda, carefully putting before what he is saying an *if for instance one happened to* . . . ?

But, no. At last the spectacles were removed and the deep-set eyes focused on him.

'Yes, Inspector, I see that here is something

164

that needs looking into. To be frank, I do not think at the present stage it is a matter for Delhi and the Central Vigilance Commission. It may come to that, though we in Bengal prefer to tidy up our own messes. I can see, however, that it could well be something that may reach up to the highest levels in the West Bengal Government. So, as you will understand, it will be necessary to move with extreme care.'

He sighed. A burden settling.

'However, Inspector, all that will hardly concern you. Your task is done. You have seen what was wrong. You have found someone of standing to tell what you know. You may safely set it all aside now. You are here in Calcutta — my cousin's letter said — with a view to retiring from the police and living in our city with your Bengali wife.'

'Yes, sir.'

But am I? In Protima's view, yes, I am. But in my view? Each time ACP Sahib was calling me *Inspector* just now I was feeling one small jump of pride. I am here, I was feeling, where I ought to be. In a police headquarters.

But now . . . Now he is saying to me, *Your task is done.* I am to go back to being Ghote Babu, plastic Bengali.

Suddenly he saw that ACP Bhowmick

had unlocked a drawer in his desk and was folding up the *Memorandum of a Confidential Conversation* with the evident intention of putting it away there.

'Sir, no,' he blurted out.

'No? What — '

'Sir, I would wish to retain that document.'

The Assistant Commissioner looked at him. The faint air of surprise on his long, grave face plain to see.

'But surely you realize that this is evidence?'

'Yes, sir. Yes, I do. What else was I — Why else was I obtaining? But, sir, I do not think it is evidence for court of law. It is evidence only that some corruption matter is happening.'

'Well, yes, I suppose you're correct. Strictly speaking. But all the same I think I ought to keep it.'

He pulled the drawer further open.

'Sir, you do not need. Sir, you have seen what is written there. You must be able to remember same. You can tell whomsoever you need what it is. But, sir . . . Sir, I must confess I was obtaining that document through some bribery, and I would not wish that to be more known. So, sir, I am thinking it is best if I retain same.'

The ACP looked at him, long and steadily.

166

'Mr Ghote, you are sure of this?'

So, no more Inspector. For this man of principle the offerer of bribes is just only Mr Ghote.

'Yes, sir,' he said, despite that judgement. 'I am one hundred per cent sure.'

The ACP gave a long, long sigh.

'Very well, Mr Ghote. Keep the paper. But keep it safe. On your head be it.'

'Yes, sir.'

'Well, thank you again for coming to me. Not every Ram or Shyam, as we say, would do as much.'

Ghote felt a little less unhappy. But not much. It seemed a far step down from Inspector to being just the common man dressed in the common man's simple shirt and trousers. Not that he was not a little glad that the shirt happened to be, if not his best, at least a decent one, in a green-and-yellow check that toned in with his green trousers.

He took up the smudgily typed document, gave it one more fold, stuffed it into his wallet and buttoned that safely into his back pocket.

'So, off you go now and enjoy yourself, enjoy our splendid city,' the ACP said. 'Have you seen much of it as yet?'

'No, sir. My wife was showing me the St John's Church and also the Hastings

House. Most historical.'

'Hastings, yes. A great man, a great man. Imagine. Coming all the way from the small island of Britain, on the edge of Europe, and ending by establishing British India, its first Governor-General ruling many millions of people from here in Calcutta, a remarkable achievement.'

And this Hastings also a bribe taker, Ghote thought to himself, the sourness of his verbal demotion from Inspector still rankling.

'And where else in the city have you been?'

No doubt this Assistant Commissioner is stepping down to be talking man-to-man with a mere Inspector, soon to be ex-Inspector. But it is stepping down, and he is knowing he is doing it.

'I have not had time for elsewhere,' he answered dourly.

'Ah, but you should make time. Calcutta has so much to offer. It is not for nothing, you know, that we were once called the City of Palaces. You should see the Marble Palace. Subject to some decay, of course. But in many ways all the more interesting for that. You should wander the streets round here, in Lalbag, in Bow Bazaar, and look at the variety of our old buildings, the true Bengali, the Palladian, the neo-Gothic, the

Art Nouveau and Art Deco, all painted and painted over and over again and then washed and washed by our tumultuous monsoon rains until they show to the full the beauty of decay. And, yes, visit the Park Street Cemetery, all those graves of Englishmen who laid their bones here, the father of William Makepeace Thackeray, a son of Charles Dickens, Rose Aylmer to whom the poem was written. *Ah what avails the sceptred race, Ah what the form divine! What every virtue, every grace! Rose Aylmer, all were thine.*'

Ghote, inwardly groaning at yet another outburst of Bengali self-love, thought he could see, just, a tear at the corner of one of ACP Bhowmick's eyes.

'Yes. And then there are our painters. You must see what you can of their art. Our musicians. You enjoy music?'

'No, sir. Not very very much.'

'Pity. Well, what are your interests then?'

He thought.

What to say? Something must be said.

'Sir, I have always very much wanted to see the banyan in the Botanical Gardens. Oldest in the world, biggest also, isn't it?'

'Yes. Yes, you should certainly see that.' The ACP pursed his lips in thought for a moment. 'I tell you what. Go now. Go this very afternoon. The Gardens are wonderful, hard to find better anywhere in the world. Been there since seventeen-eighty something. Beautiful, tranquil, interesting. You've done a good job, Mr Ghote. You should have some reward at least. I'll get a jeep to take you to Chandpal Ghat. From there you can go by the ferry along the Hooghly to the Gardens. Another of Calcutta's pleasures.'

'Thank you, sir.'

It was all he could say.

But, as he went out, he saw ACP Bhowmick reaching for one of the telephones on his wide desk. The look on his face was even more gravely thoughtful than it had been. Was he making the call that would be the first step towards bringing down the tower of corruption that A. K. Dutt-Dastar's one small lie about Amit Chattopadhyay's intentions had given the first glimpse of?

★ ★ ★

Slowly moving southwards as the crowded ferry pushed its way along the swift-flowing, khaki-coloured Hooghly, Ghote found he could not throw off his feelings of disappointment. He had been once again, if only unofficially and intermittently, an investigating officer. He had had a case. That was what his work

170

in the world was, for better or worse. His dharma. To be a police officer. A detective. But then it had all been snatched away from him.

He had been sent off to go and moon about in the Botanical Gardens. As if he had had some breakdown. As if, at best, he was on sick leave. What did it matter now that he had been whisked in a police jeep, swerving through the traffic, furiously hooting, to the Chandpal Ghat? All right, then for a few minutes, a very few minutes, he had felt a last touch of respect. But, once at the Ghat, what had happened? Nothing. A long wait to get on board the ferry, pushed and tugged at like any other no-account passenger. One of Calcutta's faceless millions. Not by any manner of means an Inspector of Police.

And never more to be one.

He stared at the rippling, sun-struck sparkling surface of the river as the ferry made its laborious way along against the current. And all he saw were the dead dogs floating alongside. And even these made him think, with a dagger pang, of his case. No doubt their rotting flesh was soon to contribute to the rich silt that was somewhere being pumped out of the river and off to the eutrophic lakes, there to feed the fish that existed to feed the Bengali

171

fish-lovers. The Sikh taxiwalla's U-traffic lakes, which someone was planning to fill with truckloads of earth, taken on a wide new road that would begin its route through the ruin of Protima's house. And on the solid land created there someone intended houses, shops, apartment blocks to rise and would line his pockets deep and deep. Unless ACP Bhowmick was able to put some spoke in the wheels.

ACP Bhowmick. Not Inspector Ghote.

Slowly the ferry made its way onwards. Along the bank nearest to him Ghote saw the remains of the fine buildings that had once made Calcutta the second city of the British Empire. And, despite his gloom, found he was admiring them.

Could I get to like this place after all? Even if it is what is expected of me? Will old Calcutta at last work her charms upon myself? And if she does, will I really be happy to be her kept man?

Then ahead there loomed the new high and elegant Vivekananda Setu Bridge. 'It was twenty years to be made,' he heard a voice from the packed deck beside him say. He turned and saw behind, still just in sight as the river bent, the high, criss-cross steel girders of the old Howrah Bridge, reaching up into the hazed-over sky, glinting like silver in the sun, dominating the whole river behind him, symbol of Calcutta in a thousand photographs.

And he wished and wished then that the sight in his eyes was the symbol of Bombay, the arch of the Gateway of India, even if nowadays it lead to nowhere in particular.

A barge loaded with straw till it looked like a floating stack went past, swept onwards by the current twice as fast, it seemed, as his chugging ferry. An inlet on the left with, behind it, a diverging waterway. And that same high-pitched informative voice from somewhere inside the knot of pleasure-goers nearby saying, 'Tolly's Nullah. Same was dredged in year 1775 by one Major Tolly, first-class chap, so that pilgrims at Kalighat Temple may immerse in pure Ganga water, since Hooghly River itself is branch only of Mother Ganga.'

Someone else getting a history lecture, he thought maliciously. And then with a quick flowering of guilt he regretted that he had not told ACP Bhowmick he would wait to visit the Botanical Gardens until Protima could accompany him.

The river broadened and he saw the masts and moored ships of Kidderpore Docks. Little white birds were diving into the thickly turbid water.

Oh why am I going to see this banyan? Do I really want? I did once, yes, when I was here before and could not get to see it. And I thought I did again when I was at last getting on to this ferry. But now, do I want? Today, when some hopes have been trodden down into mud?

Well, I am not able to step off this ferry. So I will at least get to the Gardens, and when I am landing at the ghat there I can decide not to go in or to go in. Whichever I am wanting.

At last the ferry docked, with Ghote still feeling uneasily that he did not really want to have arrived, that ACP Bhowmick had somehow, with Bengali enthusiasm, rushed him into making the trip. Why had he ever told him that he wanted to see the Great Banyan? All he needed to have said when he was asked what his interests were was something like *Oh, sir, there are so many things to see in your wonderful city of Calcutta.* Something just only to satisfy an avid Bengali.

So, as he followed the eager crowd, freed from their cripplingly slow passage, tumbling down the ferry's gangplank, it was only because he could not prevent himself being swept along.

A good many of the freed passengers at

once surrounded the refreshment stall near the gate. But one group moved on. Idly he followed them, followed in turn, equally idly, by a few others, either from the ferry or from coaches that had crossed the Vivekananda Setu Bridge. And the Gardens, he grudgingly conceded before long, were as beautiful as ACP Bhowmick had claimed. Tall palms against the blue sky, a true blue here, this far removed from the city's dust and petrolfume haze. Lakes, glinting in the sun and promising coolness. Long shaded paths. Glasshouses with glimpses of vivid orchids inside, of monstrously shaped cactus plants.

And then there in front of him suddenly was the Great Banyan.

It was, yes, immense. A whole forest in itself. A huge umbrella of dangling roots, some still only rope-thick and pale, others over the tree's two hundred and fifty years of life grown into sturdy twisted trunks. And high. The dome at its peak, he calculated, a good thirty metres above the level ground. Altogether more gripping to the imagination than old Mr Bhattacharya's mildly boastful talk about its huge circumference, its missing central mother-trunk. The missing centre. Perhaps, he thought, that is like Calcutta itself now, all busyness and no core.

But, in a sudden shift of sentiment, he

ceased abruptly to feel he did not want to let the huge old tree become an abiding memory. No, suddenly now he wanted to step underneath its generous shade. To savour it all. To fulfil completely the ambition he had once had. To taste to the full the pleasure he saw the great overhanging umbrella as offering.

So he did it. He walked into gloom. And found it delightfully cool, wonderfully restful, twinklingly alive with the whistlings of the dozens, the hundreds, of mynah birds hopping here and there among the interlaced tangle of the branches. He breathed a deep sigh of contentment.

Here, if I can, he thought, I will finally accept staying all my life in Calcutta, to being not-Inspector Ghote, to being a somehow Bengali. To being just only a person. A person living in this city, this city with, yes, its pleasures. To not being a police officer.

And then, instant as a thunderbolt, from somewhere above in the darkness of the close interwoven branches something, someone, dropped down on to him with crushing force. He was flattened into the soft leaf-mould of the ground at his feet. Breath squirted out of his lungs. Pain shot up and down inside him.

He was aware after a moment that there

were two men, not one, on top of him. One had a sharp knee in the small of his back and clawing hands holding down his shoulders. And the other — were there even only two? — seemed to be tugging and tearing at the back of his trousers.

Then, as suddenly as the attack had come, the pressure was lifted. A moment later he was just aware of the two attackers running off in the under-tree gloom.

He lay where he was. Shocked. Hurting. Dazed. Puzzled.

Cautiously he began at last to feel at his body where he could, not daring to roll over. And then he made his discovery.

His wallet was missing. Gone.

12

Lying there, face-down, in the Great Banyan's shade, the uninterrupted whistlings and chatter of the mynahs in his ears, the sharp smell of the soft earth in his nostrils, Ghote slowly began to piece things together.

Of course, it may have been just only a chance attack. ACP Bhowmick was talking about Calcutta's anti-socials. But it was hardly a pair of child kingalis who dropped down on to me from some hiding-place in those criss-crossed dark branches up there. And if I was no more than the victim of pickpockets, chhentais, their work would have been cleverer. In the crowd hurrying off the ferry easy to cut off the button of my trouser pocket with a razor blade, slide out my wallet. No, this was goonda work. A pair of Calcutta's goondas, the goondas ACP Bhowmick almost boasted were not afraid to kill just to get hold of any tiny sum.

To kill. But I was not killed. Not even much hurt.

He rolled over now and, with care, sat up.

And, something more, that attack ended

altogether suddenly. As if, task completed, the goondas at once hurried off.

So surely their aim was not just only to take what rupee notes I had. Dressed as I am in my commonman's cotton shirt and green cotton trousers, I do not at all have the look of someone who would be carrying one fatly stuffed wallet. And, in fact, despite those folded and re-folded sheets of A. K. Dutt-Dastar's document, my wallet did not make a heavy bulge on my hip.

So, what is the conclusion?

That I was marked out as those fellows' victim? That it was not any passing stranger who was ambushed in that way? That it was just only a man definitely dressed in a green-and-yellow check shirt and matching green trousers. A man not difficult to spot coming off the ferry after that long, long, slow journey from the Chandpal Ghat. A typical Maharashtrian it would not be too difficult to describe over the telephone to someone who had a pair of useful Bengali goondas at his disposal.

The man only one person knew would be at the Botanical Gardens and wanting to visit the Great Banyan at just the time I was there.

ACP Bhowmick. He alone knew that.

Is it possible? ACP Bhowmick? But, yes,

even as I was leaving his cabin he had been reaching for his telephone. Was it not just only to order up a police vehicle for myself? Was it not even to start the machinery that would bring about the end of this road-building scam I had put my finger on?

And, yes, he had seemed for a long moment lost in thought when in answer to his pressing question I was saying I wanted to see this tree. Had he been saying to himself *Ah. My chance. Get this nose-poking fellow pickpocketed out there. Get back that document leading to the person whose good friend I am*?

And old Mr Bhattacharya, he had said it would be necessary to go carefully in trying to push this matter higher up, yes? That you could never be sure every senior officer in the police was free from taint of corruption? Could be bribed with rapid promotions or a good posting or with large sums of money brought to them in crammed briefcases?

Yes. Question asking finished. Facts no longer to be doubted. Assistant Commissioner Bhowmick must be some friend of the hidden figure behind the wet-lands scam. And now . . . Now the only real hard evidence that the scam is there, one document headed *Memorandum of Confidential Conversation*

180

Between A. K. Dutt-Dastar and the Eventual Assignee is once again out of reach, not any more hidden in A. K. Dutt-Dastar's old filing cabinets. But hidden as effectively somewhere else. If not totally destroyed.

★ ★ ★

The gate of the Fairlawn was closed, shutting out the bustle of still lively Sudder Street, the backpack young tourists, the brown-sugar sellers, the shouting taxiwallas, the beggars and the vendors. It was early evening, not long dark. Only later would the cycle rickshawallas who spend the night on the pavement just outside the locked gate arrive. Inside, in the courtyard it was cool and pleasant. Ghote and Protima, her forehead once again heavily smudged with a tikka from the Kalighat Temple brahmins, had secured a table and were sitting with cold drinks.

A calm and peaceful scene.

'This afternoon, after I was talking with ACP Bhowmick,' Ghote said slowly and carefully, easing his bruised back against the hard plastic chair, 'I was visiting the Botanical Gardens.'

'I remember afternoons there with my mother. It is a wonderful place. Only in Calcutta can you — '

'Not one hundred per cent wonderful.'

'Oh, you are always and always trying to make out Calcutta is not as good as it is. You cannot compare Calcutta with Bombay. Never.'

'No. I was not saying Calcutta is not wonderful. I was saying just only that the Botanical Gardens were not as wonderful for me as they were for yourself as a child.'

'Nonsense. Somewhere like that does not change. They have been there for hundreds of years.'

'Since seventeen-eighty something. ACP Bhowmick was telling that.'

'There. You see. A man like him. A true bhadrolok. He would not say what is not true.'

'Oh, but he did. Let me tell just exactly what he was doing.'

Protima took more than a little convincing. But in the end, by simply putting each fact and inference quietly before her, he persuaded her that the wallet with the document which he had bribed birthmarked Shibu to give him had been stolen because it had in it that document.

She sat in silence for some long moments.

'So what to do?' she said at last. 'Something must be done. I will not lose my house.'

'I have been thinking.'

'Yes? What it is?'

Suddenly she was all eagerness. Trusting him. Trusting, he thought, Inspector Ghote, Bombay CID. As she had done, unthinkingly, for so many years. Until she had come to Calcutta.

'Do you remember Mr Bhattacharya talking about one suggestion some friend of his was making at what he was calling an adda?'

'But he was suggesting you should tell to Assistant Commissioner Bhowmick what you had so far found out. Are you going to Bhattacharya Babu now to tell what bad advice he has given?'

'No, no. All that adda-padda was so much uselessness. I am not going back to him.'

He regretted at once that he had jumped at that chance of putting down Bengali ways. But it seemed that Protima, seeing perhaps how much truth there was in what he had said, was ready for once to pass over the slur.

'So what it is you are planning to do?'

'It is this itself. They were talking at that adda, Mr Bhattacharya said, about Calcutta's newspapers. He was telling, wasn't it, that an editor there was giving some good advice. To go to a certain paper, the one you were saying would knock into very much a cocked hat even the *Blitz*.'

'Yes, *The Sentinel*.'

'Well, first thing tomorrow I am going to go to *The Sentinel*. Yes, I no longer have the firm evidences that A. K. Dutt-Dastar's document was providing. But a paper like *The Sentinel* will not be requiring firm evidences. A smell only of corruption may be enough for them.'

'Yes, yes. Good. Good. Go as soon as you are able.'

★ ★ ★

The offices of *The Sentinel* turned out to be squeezed into a narrow old house behind the Writers' Building.

However, the Bihari cycle-rickshawalla who had threaded his way through tram-clanging BBD Bagh to bring Ghote to the area had contrived, despite speaking Hindi rather than Bengali, to put him down at the wrong place. With many assurances of *Is jagah, is jagah*, here, here, he had then promptly vanished into the dust-choked tangle of traffic.

Clutching the file Shibu had sold him, deprived though it was of its key document, and searching among the bustling streets of this commercial hub of Calcutta — pavements

184

crammed and crowded with hawkers and vendors, selling office supplies, images of the gods, cigarettes, pornographic books — he came at last upon something Protima had told him about, the Memorial to the Dead Telephone. What little experience he had had of Calcutta's phones had proved that nowadays they were just as efficient as Bombay's. But here solemnly recorded were the errors and complications of the recent past. An upright stone slab on a plinth dated 1984 held a picture of an old-style dial phone in shiny black and underneath

Oh! Child of Communication
You were born to bridge the gap.
But corruption has caused a mishap.
Inefficiency and procrastination
Caused the telephone lines to go
— 'SNAP'

Well, he thought, Calcutta wit hundred per cent, if not as good Calcutta poetry. And trust a Bengali to use one long word, *procrastination*, where one short one would do.

Then, moving on a little, he saw beside a battered old doorway a small brass plaque with on it just two words, *The Sentinel*.

All right, go in.

Five minutes later he was sitting at an old, scarred and ink-blotched table, which incongruously held two shining VDUs and three differently coloured telephones, a far cry from *inefficiency and procrastination*. Above, a fan dating from another age slowly creaked its way round and round. A sharply black rim of concentrated dust edged its pale blades.

Facing him was the paper's assistant editor, Khokon Roy. Young — thirty or so, Ghote guessed — dressed rather smartly in a boldly striped black-and-white shirt, open at the neck. And he was smiling.

He had smiled when Ghote had been shown into his room — bare, stained walls — and at intervals as Ghote told his story he broke into more smiles, cheerful, quick, come-and-go.

'Right, Inspector,' he said at last. 'But do you mind me calling you Inspector? You are not one of those police officers who are ashamed of what they do? I know you are not one of those who are ashamed because they ought to be. From what you've been saying I put you down as no bribe taker. And not much of a bribe giver either, actually, to judge from your handling of that peon from A. K. Dutt-Dastar's chamber. And there's a nasty bit of work, that Dutt-Dastar, I know more than a few things to his detriment. But, really, Inspector, you shouldn't give a bribe of whatever sum's first asked. All very well to oil the wheels, but use oil that's too thick and you clog up the works. Oh, forgive me. I've been rattling on and on and haven't given you a chance even to object to being called Inspector.'

'No,' Ghote said, reflecting that here was another Bengali who *rattled on and on,* though one with the grace to admit it. 'No, I am not at all objecting to being called as Inspector.'

He felt, in fact, a puffing-up of pride at having been once more awarded his proper title. It meant that this clever young man — and he had no doubt that Khokon Roy was clever — had judged that what he had said was indication enough that there was a major corruption affair in his sights. So in a way he himself was on a case again. As he ought to be.

The crusading journalist at once confirmed his feeling.

'Yes, Inspector, I have no doubts about it. The fragments of evidence you have produced, pieced together, seem absolutely to support just one explanation. Corruption.' A quick, flashing smile. 'You know the old joke? *A corrupt deal is exposed: a Russian commits suicide, a Chinese is executed and an Indian . . . becomes a Member of Parliament.'*

Ghote laughed. Not so much because the joke was funny, but because of the bouncing enthusiasm with which Khokon Roy had told it.

'And you are thinking this is matter that definitely goes up to MP level? ACP Bhowmick was saying as much.'

Another flash-of-light smile.

'Well, he would, wouldn't he? True, he's not someone I've heard anything iffy about. But, as you say, he must be in the pocket of some high-up somewhere to have arranged for you to be robbed of that document. After all, how does he come to have that nice posting of his? Sitting in comfort, fat salary, and having to do no more than ponder Calcutta's traffic problems. And those won't be shifted by any amount of ponder, believe you me.'

Thinking of the traffic chaos he had just witnessed in BBD Bagh, somehow worse than that in Bombay, more excitable, more cheerful, more angry, Ghote felt a jab of righteous anger. The people who had to dodge the lumbering, clanking two-car trams. The people coughing and spluttering as they ducked through the buses' outpourings of filthy grey exhaust, with the yellow-topped taxis weaving and jostling with no thought of rules or regulations. Something should be being done about it all. The utmost possible should be being done. And it was not. Because of bribery, corruption also. The traffic cops taking chai-pani for ignoring regulations. Senior officers sitting idle because they had won their postings by becoming the tools of corrupt high-ups.

'So what can *The Sentinel* do?' he asked Khokon Roy.

'No guarantees,' the young journalist cheerfully replied. 'You have to understand this. *The Sentinel* investigates perhaps two-three hundred corruption allegations per annum, some well backed-up, others of course merely fanciful, or spiteful. And how many of them result in action? Well, a few do. A few is the best we can rise to. But that's worth doing. It's what we exist for. What I exist for, to tell you the truth.'

Another brilliant smile. But a smile deprecating that declaration rather than mocking the process.

'Very well, no guarantees. I am able to understand that. But some action, yes?'

'Oh yes. Action. You see, I think there must be some urgency about this whole scam. There's been a good deal of agitation recently,

you know, about saving the wetlands. Or, to
be rather more cynical, about saving those
eutrophic lakes that supply us Bengalis with
so much of our beloved fish. And if that
agitation produces results, then this plan to
build a whole new colony in the wetlands will
fall through. So whoever is behind it must
be in a hurry. In a hurry to have the plan
approved, and in a hurry also to get hold
of your wife's house so as to build a road
through it. Well, therefore we also should be
in a hurry.'

Another quick, eyes-alight smile.

'Yes, it is action now. Action for me, and
I rather think action for you too, Inspector.
I'm delighted, to tell you the truth, to have
a trustworthy police officer to work with. I
well understand, of course, that you are out
of your territory here in Calcutta. Reduced
to being, if you like, just the common
man. But there are things, it occurs to
me, to which you can bring your detective
skills. Apart from that, I need the sort of
advice you can probably give me. There
have been stories in the past that I might
have brought to front page status, and I've
had to watch them being forgotten because
I just didn't know enough about the criminal
world.'

'But, please,' Ghote exclaimed, breaking

in on yet another bout of Bengali word-spinning, 'what it is I can do?'

Khokon Roy gave a broad grin.

'Ah ha, the Bombay spirit. Cut out our Bengali crap, get down to business. Right. So this is what I have in mind. What that document of yours called, if you've remembered it rightly, the Eventual Assignee. He's the fellow we've got to ferret out. To ferret out and blasted well name in the pages of *The Sentinel*. On the front page. Over the whole of the front page. And in our boldest type.'

'But how? And, most of all, how can I do this ferreting?'

'Oh, Bombay. Bombay, Bombay. Absolute Bombay-style. Right to the nub. No chatter, no patter. No. But you want your answer. And here it is. You can simply go to our friend tricky old Dutt-Dastar and tell him a black lie. You know, lie-telling is a great old Calcutta tradition. And I'm delighted to induct you into it. There's a rhyme we used to have *Jai, juochuri, mithye katha, Ei tin niye Kolikata.* Your Bengali up to that?'

'I am not altogether sure.'

'Well, let me translate. Into good English. Or bad English. Well, never mind which. Here we go: *Forgery, swindling, telling lies, the three that add up to Calcutta.*'

'Yes, but please,' he was beginning to find words-tumbling Khokon Roy a little trying. 'Please, what lie am I to tell?'

The young journalist burst into laughter.

'My fault, my fault. No. Let me spit it out straight away. The lie you are to tell, Inspector, is that your wife is now willing to sell her house.'

'To sell — But she — Ah, no, I see it. If I am telling A. K. Dutt-Dastar that lie, I can perhaps get him to say who she is to sell to. The Eventual Assignee. But, no. No, that man is knowing now that I have got this.'

He slapped the buff file with the green-ink words *Mrs Protima Ghote — Bombay* scrawled across it.

Khokon Roy looked at it.

'You're right, of course,' he said. 'I'm afraid I was rushing into things altogether too fast. A fault of mine. A bad fault.' He brightened abruptly. 'A Bengali failing, I have to say. We're too enthusiastic, and that's a fact. I dare say, if we were not, Calcutta would still be the capital of India, as it ought to be. The British would never have gone and built that appalling New Delhi just to get away from us if we had not given them such a hard time.'

'But it is A. K. Dutt-Dastar and whosoever

is behind him we are wishing now to give one hard time to.'

Khokon Roy grinned sheepishly.

'Quite right to pull me up again, Inspector. I see you've had rather too much of Calcutta boasting in your time here. Right, the question now is: how can we possibly extract from Dutt-Dastar the name of — Wait. Wait. No. Yes. Yes, I've got it.'

He stopped. And grinned.

'Look, let me put it this way,' he said. 'I think I may see how to get out of our dilemma. And, if we don't rush into it, we may yet pull it off. So, listen and give me the benefit of your Bombay hard-headedness.'

Ghote felt the responsibility.

'Very good,' he said. 'Tell me what-all you are thinking.'

'Just this. Say you go to Dutt-Dastar, but instead of simply telling him your wife has suddenly changed her mind and wants to sell the house after all, something which — you're right — he'll never believe for a moment, say to him instead that you have been well frightened by that attack on you in the Botanical Gardens. You can add that your wife is yet more frightened. That's something he'll almost certainly believe, if you can say it with enough conviction. And I have no doubt that a Bombay detective can summon up a certain amount of deception without too much trouble. Well, I dare say a Calcutta detective would be — '

'Mr Roy, kindly tell what exactly is your plan.'

'Oh, my dear fellow, you do well to check me. Impetuous Bengali that I — No. No, I'll get on with it. I really will. It's just this, old chap. What if you go to Dutt-Dastar, say your wife is scared, and yourself too if you can bring yourself to it, and that you're both willing to call it a day? Say that you're willing to sell the house and its compound, and that you'll go back to Bombay and count yourselves lucky?'

Well, Ghote thought, if we were to go back to Bombay I would count myself lucky, yes. But . . . But I do not all the same like to be beaten. So it is one damn good thing that this is just only a clever move and not simple truth.

'Yes,' he said. 'Yes, I am thinking that, if I am able to make A. K. Dutt-Dastar think my wife is very much frightened, it may be enough.'

'And will tell you then who he means to be the buyer of that house.'

Khokon Roy looked as if the triumph had already been achieved.

'If,' said Ghote.

'Well, all right, if we are lucky. But, yes, if you can really trick Dutt-Dastar into producing a name we'll be on our way. At least by a good margin. You may not actually hear who this Eventual Assignee is. People like Dutt-Dastar are a good deal more devious than that. He'll quite possibly have a nominee ready to hand. But if you can just get one name out of him, we could run the story with that and see if it brings a few rats out of their holes.'

And, with sharp in his mind the image of snouts poking out of the tunnels of the Rat Colony, Ghote left with his new ally the buff file, sole tangible evidence of A. K. Dutt-Dastar's deviousness, and set out back to the Fairlawn.

13

Ghote did not tell his wife that he was going to see A. K. Dutt-Dastar once more. Before leaving *The Sentinel* he had made use of Calcutta's nowadays efficient telephone system. But, he had wondered as he punched out the number, was that *child of communication* even now altogether free of the corruption that *caused a mishap*? What chance was there that it could be? In Bombay or Delhi, it was well known, if you wanted a new connection or in an office an extra line you very seldom got it without paying out money to some officer, and yet more to the linesman when he came. But his quick call from one of Khokon Roy's coloured phones had got him an appointment with the lawyer for that afternoon.

Eating the curry lunch the Fairlawn invariably served — no question of fish heads, he thought, some good coming out of this British atmosphere — he told Protima how his visit to *The Sentinel* had gone. Until the moment it came to saying that, as a result of it, he was about to join battle once more with wily A. K. Dutt-Dastar. Then he suddenly baulked.

He did not immediately realize what it was that had motivated him. But, once he had told Protima his lie, or had told it by omission — Am I falling into one of those three *jai, juochuri, mithye katha* that add up to Calcutta? — he knew why he had allowed it to come into existence. When he went to A. K. Dutt-Dastar he wanted to be a Bombay detective.

It might, he thought, be the last time he was to be one. If the coming interview eventually led to *The Sentinel* exposing whatever huge scam was taking place, Protima would keep her house. And make her husband into a half-Bengali. But to have his Bengali wife there as he attempted to deceive A. K. Dutt-Dastar would, he felt sure, blunt his edge. He would find himself indulging in long-winded Bengali excuses. And would fail to get out of the fellow the name of the prospective purchaser. Who might, just possibly, even prove to be the mysterious Eventual Assignee.

So, when he had seen that Protima was content that the business was in the hands of *The Sentinel*, he simply asked her if she had any plans for the afternoon. Yes, she said. She was going to Rash Behari Avenue to see if she could track down the house where she had lived as a girl 'among all the many, many shops for underwears. Rash Behari Avenue, you know, used to be famous for having the largest number of underwears shops in the whole world. And music shops also. More than you could count. But, of course, Calcutta is the most musical city in India. Everyone in the city can sing Tagore's songs. *Rabindrageet*, we call them in Bengali.'

She fell silent for a moment.

'Somehow in Bombay I never used to sing,' she said.

Surely she sang sometimes in the flat in Bombay, he thought? Surely she had. Hadn't she?

But she made no demand for him to go with her on her expedition. Perhaps, he thought, she is wanting, if she is able to find the place, to remember on her own the events of her life there.

'It would be very fine if you would get to see inside,' he offered.

And put her into a taxi.

★ ★ ★

The peon Shibu was no longer at A. K. Dutt-Dastar's chamber to admit him. His place had been taken by an individual almost as shamblingly awkward, if without a disfiguring snake-like birthmark. It was easy enough to draw the right conclusion from bribe-taking Shibu's departure. A. K. Dutt-Dastar must have been told that the file he had had 'mislaid' had got into the hands of this too inquisitive Bombay police officer. And Shibu had paid the penalty. But who was it who had told the lawyer? ACP Bhowmick directly? Or the person ACP Bhowmick had reported the loss of that dangerous document to, and who then had either instructed him to arrange to get it back or had arranged to do so himself?

No matter. What had now been doubly confirmed was that A. K. Dutt-Dastar was the initiator of the corruption affair, and that he was in communication with the ACP about it, either directly or through some other channel.

So, sitting facing him, Ghote saw no reason not to tell his probing lie straightaway.

'Sir, I am happy to tell that my wife has now, for certain reasons, decided it would be best to sell the house. Calcutta is no longer so pleasing to her.'

He saw the lawyer's head lift up. Because he had heard something unexpected? Or in a sudden dart of suspicion? He cursed him for still wearing his impenetrable wrap-around glare glasses.

'So, sir,' he went cautiously on, 'if you would be so good as to let me have the name of the purchaser you have in mind . . . '

'Ah, there, my dear Mr Ghote, I must disappoint you.'

'But, Mr Dutt-Dastar, how can my wife sell her house if she is not at all knowing who is to buy?'

'Perfectly simple. I will conduct the whole transaction.'

How to get round this wall?

'But — But, yes, Mr Dutt-Dastar, I do not think it right, when you are representing my wife, that you should also represent the buyer she would be selling to.'

The lawyer slowly removed his concealing band of dark glass.

Anything now to be seen from his eyes?

Inscrutable. Looking straight ahead into nothingness. As blank as the inflexible gaze of the clerk Haripada pounding his ancient typewriter outside.

'Very well, Mr Ghote. Then let me find your wife another lawyer. I can recommend three or four excellent men. Off the top of my head.'

No, must not let him get away with that.

'Mr Dutt-Dastar, I have no doubt that you must have many acquaintances in legal profession. But somehow . . . '

'You are not doubting my integrity?'

The doubtful lawyer sat up in his big chair, the very picture of affrontedness.

And then in an instant Ghote saw his way ahead.

'Dutt-Dastar Babu, I have only the highest respect for you. Everything you have done for my wife has been carried out in the most efficient manner. We have complete trust in you.'

Now the eyes, no longer protected by that strip of black glass, did give away something. It was only for a moment. But to Ghote sitting opposite, looking meek as he could but unrelentingly observing, it was clear enough. An expression of malicious glee. It said, as clearly as if A. K. Dutt-Dastar had mockingly laughed aloud: I have fooled this Bombay-side fellow through and through.

He felt just a little put out, despite his having gone to such lengths to make the lawyer believe him a fool. That he should be seen as someone who could believe, despite that attack under the Great Banyan, that he was still dealing with a reputable man: it hurt.

Quickly, however, he took advantage of the situation he had gone to such pains to create.

'But if you are passing us to some other

lawyer, then that individual must be telling us who will be buying the house. So, sir, would it not be altogether better if it was you who represented my wife, and if you then passed on this buyer you are having to one of your trusted legal friends?'

And he saw that he had caught his man on the hop. If only because those black glare glasses were hastily resumed.

'Well, Mr Ghote . . . Well, I do see certain objections to that course.'

'But, Mr Dutt-Dastar, you cannot represent both parties.'

'No, no. That is correct. Of course.'

Another pause for thought behind the protection of his black shield.

'Yes, Mr Ghote, you are right. It would be simplest if I did continue to represent you, and another lawyer represented the buyer.'

'In that case, sir,' he jumped in, 'there can surely be no objection to telling me now his name since he will not be a client of yours?'

'Yes. Yes. Well, I am certainly ready to do that.'

Now? Now? Am I now going to hear that name?

He fixed his gaze on the black glasses in front of him.

'Yes, Mr Ghote, there is no reason at all

not to give you that gentleman's name. He is a person you are hardly likely to know, after all.'

Know or not know, am I really now going to be given that name?

'So, sir?'

'It is a certain Mr Gopal Deb.'

Gopal Deb, he thought, typical Bengali name. Curse it. There may well be dozens of Gopal Debs in Calcutta. And, yes, I was even catching Dutt-Dastar saying more or less to himself that I would be *hardly likely to know* him. So have I been so much of clever? Have I in fact learnt any more than I knew before? When all I am knowing is that the house is to be bought by one among all the many, many Gopal Debs in Calcutta, among perhaps hundreds in Bengal? And is my Gopal Deb, whoever he may be, actually the Eventual Assignee?

He thought.

And thought he had hit on one way perhaps to advance a little.

'This Mr Gopal Deb,' he said, 'can my wife be assured he has enough of funds to buy the house? She is expecting to get an altogether decent sum. If we are to retire, as you were yourself recommending, to a fine bungalow outside Bombay in the cool heights of Mahableshwar, we would require a considerable amount.'

'Oh, I don't think you need concern yourself over that. Mr Gopal Deb is a retired senior ICS officer. No family. Only himself to please. Looking for a business opportunity. And, as you must know, the Civil Service not only provides good salaries, but — Well, shall we say opportunities as well?'

And A. K. Dutt-Dastar favoured him with a smile that was more of a leer.

Money from above once more?

But he must not trust much longer to this picture of a simple Bombaywalla he had made out of himself. Surely now, with the additional information A. K. Dutt-Dastar had let slip, it would not be too difficult for Khokon Roy at *The Sentinel* to trace a Gopal Deb who was also a retired Civil Service officer.

* * *

Khokon Roy, face alight with pleasure when Ghote triumphantly told him what he had learnt, had simply said: 'Senior ex-ICS man, easy enough to find. There are lists of such fellows. So wait to see his name and address on our front page tomorrow.'

But when at the Fairlawn he greeted Protima, back from Rash Behari Avenue, his feeling of triumph at once evaporated.

'Yes,' Protima said, eyes alight with her own triumph, 'I was finding our old house. Outside is no longer pink but a nice yellow. A family by the name of Chatterjee is there, good bhadrolok stock. Mrs Chatterjee was showing me every nook and corner. And so many memories were coming back. I even saw the old table we had left, and remembered sitting at it, with my father bribing me each evening with the promise of a biscuit if I would drink all my milk. Oh, I cannot wait to settle in Calcutta once again.'

He felt a tumble of misery. Not at having to decide whether bribing a little girl to drink her milk was setting her on a bad course, but because he saw Protima so was locked in her hope of becoming a full Bengali again. When *The Sentinel* broke the story and this Gopal Deb, ICS retired, bank account full no doubt from years of money from above, was prevented from buying her house she would be able to enter into full possession.

Then I myself would do what? Take a walk in the morning like Mr Bhattacharya? Take another in the afternoon? Improve my Bengali? Go in the evenings to all these culture-pulture events Calcutta is so proud of? Or sit and fall into just only a doze?

'You know,' he said, the thought of Mr Bhattacharya reminding him of the promise he had made him, 'one thing we must do is to tell your uncle's good friend what was the result of the advices he was giving. He has a right to know even that ACP Bhowmick is not the man he was believing.'

★ ★ ★

They went to see Mr Bhattacharya early next morning, starting out even before *The Sentinel* with its promised denunciation of the unmasked Gopal Deb was on the streets. For a moment or two Ghote had wondered whether to wait till he could see it, till he could experience the first thrill of the ever more rapid hunt. But in what might be a newborn upspringing in himself of bhadrolok civility, he felt that, as he had remembered his promise to tell the kindly old man what had happened, it was his duty to do so without any delay.

They found him sitting on his roof. Seen from the back, he had his full weight resting on his left hip in that typical Bengali way, with his right knee raised high and the folds of his pure white dhoti cascading down from it. He was looking out into the distance.

And singing.

Well, hadn't Protima said everyone in Calcutta could sing?

She put a hand now on Ghote's sleeve as they were about to emerge fully on to the roof and with her other hand motioned the servant who had led them up not to stay. They stood then listening.

Listening, to Ghote's blossoming pleasure, to the old man's gentle but beautifully expressive voice.

'Tagore song,' Protima whispered after a minute. 'One I am well knowing.'

He stayed beside her, unwilling by even the slightest sound to bring the song, whose Bengali words he barely grasped, to an end.

The fluting voice rose into the clear blue sky above.

He caught a phrase or two. *The night the storm blew open my doors . . . Little did I know you would come in . . .*

He stood there caught up, ravished away. He hardly dared even to breathe.

In the smallest of whispers Protima translated a word or two here and there.

'*I reached to the heavens not knowing why . . . Restless I lay dreaming . . . The storm was the flag of your triumph.*'

Soon he forgot everything in the trance of the solitary floating music of that pure quiet voice until something momentarily tickled at the back of his mind. Yes, the Tagore poem Protima had quoted about the clerk Haripada, *The Flute*. This was like just such tears-bringing lonely flute music. He forgot altogether why they had come out here. He forgot about his own triumph in getting hold of that name *Gopal Deb*. Now all that busyness seemed blankly insignificant. A scratch upon the surface. He forgot even his doubts and fears about coming to this alien city.

Then at last the old man's clear voice faded into silence.

Still they waited where they were.

Eventually Protima whispered, 'I think in the words of that Rabindrageet he must have been remembering his own wife. Yes, I am sure of it.'

'Yes,' he said.

There seemed to be no more to say.

Then, seeing the old man was not going to repeat the song, Ghote gave a small cough and led Protima on to the wide expanse of the roof.

'Mrs Ghote,' Mr Bhattacharya exclaimed as he saw them, grasping his silver-topped stick and pushing himself to his feet. 'A most pleasant surprise. And Mr Ghote. Or ought I to call you Inspector? Ought I all along to have been calling you Inspector? Is that a title you cling to? Or are you anxious to throw it off and live the life I do? A life, I may say, of idleness. What do I do, after all? No more than keep the world turning by writing letters to the newspapers.'

He dropped back on to his broad bench and patted the sprawled heap beside him, *The Statesman, The Telegraph, Amrita Bazaar Patrika*. But not *The Sentinel*, Ghote saw, coming slowly back to where he had been before he had heard the old bhadrolok sing.

'And when I say *the world*,' Mr Bhattacharya added with a chuckle. 'I mean, of course, Calcutta. Where else? But I am failing in my duty. You must tell me at once how your battle with corruption has gone. Did Assistant Commissioner Bhowmick feel there were steps that he could take?'

'Yes, sir,' Ghote could not prevent himself saying. 'I am sorry to tell he was very much finding steps. He was having me assaulted. In the Botanical Gardens. Under the Great Banyan itself. So as to rob me of — '

He broke off. Had he got to confess now to Bhattacharya Babu that he had bribed A. K. Dutt-Dastar's peon to give him the 'mislaid' file?

Yes, he had to. He had gone too far.

'Sir, to rob me of a document which I had

given one heavy bribe to A. K. Dutt-Dastar's peon in order to obtain. A document making it finally clear there is a plan to buy my wife's house, even against her will, and then to drive through it a road to the big new colony they are proposing to build over there.'

He flung out an arm towards the distant glitter of the eutrophic lakes.

Mr Bhattacharya, picking up his stick, leant forward with his full weight on it.

'My good friend,' he said, 'I too must make a confession. When we first met I saw you as a newcomer to our city, and I am afraid I allowed myself to be led away in praising it as a place above and beyond every other city in India. Almost, so keen was my desire to welcome you, I portrayed it, did I not, as beyond any city in the world for integrity, beauty, civilized life. But I was wrong. Wrong, wrong, wrong. Let me tell you now the truth as I see it.'

He was so earnest, looked so sad as he spoke, that Ghote would have liked to halt this flow of remorse. To say, *Bhattacharya Babu, I understand. Please do not apologize. No need to utter one word more.* But he knew, too, that he must not prevent the old bhadrolok from saying what plainly he so urgently wanted to say.

He pressed his lips hard together.

'Yes, the truth. The bitter truth. Calcutta, my dear Mr Ghote, is no different from every big city in the world. No different? Yes, perhaps it is different in that more than any other city in India it is the victim of corruption. But you must understand what I mean by corruption. It is not perhaps what is ordinarily thought of under that heading. It is something deeper, and more to be feared. When you first told me about this business I went, as perhaps I told you, to the library at the Bengal Club in an effort to clarify my ideas, an effort which, I rather believe, the subsequent plethora of differing views I was offered by my adda friends somewhat nullified.'

A cough. And a continuation.

'However, in my preliminary researches, if that is not too much dignifying the process, I chanced to look up in the Oxford Dictionary, that well of English undefiled, the definition of corrupt. And this, to the best of my recollection, is what I found: *Changed from the naturally sound condition, especially by decomposition or putrefaction, infected or defiled by that which causes decay.* The word comes, I saw, from the Latin *corrumpere*, to break into pieces and also, significantly I believe, to bribe. Now, I do not need to point out to you, I am sure, how aptly that description of decay and putrefaction fits our poor Calcutta.'

Ghote acknowledged this, thinking of the huge garbage heap he had watched over from his hotel window. But he could not help wondering, too, whether Mr Bhattacharya was ever going to get back to what had so disturbed him at the outset.

'So you see,' the old bhadrolok went on, 'when I speak of Calcutta as the victim of corruption I do not mean only the sort of corruption which your arrival amongst us, with your charming wife, has unexpectedly revealed. Oh, that is bad enough. Bad enough. But Calcutta, as I see her, is attacked in her every aspect by corruption. We are used to thinking that the corrupters are the rich wishing to get yet richer. And so they are, let me not baulk from saying that. But there are other corrupters. Even the very poor, even the poorest. Because, my dear Mr Ghote, think what it is that the thousands, the hundreds of thousands, the millions even, who have come pouring into my city over the past twenty years have done. They have battened on her. Yes, that is the word. Battened. They have eaten away at her flesh. Corrupted it. With their demands. Their just demands, oh, yes. But

212

demands none the less. For food, for water, for shelter.'

A demonstrative gesture to where Protima's house stood.

'Yes, you have seen that corrupting at work. There. There in the house you have inherited, my dear Mrs Ghote. You have seen how those refugees have eaten away at it. Have stripped it. Have corrupted its very structure. And what has happened to your house has happened ten times over to others. The City of Palaces. That is what they once called Calcutta. And look at those palaces today. Some ground right down to dust. Some still surviving in an almost ruined state. A few still inhabitable and inhabited. But all corroded and corrupted. Allowed to rot in the rains of each monsoon, unrepaired, unpainted, unkempt.'

'But, sir, no.' The protest broke from Ghote, however much he had resolved to let Mr Bhattacharya have his say. 'Sir, you were before painting one fine picture of Calcutta for me, and I must tell you that I have found it is true. Oh, yes, I am fully a Bombayman, and I will admit that not everything in Calcutta is what I like. But, sir, I have seen in these last days what a fine city it is. Yes, even when under that Great Banyan I was set on and robbed I had just only seen

213

those magnificent Botanical Gardens, I had just only sailed along the Hooghly and seen, despite the dead dogs that were floating by, the splendour of its wide sweeps, the still fine remains of the buildings on its banks. And I have seen the way you Bengalis jump at life. The joy you are showing. Sir, Calcutta has not just only been called City of Palaces, it has been called City of Joy also. When I was first coming I was thinking that was a cruel joke when there is so much of death and destruction, of poverty and degradation to be seen in the streets wheresoever you are going. But soon I was coming to see also that there is very much of life here. Of joy. So, please, sir, do not think you have deceived me with your praises.'

'No, no, no. You are kind, my dear fellow. But I insist on telling you the truth. Yes, we in Calcutta make light of what is happening to our city. It is all we can do perhaps so as to keep our sanity. But nevertheless it is true: Calcutta is a victim city. Corrupted. Corrupted by its rich who bribe and connive to get richer at her expense. Corrupted from its very earliest days of the British, living to the top of their bent, drunken and lecherous. Can it be something in our air? Even the always present imminence of death from the unhealthiness of the terrain? Corrupted, too, by all her old inhabitants, however lowly, who do not put back one tenth of what they take from her, who bribe and pillage in their smaller way with the best of the corrupt businessmen, the corrupt civil servants, the corrupt ministers. And corrupted even, as I have said, by the very poorest refugees whom we have welcomed and allowed to scrape and eat away at our heritage until, as you must have seen, the dust of their depredation hangs over us all in a dreadful, never dispersing pall and the filthy remains that even they cast away lie stinking in garbage heaps everywhere, garbage heaps our Corporation is too corrupt from the top to the bottom ever to get rid of. Ever to allow us to breathe.'

'Sir — '

'No, let me finish. Goddess Kali is, as you know, our tutelary goddess. And she is a goddess of destruction. The ten blood-dripping heads she holds in her hand are not there without a purpose. Oh yes, people will tell you that Kali is the goddess of destruction of the wrongdoers, and so she is. But she is also the goddess of the destruction of the city she presides over. A destruction she lets us bring down upon our own heads.'

14

There was no story in *The Sentinel*. They
had had to wait almost the full length of
the long taxi ride back — Mr Bhattacharya's
sombre words echoing and re-echoing in
Ghote's head — before they saw any street
trader with newspapers. As soon as they
found one Ghote stopped the taxi, darted
out and bought *The Sentinel*. Nothing on
the front page. Nothing, search as they both
might, each disbelieving the other, on any
of the sheet's scanty inside pages. They sat
there in the stationary taxi in bewildered
despondency.

There had been nothing more to say at
Bhattacharya Babu's. The old man had stayed
where he was on his broad bench, drooped
in silence, until recollecting his bhadrolok
obligations, he had rung a little bell for a
servant and, with profuse apologies, offered
tea. They could not, of course, do other
than accept it. And so they sat, all three,
in exhausted silence relieved just occasionally
by some comment on the weather or the
excellence of the sandesh the servant had also
brought up. 'We in Calcutta have the sweetest

tooth in all . . . ' Mr Bhattacharya had begun but, catching himself once more praising his native city, he abandoned the thought with a gesture of complex ambiguity.

Soon afterwards they had left. And now, arriving at the Fairlawn with the prospect, after a wait of precisely thirty-five minutes until the gong would boom, of another large pallid curry lunch, they retreated to their room like a pair of vanquished mud-covered wrestlers from the shore of the Hooghly underneath the Howrah Bridge.

Once more they searched the few pages of their now tattered *Sentinel*.

'Nothing,' Protima admitted at last. 'What devils some people are. Promising and promising. Or did you misunderstand what you were told?'

'No. I am not making such mistakes.'

'You are sure? Was that Mr Roy speaking Bengali? You do so little to master it.'

'He was not speaking Bengali. He was speaking good English. He promised that in the paper today there would be a story naming this Mr Gopal Deb, mentioning also the wetlands.'

'Then it is where?'

He felt a spurt of anger.

'I am going now to telephone and ask.' He checked himself. 'No. No, I will go round there itself. At once.'

'Are you now saying Calcutta phones are no good? Yes, I was telling you about our famous memorial to the Dead Telephone. But, you duffer, that was from long ago.'

'No, I am saying nothing about Calcutta telephones. I am just only wanting to see Mr Khokon Roy face to face.'

'But lunch. We have paid for all meals.'

'To hell with lunching and munching. I am going now, this instant.'

★ ★ ★

Twenty minutes later — for speed's sake he had let himself be carried through the jammed traffic by a running, dodging barefoot rickshawalla — he was facing the young journalist across his ancient table with its two VDUs and its three coloured telephones.

'Mr Roy, you were promising something to me yesterday.'

'My dear chap, I know I was. I told you in good faith that we would run a story about Gopal Deb, ICS retired, as forced purchaser of a house, plus a paragraph mentioning a proposed new colony in the wetlands.'

'And . . . ?'

'And, after I had made all necessary

218

inquiries with my editor's full backing, this telephone rang' — he gave his green one a sharply infuriated tap — 'and he told me to spike the whole damn thing.'

'But why? And what is *spike*? It is cancel?'

'Yes. Cancel. I've been ordered to cancel the whole operation.'

'Once more I am asking why?'

Khokon Roy bit his underlip.

'I'm afraid I can't tell you. Officially, in fact, I don't even know myself. I can only guess. And I may have guessed wrong. All I know is that when my editor gives me instructions in a certain way there is no point in questioning and arguing. There it is.'

For two seconds Ghote sat, taut with baulked fury.

'Very well,' he exploded at last. 'I am going to see your editor. Now.'

'Old man, best of luck. But I doubt if you'll get to learn from Soumitra Mukerjee, good man that he is — and he is that, believe me — one bit more than I have.'

The editor of *The Sentinel* sat in a room higher up in the narrow old building and rather less bare than that alloted to Khokon Roy on the ground floor. It was poky enough, however, although there were here and there touches of, not luxury, but a certain artistic display. Behind the desk there hung in an ornate frame a painting of the great Rabindranath Tagore, all flowing white hair, flowing white beard, long sombre robe. Poet, novelist, painter, sage and rebel, too. Behind, as Ghote was shown in, on the wall by the door where the man sitting at the desk could see them at every instant were four posters, curling with age at their edges, pinned at their corners to the otherwise bare dust-dimmed white wall. Ghote, glancing back, had recognized from the statue he had seen on the Maidan the topmost one as Netaji Subhas Bose, Calcutta's fighting hero, revered in the exuberant city high above peace-loving Gandhi. A round, fattish face, faintly double-chinned, with typical Bengali rounded nose and eyes fire-flashing behind ever-present spectacles.

Then, since he felt his looking at the poster was winning the approval of Soumitra Mukerjee, who in fact rather resembled Bose himself, he took a good look at the three posters below. And saw at once the names printed in the Bengali script he could just make out, *Binoy — Badal — Dinesh*, the three martyrs of revolution for ever commemorated in the name of BBD Bagh.

'Yes,' came the editor's voice from behind him, 'four heroic men who look me sternly in the face if ever I am inclined to falter in my pursuit of truth and justice. But please be seated, my dear sir. How may I help you?'

Ghote was tempted not to sit but to stand there, accusingly. Just the day before, according to Khokon Roy, Soumitra Mukerjee had faltered more than a little in his pursuit of truth. Time to tell him so, blunt Bombay fashion. But he let second thoughts prevail.

If I am to get this man to change his mind and put out a story naming Mr Gopal Deb, he thought, then I must go about it in some more cunning way.

'Sir,' he said, introducing himself as he settled into the middle one of the three chairs lined up in front of the desk, 'I have not been very long in Calcutta but I have heard nothing but praise itself for you and your paper.'

On the editor's distinctly double-chinned face a look of unconcealed pleasure appeared behind his round spectacles.

'Well, Mr Ghote, young Khokon has told me about the business that has brought you to us, and let me say at once how much I sympathize with the difficulties yourself and your wife have got into. They cannot have made Calcutta seem as welcoming as she always is.'

'No, sir, I must admit, Calcutta has not

been altogether welcoming. But I had thought that was changing when Mr Khokon Roy was so helpful to me.'

Soumitra Mukerjee's face swiftly took on a look of comprehensive vagueness.

Ghote, taking this in, almost gave up there and then. Plainly the man was anxious to avoid considering the plea he guessed was coming. But he was not going to let himself be easily fobbed off.

'Sir,' he went on, 'it was, I must confess, something of shock to me, to my wife also, when we were not reading in *The Sentinel* this morning a story with in it the name of a certain Mr Gopal Deb.'

'Yes,' the editor replied with evident reluctance. 'Yes, well, I am afraid that Khokon, who is full of true Bengali enthusiasm, does sometimes promise rather more than he can perform.'

No, again I am not going to let him off the hooks so easily.

'But, sir, I am understanding that he was altogether ready with that story, and that he was finding same had to be — is it? — spiked.'

'Spiked, yes. Mr Ghote, you have picked up with admirable rapidity the jargon of our unholy trade.'

And that appeared to be all the comment

the editor of *The Sentinel* was willing to make. But, again, Ghote pursued him.

'Sir, I must be blunt. Kindly put it down to Bombay directness. But it was you yourself, yes, who was spiking?'

For a long moment Soumitra Mukerjee sat in silence. Ghote noticed that he was looking, not at the array of heroic figures on the wall opposite him, but down at whatever papers he had on his desk.

But at last he spoke.

'Mr Ghote, I do not know whether you will understand. But let me tell you something of the situation this paper finds itself in. You see, we have no financial backing. We are not a paper like *The Statesman*, in existence for many, many years, read and bought by thousands in Calcutta and sought out in consequence by advertisers by the score. No, *The Sentinel* lives almost hand-to-mouth. But nevertheless we do not hesitate — no, no, I must correct myself — *The Sentinel* does not often hesitate to expose the evils in our midst. And sometimes, I flatter myself, we are successful. An evil is wiped out.'

Now he did look up, for just a moment, to Binoy, Badal and Dinesh.

'But, Mr Ghote, there are areas when, if it gets known that we are on the verge — how shall I put it? — of putting our finger on too tender a place, well, then we get to learn that there are limits we must not cross. Limits which we must respect, or risk even extinction. Mr Ghote, let me put it this way: is it better to have in Calcutta a crusading paper which sometimes does not crusade, or not to have any such journal at all?'

It was plain that he did not really expect an answer to the question, and Ghote did not give him one directly. Instead he got up from his chair.

'So *The Sentinel* will not be using any story with in it the name of Mr Gopal Deb,' he said.

'Mr Ghote, I am sorry that I have not been able to be more helpful.'

★ ★ ★

On his way out Ghote looked in on Khokon Roy, who grinned at him, if wryly.

'Well, I see by your face that I was right. You got nowhere.'

'True. So there is one thing I am asking.'

'Yes? My dear chap, ask. Ask, ask, ask. And, I trust, receive, receive, receive.'

'The address of one Mr Gopal Deb, ICS retired.'

'Oh, my dear fellow, no. No, no, no. You cannot have any idea what going further with this business may bring down on you. I say no more. But I do say *Don't*. Be sensible, don't go one step further.'

Ghote heard him without interrupting. Then he spoke up.

'Mr Roy, kindly give me that address. I am not your editor, even if I may perhaps somewhere in me like to be such a man as I have found him to be.'

Khokon Roy shook his head.

'My dear chap, you may at this moment have a somewhat low opinion of the courage and resolution of my esteemed editor. But let me tell you: a pretty grave threat has to be made before he at last gives in. A very grave threat.'

'And you are thinking that one grave threat has been made to him just now?'

'I know no details. But I can deduce. And that is what I believe has happened.'

'But that threat was just only to the future of your paper, yes? Not the kind of threat you are hinting would be made to myself?'

'Listen to me, I beg of you. There are people who are ready to threaten the existence of *The Sentinel*. And those same people are very likely to threaten the existence of an individual, of any individual who offers to trouble them as much as you seem minded to do.'

He looked up at Ghote, his hitherto smiling face abruptly grim.

'Listen,' he said, 'Mr Gopal Deb may be no more than a nominee there to conceal the identity of whoever so desperately wants to get hold of your wife's house. But he will be some sort of associate of Dutt-Dastar's, if not of the person behind him. Let him so much as guess you are poking and prying into this affair, even though *The Sentinel* has been silenced, and he will let those whose cat's-paw he is know. And then you will be in the gravest danger, my good chap. So think, I beg you. Think.'

'Mr Roy, thank you for saying that. Not every person would venture so much for a stranger. But nevertheless I am asking once more. What is the address you have found for Mr Gopal Deb?'

Khokon Roy, unsmiling, sighed.

'Try Apartment 93, Blue Haven, Lord Sinha Road.'

He looked as if he wished he had not uttered the words.

15

Ghote went straight to Lord Sinha Road, which the driver of the taxi he hailed had no difficulty in locating. Briefly he wondered if every taxiwalla in Calcutta knew and loved the city so well that its every street was familiar to them, as was certainly not the case in Bombay where sometimes it seemed every ride ended with directions being asked for, in loud shouts, from every passer-by. Lord Sinha Road was not far off Chowringhee at the southern end of the Maidan, a short street looming with tall buildings, mostly dating, he guessed, from the 1960s.

In no time at all, swept up in the lift — handsome fountain in the front courtyard, but dry — he was ringing at the bell of Apartment 93 and hearing from inside a melodious chime. He looked at the solid dark-wood door in front of him, stainless steel letters on its plaque spelling out *GOPAL DEB*. What would this man be like? The nominee ready to buy Protima's house so as to pass it to the person, whoever he was, who intended to build a road over it to the wetlands site for a new colony productive eventually of vast wealth? More, this Gopal Deb must be a man who would not hesitate to pass a warning to his mysterious backer, the person who had given instructions after hearing from ACP Bhowmick, to have me attacked there in the Botanical Gardens? To spare me my life then. But is it to be spared now?

Or was stainless-steel Gopal Deb not just the nominee but the Eventual Assignee himself? It might be. It might be.

He felt in the pit of his stomach a hollow ball of apprehension.

A servant swept open the door in front of him.

He straightened his shoulders.

'I am wishing to see Mr Gopal Deb.'

Would the fellow answer *Sahib, not at home*? He half-wished he would.

'Your good name please? I will ask Deb Babu.'

And then there was the man himself. He was standing against a big window leading on to a balcony with, behind, a widespread panorama of Calcutta, distant and magical in its shroud of dust. Dressed in tweed jacket, white shirt, quietly striped tie and grey trousers, just wearable at the onset of winter, stern pipe in mouth, heavy spectacles on nose, he was the very picture of an almost British respectability. A man of sombre, settled look. A deceptive look?

'Mr Ghote, did my servant say? I don't believe we have met.'

His English was clipped, almost as if he was in fact someone from the distant days of the British Raj.

'No, sir,' Ghote replied, conscious that his very next words would be the first signs to this man that he was being probed about the house, the wetlands, the new colony. 'But perhaps you are knowing the matter of business that is bringing me.'

'Business? Well, I don't have much to do with business. You aren't going to try to sell me something? A car? Life insurance?'

A sharp look.

'No, no, sir, not at all. It is — It is this. I understand you are interested in buying a certain house.'

Sharp look for sharp look. But no apparent response.

Surely he must be alerted? If he is attempting to buy Protima's inheritance to advance that corrupt plan, then when I was mentioning *a certain house* he must have realized who I am. Even if at first the name Ghote did not mean anything to him.

'Yes, it is true, Mr Ghote, I am — Ah, wait, yes. I believe Mr Dutt-Dastar told me that the name of the seller of the house he was advising me to acquire was Ghote. But didn't he say it was a Mrs Ghote?'

'My wife.'

'Ah, yes, I see. Of course. But what is it you want with me, sir? I expected the whole transaction to be dealt with by Dutt-Dastar.'

Either he is being one hundred per cent cunning, or there is some mistake. Certainly he is not at all sounding like the Eventual Assignee I had hoped to reach.

'Yes, sir,' he answered with care, measuring out each word. 'Mr Dutt-Dastar is the person who was approaching my wife hoping to induce her to sell. But, sir, kindly understand. She has no desire to sell. She wishes to have the house put in order, to have some squatters that are there sent away. And then she is wishing for us to live there for the whole remainder of our days.'

Well, that is what she is wishing, and no point to say my wishes may be different.

But Gopal Deb was frowning in what seemed to be a wholly puzzled way.

'You say your wife does not wish to sell? You are sure? It was certainly my impression that she was eager to disembarrass herself of a place presenting nothing but problems for her.'

'Sir, no. She is very much keen to stay.'

Another puzzled frown.

'Sit down, Mr Ghote. Sit down. I see we shall have to go into this at some length. There seems to have been a considerable misunderstanding.'

Ghote sat down on, almost collapsed on to, the soft armchair behind him. Gopal Deb, face pursed in a look of dawning worry, took a chair opposite.

Can it possibly still be the Eventual Assignee I am sitting with, Ghote asked himself? If he is, this sitting together and *considerable misunderstanding* talk is playing one very deep game. And I am not at all seeing why. Look at it. He is intending to buy Protima's house to use it for that road to the wetlands. He has gone to some lengths to make sure he is getting, and keeping his secret also, even to the extent of having me robbed of that document. Then I myself am coming here and beginning to question. Surely he must then deny everything, turn myself out of his apartment and then call in some goondas to me? He would have to deny everything also even if he is just a man put there by the Eventual Assignee, and pass on the warning that will see myself dealt with. But he is showing no signs of doing any of those things. Why?

And no answer coming.

'Let me tell you something of myself,' Gopal Deb said, settling in his chair, knocking the ashes from his pipe into a large ashtray beside him, then taking from his jacket pocket a yellow pouch and slowly stuffing the pipe with tobacco. 'I often find it necessary to go back to beginnings whenever I am faced with some more or less intractable problem. It's a method I frequently found useful in my working life as a Government officer.'

Another roundabout, talk-talk-talk Bengali, Ghote thought.

But he said nothing.

'So,' Gopal Deb went on, 'let me start indeed from that. My life as a civil servant. Because until something over a year ago that was all my life. I was left a widower at an early age, a widower with just one daughter whom I had to send away to be looked after by her mother's family. So I devoted all my days and all my efforts to doing my duty to the Indian Civil Service, to my fellow countrymen. A limited life, you will say. And I have to admit now, looking back, that it was such, though I hope that by it I made the lives of those it was given to me to affect somewhat better. But it was a life that taught me little of what the lives of those outside my circle were like.'

He leant forward, took the now smoke-drifting pipe from his mouth.

'It is only now, in my retirement, that I have really seen the mess that many people live in. Oh, of course, I had had glimpses of that world. An officer in Government service cannot go for long without being offered some sort of bribe. But, well, I was brought up in the shadow of what we thought of as the strict code of the British. I have always been punctual to the dot. I have always known what is right. I never had any difficulty in rejecting such approaches. I have always kept my conscience clear. My father, an ICS man like myself, and in the days when there were precious few Indians in the service, used to say to me that if you had a good conscience you could digest what you ate. He used to cite Henry Ford in America saying that there was a man so single-minded in building up his motor-car empire that he ended by not being able to digest even a simple boiled egg. Wheras the Viceroy of his day, Lord Linlithgow, always had two quarter-boiled eggs for his breakfast, and never suffered so much as a pang of indigestion. And so my father, too, ate his quarter-boiled eggs every morning and saw to it that there was nothing on his conscience to disturb his digestion. And, yes, I have always eaten two quarter-boiled breakfast eggs.'

A sudden smile as the pipe was removed from between his teeth.

'And I digest them. But just now, when you told me what you did, I begin to wonder whether tomorrow morning those eggs will digest quite as easily as they usually do.'

Ghote felt puzzled. And not only by all the Bengali nonsense about quarter-boiled eggs. Gopal Deb was giving a wholly unexpected picture of himself. And how was all this talk-talk going to lead to A. K. Dutt-Dastar having apparently offered Protima's house to this brown sahib, as he and his like were often called?

But it seemed he was about to get the answer.

'Well now, that much said, let me move on to this house of your wife's. Believe me, Mr Ghote, I had no idea when I learnt that it was for sale that anything underhand was involved. Dutt-Dastar was someone I had simply met playing golf at the Tollygunge Club. I had mentioned to him that with my retirement I had some funds at my disposal and felt I ought to put them to use for my daughter's benefit. You know, I have seen fellow officers of mine, men I had thought of as beyond reproach, when they were getting

234

to within, say, five years of the end of their service, yielding suddenly, with sons to send to college, daughters to get married, to the temptation of receiving money. Holding out their hands, even. But I had been brought up with certain principles and wouldn't take a step down that primrose path. However, when Dutt-Dastar told me he could put me in the way of a good investment that might yield a quick return, I simply said I was willing to go ahead. I had no idea you and your wife had such a strong attachment to the house in question.'

And now, against his better judgment, Ghote did break in.

'Not myself, sir.' The words tumbled involuntarily out. 'It is not my wish to live there.'

'No? But it is your wife's I believe you said. Her earnest wish. Very well. Let me say that, had I known that, I would never have said for a moment I would buy the place. Dutt-Dastar told me your wife had unexpectedly inherited it and had no idea what to do with it. He said it would be a service to her to buy it for a reasonable sum, and added in strict confidence that he had a possible further buyer, someone not wanting to lay out money at this particular juncture.'

A possible buyer.

Ghote thought he was beginning to see the light. The Eventual Assignee, whom he had thought he was about to confront as he stood outside the door of the apartment, was certainly not this quarter-boiled-egg-eating brown sahib. Gopal Deb was no more than the innocent nominee buyer Khokon Roy had talked of. But the Eventual Assignee? That could be the man A. K. Dutt-Dastar, doubly proven liar, had said did not want to pay for the house at *this particular juncture*.

How these Bengalis loved their long words and roundabout expressions.

But, more important by far, can I to get from this brown sahib, who has been told that name *in strict confidence*, who it is?

Try.

'Sir, thank you for telling me so much as you have done. And I begin to see that, yes, you have been in good faith involved in what I am thinking is a hundred per cent serious matter. Sir, I have to tell you I believe the person Mr Dutt-Dastar found for you to sell my wife's house to is wanting same not at all to be his home. Sir, I do not know if you are aware of what is proposed for the wetlands beyond the house?'

'Wetlands? I know nothing about the

wetlands. Beyond the fact every Calcuttan knows. That they exist.'

'Then, sir, let me inform. There is a plan, as yet just only some possibility, to create in the wetlands a new colony. Sir, it is a scheme that may bring crores of rupees in profits to whoever is controlling it. And it is vitally depending, I believe, on being able to make a major road where my wife's house is standing, by some chance on the only easy route to where that colony may be built. Sir, there is happening, I am certain, one dirty business. Even to the extent that I myself have been attacked when I had obtained a certain paper that was giving a clue to it.'

Watching closely, he saw dawning in the eyes behind the heavy spectacles a look of understanding.

'Corruption.'

The word fell into the quiet of the big room high above Calcutta's roar of distant noise like a sentence from the judge's bench.

'Yes, I see now, Mr Ghote, that I have been duped. To be frank, I never wholly liked Dutt-Dastar. But I saw no reason to let what I thought of as mere prejudice — the fellow's not exactly a gentleman, you know — stand in the way of a piece of legitimate business. But I see now it was far from legitimate. Someone plainly intends to get his hands on your wife's house by buying it, *sub rosa* as they say, through me for what must amount to a song, in anticipation of permission being granted to build this colony you speak of. Yes, corruption. The business stinks of it. And in high places, I don't doubt. A scheme like this would never have been entered upon unless it was known that there was someone at least in the higher reaches of West Bengal Government who was susceptible to bribery. Who, yes, could be bribed into granting whatever permissions may be necessary. This country, Mr Ghote. This country of ours. Undermined. Prey to greed of every sort.'

'Sir, I am certain now that you are right. You have mentioned highest places. Let me tell you, sir, that I was trying to get this business stopped by going to that paper *The Sentinel* — '

'Bit of a rag. But, yes, I believe it has exposed corruption cases in the past. Go on.'

'Well, sir, all was going very well, until suddenly the editor there was receiving orders from some altogether mysterious person that, as they are saying, the story was to be spiked.'

'Spiked? Ended? Finished? Heard no more of?'

'Yes, sir.'

Gopal Deb looked at his pipe. It had long before gone out. He tapped it with a little angry tattoo on the ashtray by his side.

'What pains me, what alarms me,' he said, 'is not that bribery and corruption exist in India. They have always done that. In India and in every other country under the sun I was taught long ago, you know, to look up to the British, whatever wrongs they may have done to India, for their abhorrence of fraud and cheating in business, for their sense of fair play. But even in the UK now — you have only to read the foreign news pages of *The Statesman* — they are mired in corruption. No, what alarms me is that those at the top here in India who should know better are simply excusing corruption, justifying it on the grounds that everybody is corrupt. When I think of that I wince with shame. Yes, shame.'

Now, Ghote thought. It is now or never.

'Mr Deb,' he said, 'you can overcome such shame. I am not believing each and every person in this country is corrupt. I believe you yourself are scorning corruption. So, sir, break the strict confidence in which you were told about my wife's house. Sir, give me the name of the person who aims in the last to acquire it.'

Would the brown sahib answer?

The answer came. But it was not the one he had expected.

Gopal Deb sat in thought. Eventually he did move. But it was only to take up his pipe, look at its unlit bowl with astonishment, poke about in it with an instrument at the end of the penknife he took from his pocket, strike matches one after another and, at last, get it to draw again.

Three or four long puffs.

'May I ask, Mr Ghote, just why you want to know this name?'

Now, for a moment, it was Ghote's turn to think.

'Yes, sir, I think I may tell you. Sir, when I was standing before the door of this flat after I had rung the bell I was hoping that it would be answered by a servant who would say, *Deb Babu not at home*. Because I was almost trembling with fears. I thought I was about to face up to the man behind this corruption, the man who already had had myself attacked, who was attempting to force my wife to sell this house she was inheriting out of blue, like some three-times wonderful Diwali gift. But, sir, when I thought of that, of what he was wanting to cheat my wife out of, then, sir, I thought I must face him. I must face you, sir, as I was believing.'

'All for your wife's sake. So that she could enjoy in peace this Diwali gift, as you have called it?'

Claim the credit Gopal Deb is willing to give? No. Tell the whole truth.

'Well, sir. Although, as I have said, my wife is wishing and wishing to live here in Calcutta, a true bhadrolok lady, I myself am not wishing that. If I could do what deep down I am liking, I would return to Bombay where I am inspector of police and continue as same until day of retirement.'

'Yet you ask me for that name? Why, Inspector?'

Why? I do not know. No, I do. And I must say it.

'Sir, yes, it is partly to be making sure my wife is keeping that house because she is so much wishing for same. But it is more because I am seeing before me one piece of corruption that, if I try to do my level best, I may bring to an end.'

'Yes. Very good. Very good, Inspector. To be frank, had you replied that your sole object was to make sure your wife acquired this house, then I would have simply advised you to abandon your quest, to acknowledge that you both unfortunately have come up against forces, forces of evil, yes, that are too strong for you. I would say: cut your losses and go back to Bombay.'

Ghote, at those words *go back to Bombay*, recalled in a flash of sharp vision Khokon Roy using much the same expression when he was suggesting how he might trick the name of the buyer of the house out of A. K. Dutt-Dastar. They had been part of a piece of trickery then, but even as Khokon Roy had spoken them he had for an instant wondered whether that was what they should do. Go back to Bombay.

So should I do it now? No. No, Gopal Deb was speaking of forces of evil. And I cannot just only run back to my safe home when those are approaching. No.

'But, sir,' he said, 'you are not advising me to go back to Bombay, yes? So kindly tell me that name you were given in confidence.'

Gopal Deb gave a grunt of a laugh, through teeth clenched on his pipe stem.

'Alas, Inspector, that I cannot do. For the simple reason that I myself was never told it. Our friend Dutt-Dastar is too cunning for that. No, all I can do, I'm sorry to say, is to give you one piece of advice.'

Ghote felt a chill of despondency slowly settling down on to him. What help could he get from this brown sahib locked in his world of long-gone British values?

'I would be altogether grateful for whatever

advices you may have, sir.'

'Then simply this, Inspector. Go to *The Sentinel* once more and, using all the power at your command, all the guile if you like, squeeze out of those people who it was who ordered their report of this business to be — what was it you said? — spiked.'

16

Ghote, once more, found himself in the bare room in the dusty offices of *The Sentinel* where Khokon Roy worked, its black-rimmed fan slowly twirling above. As soon as the young journalist had finished tap-tap-tapping away at the keys of his computer he told him how his confrontation with brown sahib Gopal Deb had gone.

'At last he was giving me just only one piece advice,' he ended.

'And that was?'

'That I must come here and find out who was ordering Mr Soumitra Mukerjee to spike your story concerning himself and the wetlands.'

The cheerful smile with which Khokon Roy had asked his question slowly left his face.

'Well, yes,' he said at last. 'Good advice, all right. But easier to ask that than to get an answer.'

'I was hoping you yourself would get me same.'

A grin. A wry grin.

'Oh, yes, I could pick up this green phone,

or go tramping up the stairs, and ask. But I know very well I'd get no answer. All I would get, indeed, is a drop down in my editor's estimation, a large, large drop down. Okay, I'd gladly risk that, if I thought that it would help get me the answer you want. But it won't. It won't.'

'Then I must be myself asking.'

'I know there's nothing I can say that will stop you. But a warning nevertheless. Mukerjee Babu is a man of integrity. But only up to a certain point. You may have seen as much. However, the question for you is: up to what point? Certainly, he will not tell you the name you ask him for. He is committed to keeping that secret. He's pretty well assured that if he told you who that order came from and you then went poking your Bombay detective's nose in where it was not wanted, he himself and *The Sentinel* with him would be the ones to suffer. But will he go further than that? Will he feel that, to make sure of the paper's continued existence, it will be his duty — if that's not too high and mighty a word — to let this person, whose identity I can dimly guess at, perhaps wrongly, know that you are asking your questions. And if he does, then you can be sure that someone will take steps to see that you do not ask questions any more.'

Ghote once or twice had felt the need to interrupt this new Bengali cascade of words. But, partly because they were making sense, and partly because he liked Khokon Roy too much to be impolite to him, he had managed to check himself.

Now he no longer could.

'Mr Roy,' he said, 'kindly pick up that green telephone and inform Mr Soumitra Mukerjee that I am coming to see.'

He waited no longer after he had seen the unsmiling journalist reach out to the green phone.

★ ★ ★

He did not expect to be received with pleasure by the editor of *The Sentinel*. Nor was he.

'Mr Ghote, I heard you were making your way up here. And I note that you do so uninvited.'

Behind the editor, looking his most heroic in full Netaji Subhas Bose style, the tall imperious form of Rabindranath Tagore, white-bearded, long-robed, looked down from his ornate frame. In reproof?

Or — he thought — with encouragement? One defying an enemy to another managing to do the same.

'Mr Mukerjee, I will not beat about any bushes. When I was here before you were admitting to me that, for the sake of your paper, you had obeyed certain instructions not to continue investigating a story that was concerning one Mr Gopal Deb. Very well. I can see you may have had your reasons. But what I am here now to demand is: who it was who was giving such instruction?'

'Mr Ghote, you have no right to make any such demand. No right at all. I was good enough before to make you privy to some confidential matters concerning this journal. I do not expect to be rewarded in this way.'

The mini-Netaji Bose puffed himself up to his full heroic extent.

Ghote, anger a little added to from his not having had time to eat since the Fairlawn's porridge, kipper, toast and marmalade, struck back with fire.

'Mr Mukerjee, I am asking who it was who told you to suppress the story you were one hundred per cent ready to print.'

'Told? Told? Who said I was told? I decided it was in the ultimate interests of *The Sentinel* not to pursue a story that was almost certainly going to prove of no value. And that was all there was to it.'

'No, Mr Mukerjee. You were yourself indicating to me that you had received

247

some instruction. An instruction you were not daring to disobey. Mr Mukerjee, who was giving that instruction?'

'You — You — ' With an effort he checked himself. 'I am afraid, Mr Ghote, that you somehow received a wrong impression. There was no one. No one gives Soumitra Mukerjee orders.'

But, in the face of that blatant lie, rather than banging back another fiery rejoinder, an idea came into Ghote's head. A wondrous idea.

'Mr Mukerjee,' he said, 'I am not knowing too much about your city of Calcutta. But one thing I am knowing. It is a city of writers. Poets, yes. Novelists also. And of journalists. Mr Mukerjee, you are not the only editor of some small newspaper in Calcutta. I do not know the names of your many sister journals, but I can easily find same. And, when I have found one that may be your rival, I will be most happy to tell its editor how you yourself are succumbing to pressures. I have no doubt some way or another he will like to publish full details. Where then will be the respect *The Sentinel* has had for all its lifetime?'

He saw the look of rage on the round, double-chinned face on the other side of the desk. Of baffled rage.

For several seconds Soumitra Mukerjee

was silent. But then a small smile stole over his sagging face.

'Very well, Mr Ghote,' he said. 'I will give you the name you have asked for. But I do so in the full knowledge that if you stir so much as one finger after you have heard it, you will be crushed like a fly under a swatter. Crushed, yes. Crushed.'

'Sir, the name?'

A look of biting malice.

'Listen to this then. Mr M. F. Tuntunwala.'

★ ★ ★

Slowly descending the narrow, cobwebbed, dusty stairs of *The Sentinel's* offices, Ghote thought about the name he had been given. It was one familiar to him. Familiar indeed the length and breadth of India. M. F. Tuntunwala, descendant of Marwari traders who a century ago had come hungrily from the harsh, sun-scorched deserts of Rajasthan to the fertile valley of the Ganges, was head of a concern called simply Tuntunwala Management. But the number and variety of the firms, the factories, the shipping lines, the mills, the newspapers, the new commercial television companies that the concern managed would, Ghote knew, fill half the pages of the little crusading *Sentinel*.

No wonder that a single phone call from him to Soumitra Mukerjee had brought that order, *Spike it.*

And Ghote knew more about Tuntunwala Management than that. He knew what, years before, rival newspapers had delighted to report. At one time a dozen or more of the firms then under the Tuntunwala umbrella had been accused of tax evasion on a huge scale. But the validity of the Commission investigating these activities had promptly been challenged in the courts, and after barristers by the dozen had had their say, and pocketed their fees, it had been found that the Commission did not have the power to investigate which it believed it had possessed. The cases then had been handed back to Government officers for further action. And twenty years had passed away.

Not a man to be lightly tackled, Mr M. F. Tuntunwala.

Or, standing at the foot of the worn old staircase, Ghote began to wonder if he was a man it was possible to tackle at all.

Am I reaching to the end of it all? Should I be taking the advice that some of the other gentlemen at Bhattacharya Babu's adda were giving? To leave, as he was saying, well or ill alone? Was that a better advice than the one I was taking, to go to Assistant

Commissioner Bhowmick? Well, that could hardly have been a worse one, the way it was bringing me nearly to disaster under the shade of the Great Banyan.

So it had been Mr M. F. Tuntunwala then that ACP Bhowmick was lifting his telephone to call as I was leaving his cabin. Or perhaps, since M. F. Tuntunwala, powerful figure though he was in the world of commerce and industry, would not be able to arrange promotions and nice postings for a police officer, the ACP had been calling someone high up in the West Bengal Government. Someone who M. F. Tuntunwala had already bribed to make the decisions for a big new colony in the wetlands?

Thrusting down once again his revived pangs of hunger, he went back down to Khokon Roy's bare room.

At once the clever young journalist looked up from his VDU with a grin of welcome.

'Triumph?' he asked mischievously. 'You asked my boss a simple question and he replied straightaway with the answer you wanted?'

'Not altogether straight away.'

'What? He told you? Told you who he takes orders from? I don't believe it.'

'It is Mr M. F. Tuntunwala.'

Khokon Roy pulled a long face.

'Now I do believe you,' he said. 'If you had forced me to say who I thought it might be when you were here a few minutes ago, I would have produced that name. I had occasion some time ago to go through our back files in search of something or other, and I couldn't help noticing, as I did so, how many of the ads were from Tuntunwala companies or companies I happened to know came within his empire. With our ridiculously small circulation they could not have been commercially worthwhile. So I had said to myself, *Tuntunwala*. But I took jolly good care never to say it aloud.'

He looked up at Ghote, eyes widening in speculation.

'But how on earth did you wring Tuntunwala's name out of our look-alike Netaji Bose?'

'So you are noticing that also?'

'Doesn't everybody? But, you know, despite that pose I have quite a high opinion of my crusading editor. He does, in fact, crusade to good effect often enough. But I also recognize he has his weaknesses. Doing his best to look like our great Calcutta hero is one of them. I well remember the day he came into office with a new pair of spectacles, exact replica of those you see on Subhas Babu's pictures. He was hardly

252

able to stop himself asking me if I had noticed them. But all that doesn't mean I have forgotten my question. What is the secret of your magical powers, Mr Ghote?'

'In the end not one great secret. I was blackmailing.'

'Black — Ah, I see it now. You must have threatened to tell the world . . . But how would you be able — No. No, this will be it. You actually threatened to tell some other editor that Soumitrada — you see I still give him our Bengali affectionate *da* — has had to bow the knee to pressure. Yes, poor chap, he would not have liked that idea at all. Well done. Well done, indeed.'

'Yes, well enough done, if you are liking to say it. But, you know, after all finding out M. F. Tuntunwala's name is leaving me almost worse off than before.'

'Yes.' Smile fading. 'Yes, my dear fellow, you are not exactly happily placed, are you? I don't suppose Soumitrada will, but what if he does decide he has to tell Tuntunwala you forced him to give you his name? I don't want to scare you, but, if I were you I'd be making tracks now for your familiar Bombay. Tonight, if you can get a flight.'

'A flight? Well, yes, a flight is no problem. My wife is a first-class briber of airline ticket desks.'

'Then, and I'm serious about this, why don't you get her to go to Dum Dum and start laying down money? You may be safe, if Soumitrada hasn't used his phone. But I wouldn't like to guarantee it.'

'No. No, I will not do it. When I was coming here to Calcutta I was secretly hoping that somehow I would not have to stay in the house my wife has inherited. But now, when it is looking as if I could easily go back to Bombay, persuade her because of the dangers not after all to become a bhadrolok lady, now I am no longer wanting. I have seen in front of me one crime. And I am not willing to let it go forward.'

'Bravo, my friend. Bravo.'

Again Khokon Roy wiped the smile from his face.

'Bravo, but think. Think who you are up against. I do not know for certain that M. F. Tuntunwala is capable of having you put out of action. He may be a perfectly good man. My thoughts about him may be only the prejudices of a Bengali intellectual towards a Marwari businessman. But, all the same, I must tell you I think the warning I gave you just now is one you should pay heed to.'

'No. I cannot.'

'Then what, in God's name, do you intend to do?'

Ghote thought for a moment.

'Just now I was thinking,' he said, 'that Mr M. F. Tuntunwala cannot be the only person involved in attempting to buy my wife's house for corrupt purposes. He must have someone beside him, the person who has been putting one Assistant Commissioner Bhowmick where today he is.'

'Yes,' Khokon Roy said. 'I don't doubt you're right. There will be a shadowy figure — I could easily name two or three West Bengal politicians, more perhaps — who will be in this business with our friend Tuntunwala. Because to make a really big financial coup he needs to know just when the road he'd like to build over your wife's house will be needed. Or, indeed, if it will be needed at all. Remember what is in full swing, that agitation to save the wetlands. Well, in fact our muchloved supplies of fish. So Tuntunwala has to have someone in Government who can tell him if the plan is to be pushed through or to keep the details secret long enough for him to acquire, not just your wife's house, but all the designated area of the wetlands beyond. You know, that's a tradition in Calcutta that goes right back to our earliest days.

It was the British then who were playing the game, but it was the old Calcutta game all the same. Played, for instance, by none other than a Chief Justice of the time, one Sir Elijah Impey, lampooned in what you might call the predecessor of *The Sentinel*, something called the *Bengal Gazette*, as 'Sir Poolbundy' because — and listen to this — he gave a *pulbundi*, a contract, for river embankments to none other than his own cousin. Wonderful.'

He chuckled happily.

Ghote, reflecting sourly yet again on Calcuttans' stick-at-nothing pride, gave a sharp cough.

Khokon Roy stopped laughing.

'Listen, my dear fellow,' he said. 'Don't you see that there being someone in Assembly House involved in this business makes your plight all the worse. If the one doesn't put a stop to your interference while the scam is still on the cards, the other will. No, my dear chap, get your wife off to Dum Dum this very afternoon.'

'That might not be too easy.'

'Oh, come now. Enough modesty. When it comes to the crunch, I bet I know who in your family gives the final orders.'

Ghote did not answer for a moment.

'I suppose you may be correct,' he said at last.

'All right then, give out your orders.'

'But I do not want. Mr Roy, I am going to find out enough of this corrupt scheme to go, not to Mr Mukerjee, but to *Statesman* itself.'

'Well,' Khokon Roy said with caution, 'I suppose you might pull that off. You just might. But think what you've got to do. This is it: you've got to get to see M. F. Tuntunwala himself. He's the only person you'll ever learn enough from, trick enough out of, to have something hard to take to *The Statesman*. All right, I suppose you can appeal to him, seemingly wanting no more than to keep your wife's house intact. And he might — He just might fall for that. If he doesn't see through you within two minutes of you stepping into his office. And don't forget he didn't make himself, as we say here, so rich even God cannot buy him, without being rather more cunning than all the monkeys in India. And all this depends on you getting to see him in the first place.'

'Well, but if that is the only way — '

'No, wait. Wait. I do believe I can help you a bit here.'

'You are able to give me an introduction

to Mr Tuntunwala? One that will admit me to his office itself?'

'No, my dear fellow. I am not your favourite Bombay god, Lord Ganesh, remover of obstacles. But I do, as it happens, know something about M. F. Tuntunwala that not everybody knows. And, because of that, I think I can tell you how you can get to meet him face to face. And, what's more, in perfect safety.'

17

Khokon Roy looked at Ghote.

'Listen,' he said, 'don't be a fool after all. What business is it of yours that M. F. Tuntunwala and some Assembly House crony of his are aiming to make a lot of money, however corruptly? Let them just get on with it.'

'No. I have said.'

Another long look. No hint of the ever-ready smile now.

'All right then, have it your own way. Do you know our famous Marble Palace?'

Ghote frowned.

What was this?

'Yes,' he said, 'I am hearing about that place. One of the old palaces of the City of Palaces, yes? One famous Calcutta sight, built by some rajah, still owned by the family and in ruin altogether, no?'

'Yes. On the whole. Though it's not in ruin altogether, as you politely put it. But it is in a pretty sad state and sometimes people wonder, rightly or wrongly, how the Mullick family, for all their wealth, can continue to keep it. Which brings me to my point.

Among those who may be wondering about that, as I have chanced to find out, is our friend, M. F. Tuntunwala.'

'Yes?'

'Yes, indeed. And I'll tell you how I came to know. You see, I am one of those who has a great fondness for the Marble Palace. I like it for its decay. Decay, you may know, is sometimes seen as the essence of Calcutta. Well, I'm not sure I go that far. After all, you have only to look at buildings like the Tata Centre, just behind the Victoria Monument, or a dozen other semiskyscrapers like it, to know that we in Calcutta have our full share of twentieth century get-up-and-go.'

Oh God, Ghote thought. Just only one word triggers it off, with anybody in this city of chatterers. The full Bengali boastfulness.

'You were telling you were knowing a secret fact about Mr M. F. Tuntunwala,' he said dryly.

'My dear fellow, I've been wandering again. We Bengalis . . . Now, what was I saying? Ah, yes. That I love the old Marble Palace. So much so that, whenever I get a chance, I go off to Muktaram Babu Street, give some baksheesh to the darwan at the gate if it isn't the laid-down public visiting hours — give him a bribe, if you like — and spend an hour or so strolling round. Now, wait. Be patient, be patient. This is actually all leading up to what I'm about to tell you. You see, on one of those occasions, on more than one in fact, who should I see strolling there like myself but M. F. Tuntunwala. Only perhaps *strolling* is not quite the right word for what he was doing. Prowling, I think would be better. Yes, prowling. Prowling the way a pi-dog prowls round one of our never wholly removed rubbish heaps.'

Ghote, for a moment, saw the heap he had watched all one afternoon from his window at the Fairlawn, the crows hopping and squawking over it, the cats, lowbellied, pouncing at the crows at last, the black pig coming scavenging next and then the pi-dogs, necks extended, muzzles pointing, eyeing what was there for the snatching.

'So Mr Tuntunwala is envying the Marble Palace, yes?' he said.

'Yes. And yes again. I'm willing to bet that in secret inside the head of that monstrous millionaire thoughts are lurking. Thoughts about what one day he might do with all the valuables slowly rotting away, too many of them, there in the Marble Palace.'

'And you are thinking that if I also go there I could, if I am being lucky, find M. F. Tuntunwala?'

261

For a few instants thoughts of the triumph he might somehow achieve flashed through his mind. The monster of corruption confronted, questioned policestyle till he broke, a grovelling confession . . . And then they faded into nothingness.

'First snag,' he managed to say.

'A snag? Come, show us a little Bombay determination.'

'Well, it is just only that I have never seen Mr M. F. Tuntunwala, so how would I be able to recognize him there in the Marble Palace?'

Khokon Roy broke out in laughter.

'Trust Bombay common sense to see difficulties Calcutta high-flying had utterly overlooked,' he said. 'The police officer must have his mug-shot, yes? But perhaps Calcutta can come to your rescue over that. Let me see if I can find yesterday's *Amrita Bazaar Patrika*. They had a picture of Tuntunwala. A good full-face. Hold on a minute.'

He rummaged through the papers and files on his table, dipped down and peered underneath it. And in a moment emerged with the paper. He folded it to the right page and held it in front of Ghote.

Head and shoulders of what seemed to be a man of dark complexion. An aggressively large nose. Thinning hair oiled back from a sloping forehead. Heavy spectacles. And, most prominent of all, ears long-lobed, close to the sides of the sharply-boned face and apparently carved into a moonscape of miniature valleys and ridges.

'Yes, I would know him now,' he said. 'If I am finding him. And . . . And perhaps then, because of the secret thoughts he may be having about that palace and its many, many treasures, I would have him at one disadvantage, and if I am questioning he may let slip more than he would like.'

'Well, don't be too hopeful. It's a long shot at best, a very long shot. But I can be just a little more help to you about finding our friend. You see, for some reason no doubt connected with his schedule, or perhaps because on Thursdays the palace is not open to the public, I can tell you that Tuntunwala is very often to be found there in the morning. And I suppose that you, being an on-the-ball Bombay police officer, know what day of the week it is today.'

'It is Wednesday, of course.'

'Yes, even I, vague Calcutta walla that I am, know that. So why don't you ask your Bengali wife to take you to the Marble Palace tomorrow morning, Inspector? My small bribe for the darwan and he'll let you in. And good hunting.'

'Orphaned child of a very, very wealthy Calcutta merchant, Raja Rajendra Mullick began to build this palace in the year 1835,' Protima said.

Guidebook, guidebook, Ghote thought distantly.

For a moment he wondered, though, whether he had been right to have told Protima only that he wanted to see the Marble Palace, claiming that Khokon Roy had told him of its delights. All right, she had snapped up this sign that at last he was beginning to appreciate her Calcutta, city of palaces, city of elegance, city of softly sad decay.

But should I instead have told her why it really is that I am wanting to come here? To find moonscape-ears M. F. Tuntunwala, the man who for his corrupt purposes is wanting to get hold of her house? The man who is so powerful that, if he is wishing it, he can crush me, as Soumitra Mukerjee was threatening, like just only one fly under a swatter? But, no. No, what weakness it would be to tell one's wife one is putting one's head into danger in the hope that she would cry out so loudly that there would be nothing to do but promise not to go forwards.

But perhaps M. F. Tuntunwala will not be here, Thursday morning or no Thursday morning. But perhaps he will be.

'Rajendra, as he grew up,' Protima's voice came to him, 'was combining his fine education from his British guardian with his very great business genius to amass one first-class fortune, and he was spending and spending on acquiring many fine things. You would be able to see three paintings by famous Rubens, one statue by Michelangelo and many other costly objects. The whole building also was made from marble and the Viceroy of those times was consequently saying to Raja Mullick, *Call it the Marble Palace*, which he was at once doing.'

'Yes, yes.'

'It is stating in the guidebook' — Ah, she is admitting she is having some guidebook to her Calcutta — 'that the gatekeeper expects a donation.'

They had arrived at the closed iron gates between their two enormous, double-pillar, vase-crowned gate-posts. The darwan, hand fiercely gripping a spear, rather rusty in appearance, glowered out.

Donation equals bribe that Khokon Babu was mentioning, Ghote said to himself, thrusting a moderately generous ten-rupee note through the bars into the man's ready outstretched hand.

The gate was opened a few inches. They squeezed in, leaving behind the incessant clatter of sound in the street beyond, the calls of vendors, the shouts of laughter or of anger, the tinny music of transistors, the ting-ting-ting from rickshas, the hoot-hoot-hoot of taxis, the irritated whirring pings of bicycle bells, the thwarted rumble of car engines and the high-pitched revving of the dozens of autorickshas at a standstill in the press of traffic. And leaving behind, too, the long line of beggars waiting till noon for the Mullick family's daily gift of a meal.

Has M. F. Tuntunwala paid his bribe before me, Ghote thought? It would be a bigger one than ten rupees. Or is he still to come? Or will he not be coming today at all?

Guarded by stone lions, mouths open in silent roarings, the immense building stood before them, fluted white pillars rising high to an enormous, fantastically carved pediment.

'That is Calcutta for you,' Protima said. 'More than magnificent.'

Yes, he thought. But inside this huge place will I ever find M. F. Tuntunwala? And there are gardens also, stretching out.

Perhaps — this is a fine day — he will be there somewhere.

'I am thinking,' he said, with unusual directness, 'we must first see these gardens. I have heard that they, too, are typical beautiful Calcutta.'

Protima looked a little surprised. But pleased as well.

They set off. A tank with in the centre of its sunglinting water a much-carved tall statue, a dry fountain, with some Western sea-god, bearded, blowing some kind of horn — it looked as if it had become broken off — with behind him bare-breasted ladies upholding the fountain's basin. Ducks of a dozen different sorts swam, waddled, or sat in dozy contentment on the well-mown grass. Peacocks strutted. All round, neat paths with yet more statues beside them, a Redskin, some Chinese, Western emperors with carved wreaths on their brows.

But no head of a huge commercial empire, prowling.

'Time to go inside,' Ghote said at last.

'But it is so nice out here.'

'No, we should go in. Or we would not have time to see all that is to be seen.'

'Yes, perhaps you are right.'

A wide courtyard, looked down at from a high gallery, its floor a pattern of different coloured marbles. More statues brought from Europe. Romans in togas. And in cages all round, their narrow bars rusty, birds of various sorts, whistling, tweeting, cheeping. Shoes by direction carefully removed and added to a small collection already there, they went on into the rooms behind. A huge head of some kind of deer, its antlers spreading wide. And, yes, a label underneath, *Moose*.

Was that one of the objects M. F. Tuntunwala had looked at with lip-licking envy?

Move further on. A billiard table, covered in a heavy cloth, evidently unused for many, many years. A statue of some sort of slave girl. And everywhere dust. And stucco peeling from walls, and patches of greenish dried mould from monsoon damp after monsoon damp, and cobwebs high up in wide greyish circles and dangling in long rope-lengths.

Eaten away. Everything, everywhere, eaten away.

Oppressed, Ghote recalled Mr Bhatta-charya's long outpouring about how Calcutta was being corrupted as much by physical neglect and its scorching suns and battering monsoons as by the rapacious poor who had come flooding in, taking what they could, and the rich who had been taking yet more. Poor corrupted Calcutta.

For a moment he heard again the haunting music of the old man's quiet singing. His Tagore song.

But no place now for softly sad, Bengali thoughts. He was here for a purpose.

The next room, all red marble. Queen Victoria here, carved in wood, in wood now worm-holed almost to destruction, a young queen but, sceptre-wielding, monarch of all she surveyed. Blank white busts almost beyond counting looking back at her from shadowy nooks. And, beside him, Protima producing confused facts and guesses, only half taken-in, about what it was they were seeing.

But, at this early hour and public-barred day, no living beings except themselves. Not a sign of M. F. Tuntunwala.

And when I spot him, if I see him, Ghote thought, subduing panic, how am I to get from him whatsoever would enable *The Statesman* to start up such an investigation that even this man, unbribable by God, will at last tumble into dust?

The Paintings Room. The immensely valuable pictures, dull, gloomy, brown, their subjects hardly to be made out. One of them hopelessly cracked and bubbled. But so precious that M. F. Tuntunwala would be drawn to stand looking at them? Thinking how much was to be made if they were sold back to the countries they had come from?

The Mirror Room. Its walls covered with the hugely tall mirrors, twelve feet high and more. But all spotted and speckled. Corrupted. And, hanging from above, enormous chandeliers, some of their hundreds of glassy slivers long missing.

He thought for an instant of the hole in the ceiling of Protima's house where another chandelier must have been ripped away, to be sold or to hang from the branches of that pipal tree until a buyer appeared.

But move on, move on.

A room seemingly dedicated to the Emperor Napoleon. Two busts set up on ornate tables facing each other.

Yet Ghote hardly took them in. Because, circling round and round one of them was a man he instantly recognized. A man with a dark complexion, large prying nose, hair oiled back from a sloping forehead and, plain to see, two long thin moonscape-sculptured ears close to the skull. White shirt, pen in its pocket. A white dhoti, though by no means as beautifully pleated as Bhattacharya Babu's.

At once he turned to Protima, still murmuring to him her confused commentary.

'You were saying it was nice in the

gardens,' he said, low-voiced. 'Too hot for me, just now. I have headache. But you should go out again. I will wait here, and when you have had a walk, come and find me. We should go back to eat one paid-for Fairlawn Hotel curry lunch.'

'But — But you are all right? You are not feeling ill?'

'No, no. It is just only headache. With looking at so many beautiful things. It would go soon.'

She seemed doubtful.

'No, please. It would be better for me just to be here in the cool, and not to be trying to take in any more magnificent objects.'

'All right then.'

She left.

Over by the Napoleon bust M. F. Tuntunwala was standing now in silent contemplation of the great emperor.

What it is he is thinking? No. No, I must not be asking myself that. There is one thing only I must do. Speak. Speak to M. F. Tuntunwala, head of Tuntunwala Management, the man who wants the house Protima has inherited, the man who is planning his huge corrupt deal.

Moving silently, shoeless on the cool patterned marble of the floor, feeling as if he was one of the palace's statues not

271

come to life but suddenly endowed with the power of movement, he traversed the huge room. And then he found himself looking over the top of the white bust of Napoleon at the man he had at last hunted down.

'It is Mr Tuntunwala? Mr M. F. Tuntunwala?'

Was his voice cracked? Perhaps. He certainly could not tell.

The Marwari millionaire glanced up sharply.

'What if I am Tuntunwala?'

'Sir, I must speak with you.'

'You must? And who are you?'

'My name, sir, is Ghote. It is perhaps known to you?'

'No.'

'Then, sir, let me remind. There is a house in South Calcutta, a big old house if now in a state of eaten-away ruin, which, because it is where it is only, has become very, very valuable. Once the property of one Chattopadhyay Babu, lately deceased, now the property of my wife, Mrs Protima Ghote.'

M. F. Tuntunwala made no reply to that. But it was clear that he did have a shrewd idea now who it was who had come up to him.

'Sir, it is about that house that I am wishing to talk.'

'Well?'

'Sir, I have come to know that you are the man who, in the end, wishes to obtain possession of that property.'

He came to a halt. This was it. The point where he must turn from jamai of a Bengali lady who had inherited a certain house into — Into what? Into a police officer interrogating.

'And, sir, I am well knowing why you are determined to get hands on this property and none other.'

'Are you?'

'Sir, also I am very much aware of what steps you have so far had taken to stop my wife from continuing to keep that house. But, sir, she is wanting same. It is her lifetime's wish. Sir, why cannot she have?'

'And why should she wish to have what you have called an eaten-away ruin?'

But was this, perhaps, a thin crack. A small opening.

'Sir, it is not so much why she should wish to keep what she has in full legality inherited. It is a question of the reason that you are wanting same.'

'And why do you think that is, Mr Ghote?'

His answer banged out. For better, for worse.

'Sir, it is in furtherance of one corrupt transaction.'

There. Said. The accusation made. To his face.

'Very well, you have found out that I am engaged in what the world calls corruption. Now, let me tell you something, Mr Ghote. There is no such thing as corruption.'

Ghote felt it as a ringing slap to the face.

M. F. Tuntunwala let a small, hostile smile curve for a moment his hard, out-thrust lips.

'I see I have surprised you. But let me invite you to live if only for a moment in the world as it is. A world where the days of what they call Anglo-Saxon morality are long gone. As they are gone even in the Anglo-Saxon world, where I conduct not a little of my business. Oh yes, people still mouth the words of that morality. But it is mouthings only. I doubt if, in fact, those much-praised standards ever existed anywhere, beyond in the practice of a green-behind-the-ears handful convinced by their own preachings. As for me, when allegations are thrown at me of breaking the Anglo-Saxon taboos, those straw-and-paper or painted-clay idols, it is my policy not in any way to react.'

Ghote wanted to break in. He wanted to say that there were standards, that the old rules were more than straw idols to be sent

274

up in flames at festivals or clay ones to be immersed in the sea or the river. But he was not sure that he could put that forward with all the determination, and the truth, needed to stop M. F. Tuntunwala in his tracks.

'Yes, I see you find yourself without any good arguments,' the Marwari millionaire went on. 'As you can hardly help being. You must know in your heart that life on earth is a fight. You cannot truly believe anything else. We each of us fight against what keeps us down. Some fools fight with the strength of their arms. But men who know what it is they have to fight against fight with their brains and their wills. And if corrupting those weaker than themselves is the weapon that comes to hand, then they use it. As much and as hard as is needed. Yes, because the only weapon there is, when you get down to reality, is money. Money, Mr Ghote. You are a police officer, isn't it? An inspector, Bombay side?'

So he is knowing that. He has asked and asked about myself for his nefarious purposes.

'Yes, sir, I am a police officer.'

He had wanted to say more. But he still needed time to find the words, if find them he could. In the meanwhile that declaration would have to do. *I am a police officer.* That is what I am. That is all I am. An upholder of the laws as we have them.

And — there is something else here — M. F. Tuntunwala knows more about me than that I am one inspector from Bombay side. He has been told more about me. He knows I have seen that memorandum of A. K. Dutt-Dastar's. So I am on his list. In his field of fire. Out on the Maidan in front of his cannons.

But that means, yes, he is fearing me, however little. He is believing I can do him harm.

He felt a glow.

It was soon extinguished. Or water-showered almost to nothing.

'Yes, a police officer. So you will have little idea about money. Oh yes, you will scrape up whatsoever salary you are handed. You will argue over deductions and accretions. And I dare say you will gladly hold out your hand when there is money coming from above.'

'No — '

'But you will have no idea what money does. So let me tell you. Little good though my telling will do you. Money, Inspector, changes hands. Yes, that is what it does. It goes from one person to another. And as it goes it brings power to one person, takes power from another. So if you want in this life to make yourself safe, then you have to make the money come to you. By any means. Call that corruption, call it business, call it what you are liking to. But get the money to come into your hands, as much of it as you can. As I have got it to come to me. As I have fought with every weapon I could reach for to make it come to me. And it has. And I intend to keep it. And all those who have got it intend the same, make no mistake in that. Do you think that I am shunned in society? Or that any who are known to use the weapon of corruption are shunned? No, if they are the sort who like to belong to the clubs, they are welcomed as members. Their daughters are begged for in marriage. Their sons are courted. You know what the effect of all this money changing hands is? Quite simple. The work gets done. The world continues. And without the money going to and fro the world would come to a wretched standstill. A standstill. Without money changing hands. Without corruption, as they call it, that Anglo-Saxon relic. Yes, Inspector, corruption is necessary. Just that. Necessary.'

Necessary? He must say something in face of that.

'Sir, no. Sir, I — '

'Inspector. Go away. Leave Calcutta. Just go.'

A cold smile was set on the thrust-forward lips as the millionaire turned and walked off.

Ghote stood there where he was beside the marble-white bust of the all-conquering Emperor Napoleon.

For one moment he had thought of running after the Marwari, of seizing him by his arm, spinning him round, shouting into his face. The police officer in full pursuit.

But, no. No, he had absolutely no authority for any such action. And something worse. Far worse. He had just been told, by perhaps the man in all India with the knowledge to tell it, just exactly what corruption is.

18

He did not know how much time had passed before he became aware that Protima was once more standing beside him.

'You are looking not at all well,' he heard her say.

For a second or two he was unable to answer her. Then, as he gradually began to piece together what his situation now was, he managed to murmur a few stopgap words.

'Headache is still there.'

Yes, he confusedly thought, what has happened is that I have discovered nothing more whatsoever about the corrupt deal M. K. Tuntunwala as good as admitted he was masterminding. I was coming here to find him and to somehow get from him some fact I could be taking to *The Statesman* to be more of proof. But what it is I have succeeded to do? Nothing. Nothing. I have no more evidences than I was having before. And instead I was receiving one blister of a lecture that is making me — I cannot help it — begin to wonder if corruption can be halted anywhere at all, ever.

So what now can I do?

'Still you are not sounding like yourself.'

Shall I tell her I am truly not myself? Not the man who was saying with utmost pride to M. F. Tuntunwala *I am a police officer.* One who enforces the law. One who if he finds corruption stamps on it. But I am no more that man. I am a man who does not know what he is believing.

'No, I tell you. I am okay.'

At once he regretted that little jet of anger. It had been directed against himself, the man who did not know. But Protima had been its victim.

'No,' he lied swiftly. 'No, it is just headache. With so much of sightseeing.'

Another little upspringing of regret. I should not have said those last words. Especially when they are not at all true. And I was the one who, even if it was a lie, told her I wanted to sightsee at the Marble Palace.

But Protima did not respond to the jibe.

'Well, we should go,' she said, 'if we are to be in time for the lunch gong at the Fairlawn.'

He felt a little revived by her forbearance.

'Then we must be quick,' he managed to say with a smile. 'I do not want to have to go for fish-head eating once more. I am not yet a hundred per cent Bengali.'

She laughed.

'It will take me many years to get you even to twenty-five per cent.'

Another little bounce up the ladder from black depression. Even if she still thinks of herself as staying here in Calcutta, she is not after all determined to make her Bombay husband into a full Bengali jamai.

So it was that he decided to tell her as soon as opportunity arose the real reason that they had visited the Marble Palace and to try to get her to see what he had so painfully learnt.

* * *

It was a decision that, as they worked their way through the Fairlawn's curry lunch — it was not in any way unpleasant, he decided, just somehow too British, too solid — he very soon came to regret.

He had moved onwards, cautious step by cautious step, with what he had to tell. He had explained first how he had discovered that ex-ICS brown sahib Gopal Deb was merely a nominee as purchaser of her house and in fact perfectly ignorant of why the sale was to be made. He had gone on to say how he had gone back to *The Sentinel*, armed with Gopal Deb's advice, and had succeeded there in extracting from Soumitra Mukerjee Babu the name of the man behind the plot, M. F. Tuntunwala.

Protima had been duly shocked at hearing the great industrialist named as the man who needed right of passage through her house and its compound. Shocked and, he secretly hoped, impressed by the way her husband had found out what he had.

So, while she was thoughtfully silent, he went on to tell her that finding out about M. F. Tuntunwala was not the end of the business.

'So it became next step,' he said, 'to learn from M. F. Tuntunwala himself perhaps just only one small fact that would provide enough to make a paper as powerful as *The Statesman* take up the matter. But, you understand, I could not just only go to Tuntunwala House and demand and demand to see M. F. Tuntunwala. But then I was learning it is his habit to visit the Marble Palace almost each and every Thursday a.m. And it was in order for me to meet him face-to-face that we were there just now.'

At this Protima did look a little resentful.

'And I was succeeding to meet him,' he plunged on. 'It was when I was claiming to have headache and you were going back into those gardens.'

Now she bristled a little more.

'Being sent back into gardens, as if I was too much of a fool to be allowed to talk with a great man like M. F. Tuntunwala.'

'Well, yes. I mean, no. No. No. But I was thinking it would be easier if just only one person was trying to learn from him what I was needing.'

'Well, what did you learn?'

He had not quite expected that question, or not as soon as this in the course of his explanation. In fact, he had not really prepared himself for it.

'Well ... Well, it is not altogether simple to get from a man of the power of M. F. Tuntunwala what it is you are wanting to know. Not when he is deciding he will tell you something else.'

'So you know nothing? Nothing that is worth knowing?'

'Well ... No. I suppose I do not.'

'Then what did M. F. Tuntunwala say to you?'

This was worse.

'He was ... He was talking about corruption.'

'What else would he talk? No doubt the man is corruption itself.'

'But, yes. Yes, that is what, if you are liking, he was telling and explaining. That corruption is everywhere. That one and all are practising same. That he has no conscience about using corruption. That even it is a good thing to do for one and all.'

'It is not.'

'Oh, I am knowing that. But . . . '

He was aware that his not being able to go on was in fact an inner admission that he felt still M. F. Tuntunwala, somehow, had it right.

'What *but*?'

The question shot out.

He frowned in bewilderment.

'Somehow,' he answered slowly, 'what M. F. Tuntunwala was saying had in it very much of conviction. You yourself should have been hearing.'

'And why I was not? Because you, Inspector Ghote, Bombay Crime Branch, are believing yours is work for big-big men only and you were making sure I was just only walking in gardens looking at some ducks.'

'No, no. No, it is not at all like that.'

'Then why was I not inside Marble Palace listening to lies M. F. Tuntunwala was telling? And not, like Inspector Ghote, Bombay Crime Branch, believing each and every one of them?'

'But — '

'Then, after you had believed and

believed those lies, you were saying to M. F. Tuntunwala, *Oh, yes, maharaj, I would do whatsoever you are wishing?* Yes? Yes?'

And, yes, he inwardly admitted that was — two-three protests apart — almost what I was saying.

'No. I was not saying that.'

'So what you were saying?'

'It was more what M. F. Tuntunwala was saying.'

'And what he was?'

He sighed. Sighed to the pit of his stomach.

'He was in the end saying I should leave.'

'Leave? Leave where? Leave just only Marble Palace where you were spoiling his mood? Or leave Calcutta itself? It was that, yes? He was telling you, telling myself also, to go back to Bombay and not be like whine-whining mosquitoes troubling the great sahib?'

'Yes.'

It was all there was to say.

But not all Protima had to say.

'And you were letting him give you that order? You were willing to go? To go from Calcutta back to Bombay, and leave that man to take my house, my house, just when he is wanting?'

To go back to Bombay, where I am knowing who I am and what I am doing: yes, that is what I am very much willing to do. But . . .

'My house, my house,' Protima repeated, her voice ringing round the dining-room, now mercifully empty except for one aged, turbaned waiter dolefully clearing a distant table. 'And do you know I have not as much as seen one piece ownership paper for that house? What they are called? Deeds? Yes, deeds. That man Dutt-Dastar has been keeping and keeping from me even the deeds of my own house.'

'Yes, he could have given,' he agreed quietly.

He must make some concessions to her, even though if she got hold of those deeds they would not now do her any good. One way or another, by bribing here, by bribing there, M. F. Tuntunwala was going to get possession of her house.

'He could have given, and he should have given. He is going to give. He is going to give now, just so soon as we can get round to his chamber. And then, when I am in possession of same, you are knowing what I am going to do?'

'No,' he answered helplessly.

Protima rose from her seat at the table.

'I am going to that American gentleman who was sitting there' — She pointed with fiercely outstretched arm to the table where they had overheard occasional snatches of talk between the dog-faced American, Mr Deen Kogan, and his British friend — 'and I will ask him, as one expert on the restoring of ruined palaces, to come to see my house.'

He sat in silent misery.

How could she still think her house was going to be put into a state of repair? It was not. It was not. It was going to crumble before the mighty power of M. F. Tuntunwala. It was going, really and truly, to be ground down to nothingness. And Protima and myself are going to go, like whipped pi-dogs, back to Bombay where we came from.

'Oh, ask, ask,' he said at last. 'Ask as much as you are liking. But first see if you are able to get those deeds out of A. K. Dutt-Dastar.'

★ ★ ★

It took them, however, an infuriatingly long time to get to A. K. Dutt-Dastar's chamber. First of all, out in Sudder Street, where usually there seemed to be nothing but frantic shouts of *Want taxi? Want taxi?* there was not a taxi to be seen. At last Ghote spotted one turning in from Chowringhee at the end of the street and by pelting hard in that direction managed to grab it before anyone else.

But, coming up as it was from the Maidan, it was heading in the wrong direction for them. In consequence it took them what seemed like hours to thread their way through the tangled streets of North Calcutta, eventually to emerge into BBD Bagh, its vast Writers' Building and the glittering surface of the great tank at its centre. There they had to fight their way past buses abruptly pulling out from where they had been halted, past clanging trams and the whole jerky complexity of other traffic.

So Protima, who had begun the journey no more than tight-lipped with suppressed anger, was by the time they came to a halt in Rabindra Sarani sputtering with rage.

'How can a journey just only as short as that take so long?'

'Traffic bad,' Ghote suggested peaceably. 'In Bombay . . . '

He left it. He had been about to say that, though Bombay's traffic was seldom less than terrible, drivers there did usually manage to make reasonable, commonsense progress. But he decided comparisons in Bombay's favour were not what Protima would want to hear at this moment.

But he had left it too late.

'Bombay. Bombay. You are always and always stating how much better is Bombay. I am sick and tired to hear it.'

He shrugged.

What she had claimed was scarcely true. But it would be a good thing if she were in a little less of a fiery Bengali mood by the time they confronted A. K. Dutt-Dastar. Shouting at him was hardly likely to bring to light the deeds of the house, if the lawyer had not already been forbidden by M. F. Tuntunwala to part with them until the sale of the house was certain.

In just two minutes more, however, it looked as if they were at least on the point of being able to make their demand. The clerk Haripada, still inkily thumping away at his ancient typewriter, had gone, upright and creaky of step, to ask if his master was free. Surprisingly, it appeared that he was. They had marched then into his book-lined chamber and found him behind his wide, gleaming desk, hands spread on its big green blotter, which today did not match the pale brown shirt he was wearing. For once, too, his eyes were not hidden behind his black wrap-around glasses.

'Mrs Ghote, what a pleasure to see you.

You, too, Inspector. Delighted to see you both. If, alas, it is for the last time. Calcutta's loss, Bombay's gain.' A swift insincere smile. 'But let us get down to business. No delay. I know Bombay ways. Abandon idle Calcutta chit-chat, yes? Business before pleasure. Now, first of all I have to tell you — I am sorry indeed to say it — your purchaser is no longer as willing to pay as much as he was. You will have to accept the diminished return. But that — '

And here pent-up Protima at last burst in.

'Mr Dutt-Dastar, am I understanding you still think I am wishing to sell my house? Let me tell, you could not be more mistaken. I have never for one single moment wished to sell. And even less now do I wish.'

The lawyer's face was suddenly a whole illustration of bewilderment.

'But — But I underst — ' He licked at his lips. 'Mrs Ghote, Inspec — Mr Ghote . . . You have changed your minds? I — I — But, listen, I thought I had made it clear. Retaining possession of the house is not really an option for you. The state of the place . . . The legal difficulties . . . '

Ghote decided it was time for plain speaking.

'Mr Dutt-Dastar, we are well aware of

your attempts to trick us into parting with the house. To parting with it to a nominee purchaser. We are aware, even, who is behind such a purchaser. And we are here — My wife is here to demand from you the deeds of the house she has legally inherited. The deeds which you now, as a lawyer, hold in trust.'

'The — The deeds? You are coming here actually to request to have the deeds of that house?'

'What else?' Protima banged in. 'It is my house. You are the lawyer executing the will of my late cousin. It is your duty to pass on to me, the rightful owner, those deeds.'

'I — I shall have to think.'

'What is there to think?' Protima snapped. 'There is to give only.'

'Well . . . Well . . . Well, you see, naturally I have not been keeping such valuable and important papers here in my chamber. I would be failing in my duty had I done so. Yes, failing in my duty. The deeds, are, of course, lodged in the bank.'

He looked up now from the green blotter to which he had been addressing most of what he had said.

'And,' he added with new sharpness, 'it is now too late to retrieve them. Banking hours have come to an end. Sadly to say.'

Ghote looked at the watch on his wrist, although he had at once realized that the tricky lawyer had been speaking the truth. Yes, it was now definitely too far advanced into the afternoon. What a piece of pure bad luck. The lack of taxis in Sudder Street. The extra length of their trip here. But bad luck it was. Though good luck for A. K. Dutt-Dastar.

'Mr Dutt-Dastar — ' Protima was beginning again, but the lawyer swiftly cut in.

'However, do not worry.' He glinted out another flash of a smile. 'Tomorrow the banks are open. I can be there just as soon as the doors are parted. I can remove those deeds from the deposit-box where they are in safe keeping. You may have them at whatever hour will suit you.'

Trickery. Some trickeries only are there.

But, though this was Ghote's first thought, he could not see how A. K. Dutt-Dastar's smiling assurance was really going to help the fellow to withhold the deeds. True, earlier he had imposed delays in handing over money for Protima to pay an expert to look over the house. But, even if tomorrow he found some reason not to part with the deeds, he had admitted they were in his possession and that Protima had a right to them. So perhaps it could be only a matter of time before she

292

had them in her hands.

The deeds, he thought with a sudden inward descent, of the Calcutta house she still resolutely intends to stay in for the rest of her days. Something I must help her to do to my level best. For all that I know now M. F. Tuntunwala will, by hooks and by crooks, get his road to the wetlands through it.

And plainly much the same thoughts about the deeds had been passing through Protima's mind, if without that depressing addition.

'Very well, Mr Dutt-Dastar,' she said, laying the words down like so many winning cards, 'tomorrow at ten-thirty itself we shall be here. Here to receive those deeds.'

'Madam, it will be my pleasure.'

★ ★ ★

Protima, as soon as they had emerged from the lane into the noise and bustle of Rabindra Sarani, proposed, eyes alight with what she believed to be her triumph, that as soon as they could they should find none other than Mr Deen Kogan, American expert in restoring delapidated houses. They would arrange with him to go and inspect her house. She had not the least doubt he would agree. And then they would go that very evening to the Son-et-Lumière display at the Victoria Memorial.

'They are telling it gives a fine history of Calcutta.'

But when Ghote ventured to say he lacked the heart to go after all the turmoil of the day she agreed to postpone the outing.

'Perhaps you are right. Until and until I have those deeds in my hand I would not truly believe we are going to be able to stay here in Calcutta. And to watch that history, if somehow we are still going to be tricked, would be altogether cruel.'

'So you also are wondering if we shall be tricked?' he asked, hoping that this was her way of preparing herself for the defeat he knew was inevitable.

'With a man like Dutt-Dastar there, it is not easy to be hopeful.'

He noted with an inward jump of pleasure that from having been — what was it? — *a Bengali gentleman to the last* the lawyer had been relegated now to *a man like Dutt-Dastar*. But such pleasure as he took from this concession was before very much longer to be swept utterly from his mind.

19

They failed to find Mr Deen Kogan anywhere in the Fairlawn. So Protima declared she would abandon everything and go once more to the Kalighat Temple to beg for Goddess Kali's aid. 'She is, even you must be knowing, the destroyer of the wicked. And, if one thing only is sure, it is that M. F. Tuntunwala is wicked in wanting the house that is truly mine.'

Ghote, unwilling, as he thought of it, to sink himself to begging to a goddess he had long ceased to believe in — though in a deep corner of his mind secretly hopeful Protima's prayers would work a miracle — prepared himself to spend a dull evening amid the insistent Britishness of the hotel, the framed photographs of the Queen of England with her little dogs, of a fading Prince Charles, of the Queen with her militarily stiff husband.

For a few minutes after he had dutifully consumed the British fare at dinner, faintly spicy mulligatawny soup, lamb chops in a totally unspiced gravy, bread-and-butter pudding, he had gone out into Sudder Street, seeking distraction. But the sound of so many exuberant Bengalis talking, talking, talking in their over-excited way — Yes, in Bombay we are talking, but not as if it is our last chance to say all we have to say — filled him even more deeply with depression.

What if Protima's prayers are after all succeeding, he asked himself in a sudden spat of fury. How would I endure to stay in this place for the rest of my life itself? In that too, too big house? Doing all these damn Bengali things? Must I also come to shout out at top volume each and every thought I am having?

A terrible idea flitted into his mind then, as he stood half-watching the young foreign tourists crammed chattering in the Blue Sky Café.

Should I go back to Bombay alone? I could resume duty. Even if I was not having any share of the money she is inheriting with the house, I could live. I have my pay and allowances. I will have my pension, that I am making so much of obligatory payments towards.

But, no. No, he answered himself as quickly as the question had made its beguiling passage through his head. I could never leave Protima here, in this city. This city ruled by big men like M. F. Tuntunwala and his friends. M. F. Tuntunwala would not so easily forgive if she was succeeding somehow to keep the house against his wish. She would not be safe here. Not at all. Very well, Bombay also is a city with one full share of nefarious activities. But that is a lawlessness we are knowing how to put at a distance. But here, in this place she was once saying was so much more peaceful, it is turning out to be altogether different. No. No. No. I could not leave her here alone.

He had tramped hastily back into the hotel then. Even a British ghostliness was better than the thought of Calcutta life. And perhaps death. What else but death was it that Khokon Roy warned me of?

Glumly he sat with a sprinkling of the Fairlawn's foreign guests to watch an old black-and-white video of a film called *In Which We Serve*. Perhaps, he thought, after all I should have gone to Kalighat Temple and prayed, against all reason, that everything may turn out well.

'Our film,' announced the hotel proprietress, presiding over the showing, 'was made in days when we British set an example to the world. You know the ship that is sunk in it was based on H.M.S. *Kelly*, which went down commanded by Lord Mountbatten, last Viceroy of India?'

She was rewarded with a murmur of

appreciation from the handful of viewers. Ghote did not join in. On the small screen in front of them the video flickered by. Noel Coward proclaimed in his closed-up British voice, *If they had to die what a grand way to go . . . There isn't one of you I wouldn't be proud and honoured to serve with again.*

But, Ghote thought in the surrounding darkness, were any of those hundred per cent British gentlemen actually taking bribes in secret, or offering them? Who would know?

★ ★ ★

It was only shortly after Protima had returned with another splodgy red tilak from the temple priests on her forehead — 'I was coming back on the Metro, only one in India, very quick journey' — that they discovered that, prayers to Goddess Kali or no prayers to Goddess Kali, everything was not for the best.

The door of their room, which they had not thought of locking, was thrust unceremoniously open. And there stood Assistant Commissioner Bhowmick. In full uniform. Swagger stick under his arm.

It took Ghote a second or two, sitting unable to move for shocked surprise on the flowery-topped stool beside the dressing-table, fully to absorb what he was seeing. Then in a burst of silent rage he thought, *How is he daring to stand before me when he must be fully aware I know who set on to me those goondas under the Great Banyan.* But perhaps, perhaps, he had counted on him not making the connection between a robbed wallet and a disappeared document.

Then he thought, Protima, *she has never before seen this man, what will she be thinking? Wondering? Imagining? Fearing?*

'Mr Bhowmick,' he said, the rage taking precedence over all else, 'you are coming in here without even tapping the door. My wife is here. What are you meaning by this?'

ACP Bhowmick smiled, tigerishly.

'It is Mrs Protima Ghote I am here to see,' he said. 'More than to see. To put under arrest.'

'Arrest? Arrest?' He struggled to believe what he had heard. 'But what for would you be arresting my wife?'

'On a charge of corruptly offering money to one by name Shibu.'

Corrupt? Offer —

He almost said, *But it was myself who was offering that peon Shibu his bribe.*

But Protima had now recovered from the sudden intrusion.

'What nonsense you are talking,' she shot out. 'I am not corruptly offering whatsoever.'

'Madam, we have reason to believe differently. Unfortunately Shibu, who as you very well know was a peon employed by Mr Dutt-Dastar, a highly reputable lawyer in the city, is now deceased. Otherwise we would be able to confront you with him, and you would be already under arrest.'

Deceased. Out of the ACP's smooth talk Ghote had extracted that one word. Deceased.

With a stab of bitterness he decided not to puff out pointless questions. Deep down he knew how snake-birthmarked Shibu had not simply lost his post at Dutt-Dastar's chamber but had become deceased. Or rather why. Because he had sold that file marked *Mrs Protima Ghote — Bombay*. Had sold it to himself for the comparatively small sum of five hundred rupees. Except for that one disloyal act to A. K. Dutt-Dastar he would not have met his end. It was monstrous. Very well, Shibu was hardly a good man, no clerk Haripada. And, true, he had betrayed his master's trust, such as it was. But for that he did not deserve to die. To be brutally killed.

Then another thought. A brutal killing. That was what men of the stamp of

300

M. F. Tuntunwala and his Assembly House co-conspirator could order to be done. Perhaps they would go that far only with someone from among the hundreds of thousands of refugees who in the past had poured into the city, an almost nameless man whose death would pass unnoticed. But, pushed to an extreme, they would be willing to go further. To put an end to any life that stood in their way.

Then yet other thoughts came crowding in. Protima not just arrested but put behind bars. In the lock-up like a common woman criminal, some prostitute who had failed to pay a police jawan his weekly hafta or some petty female drug-seller of poor quality brown sugar, cramped and crowded in a hot and dirty cell. And later as an under-trial kept for years in a woman's prison, a place scarcely better. Rotting away.

Because this was no ordinary arrest, no arrest for a real crime that had been really committed. All right, Shibu had been bribed, if actually by myself, Protima's husband. But it was with only five hundred rupees, a small enough sum in this city riddled with corruption from bottom to top. And something else. The matter was hardly one to come under a senior officer whose duty it was to improve the traffic chaos of Calcutta, however that posting had been obtained.

No, it was plain. This whole business was in response to Protima's defiance this afternoon at A. K. Dutt-Dastar's chamber, her demanding the deeds of her own house. That was why she had been so easily promised them next morning. Because A. K. Dutt-Dastar had fully intended at once to report to M. F. Tuntunwala that his warning was being ignored. To report, well knowing that the Marwari millionaire would take immediate action. And now M. F. Tuntunwala through ACP Bhowmick was striking back.

And striking hard.

What to do? Really just only one answer. M. F. Tuntunwala wants the land on which Protima's house stands. It is the key to his plan to make crores of rupees out of the building of that new colony. And to get hold of that single place where a road can easily be built to the heart of the wetlands he is prepared to go to any lengths, having poor Shibu killed, putting my wife — my wife — in jail for year upon year. More, we are powerless to stop him. So it is a matter now of cowing down to ACP Bhowmick and stating we are ready to sell.

It cannot be anything else.

A tiny current of pleasure trickled then through the deepest part of his mind.

Bombay. Back to Bombay. Life to be as it was before Protima was getting that letter.

'Mr Bhowmick,' he said with extreme caution, 'is this a matter we may discuss?'

Again the ACP smiled.

But, Ghote thought, this is a smile with less of tiger.

He had not, however, reckoned with his wife. She, too, must have been thinking, and on much the same lines as himself. But she had come to a very different conclusion.

'What nonsense you are talking,' she fired off at him. 'No, Mr Bhowmick, there is nothing to discuss. I am well knowing you are making these threats so that I will agree to sell the house I am wishing from my heart's core to keep. But your threat is empty. I have bribed nobody. If you attempt to arrest me you will find yourself in trouble.'

ACP Bhowmick's eyebrows rose in his long, pale brown, oval face.

'I hardly think so,' he said. 'If it was not you yourself who handed a sum of five hundred rupees to that wretched peon, it was your money handed to him by your husband. And I can assure you that when I decide someone is to go to jail, to jail they go.'

Something in his silver-tongued certainty

must have got through to Protima.

She turned to Ghote.

'It is nonsense he is talking?' she asked, and there was not much certainty in her voice now.

He stayed silent for a moment.

How to answer? Only one way.

'No. Not nonsense. There are very few times when, if a senior police officer is prepared to go to any lengths, he cannot put someone behind the bars, convicted or not. Whether it is in Bombay or Calcutta.'

He hated to see the look on her face then. The man she had with such confidence sent off to fight her cause at *The Sentinel* after the setback under the Great Banyan.

But the look was there. Even she must now be admitting that they were defeated.

ACP Bhowmick, however, spared her putting that into words.

'Yes,' he said, 'you could, of course, be charge-sheeted with this very serious crime, an offence under Section 420 of the Indian Penal Code. However, we in the police have a certain discretion in such matters, and I think I can safely say to you that, were you to leave Calcutta once and for all, I would be able to use such influence as I happen to have to see that you would hear no more of this matter.'

'Very well,' Protima said, her voice lifeless as an answering machine's.

Ghote expected ACP Bhowmick to go then. He had achieved his object. Protima had abandoned her intention of staying in Calcutta. M. F. Tuntunwala's new nominee, whoever that might be, could buy the house whenever he pleased. But the tall, smartly uniformed assistant commissioner just stood where he was, looking thoughtful.

At last he spoke.

'You need not of course leave us this very evening, or even tomorrow morning. I hope I am able to behave like a gentleman. You can have what time you may need. I imagine, for instance, that you will wish to instruct Mr Dutt-Dastar about the sale of this house you have inherited. And there is the Kali Puja festival at the weekend. It would be a pity for you to miss that.'

What is this, Ghote asked himself? Oh, yes, I am not at all falling for *behave like a gentleman*. But why is he inviting us to delay our departure? We could instruct, as he is saying, that scamster Dutt-Dastar as easily from Bombay as from here.

'There is one thing perhaps I should add,' ACP Bhowmick went on. 'I shall feel it necessary to have a watch set on you both. I don't like to think you may still believe you can get your own way.'

He smiled. A gentle-looking smile.

'In fact,' he said, 'the watch is already in place. I hardly doubted you would agree to leave Calcutta when I made my request.'

'But then,' Ghote asked, prickling with suspicions, 'why it is you are saying we should be in no hurry to go?'

'Ah. That's acute of you. But I should expect nothing less from a Bombay Crime Branch officer.'

So he . . . ?

'Yes, Inspector, I have friends in senior Bombay police circles. I have made a few discreet inquiries.'

Absurdly Ghote felt flattered. Till he thought. To have gained the good opinion of a man like Assistant Commissioner Bhowmick, in the pocket of M. F. Tuntunwala and some pillar of West Bengal Government, what of kudos is that?

'And I am sorry to tell you,' the ACP went on, 'what I learnt about you was not what I had hoped.'

Ghote looked up, startled, from the stool where he had continued to sit.

'However, Inspector, perhaps I may find after all that my friends at your Crawford Market Headquarters have not quite plumbed your depths.'

What the hell was this damned Bengali talking about?

'How shall I put this? Mrs Ghote, you will be able tomorrow to receive from Mr Dutt-Dastar, not the deeds of the house you fondly hoped for, but at least a sum of money for its sale.'

Protima, who had been sitting cross-legged up on the bed, stirred uneasily. Ghote hoped she would not burst out again with some hopeless defiance.

'I think it may be more convenient,' ACP Bhowmick went on, 'if you were to receive that purchase price — alas, not what it would once have been — in cash. I believe, in fact, Mr Dutt-Dastar will have a suitable large briefcase in which you may carry it away.'

Ah, black money transaction, Ghote thought. He must be hoping that with a taint of illegality about this money we will be bound to keep our mouths shut. Well, we would do that in any case. This whole business is hardly a good story to be telling.

But why then is he stating that whoever he was speaking to at Headquarters in Bombay has not — what it was, his bloody Bengali expression? — *plumbed my depths*?

He soon learnt.

'Mrs Ghote,' the ACP said, 'I see a large tilak on your forehead. Am I right in thinking

307

that like a good Bengali lady you have been worshipping at the Kalighat Temple?'

'Yes . . . '

Protima sounded as puzzled, and as subdued, as he was himself.

'Good, good. So may I suggest that on Saturday, at the start of the Kali puja, you should visit the temple once more? Just before your departure from Goddess Kali's city. There is a flight to Bombay at about 9 p.m., and I have taken the liberty of getting you tickets for it. But it would be altogether appropriate, I think, for you to worship at Goddess Kali's shrine on your way to the airport, just as you are about to leave Calcutta for ever.'

Protima gave him a yet more puzzled look, as he took from his uniform jacket pocket a plain envelope and put it down among the scatter of combs, brushes and cosmetics on the dressing-table.

Ghote, reflecting for an instant that here were air tickets they would not have to pay a bribe to get, thought he was beginning to see what was coming.

'And, as you will be about to leave,' the ACP went on, 'I suppose it would be no more than a sensible precaution to take with you, besides your baggages, that large black briefcase Mr Dutt-Dastar is going to give you. Considerable sums of money should be properly looked after.'

Now Ghote saw it all. And knew why ACP Bhowmick had hoped his informant in Bombay had not *plumbed the depths* of the man they must have described to him as a hundred per cent honest officer. And he saw, too, that they had not plumbed those depths. Honest he might be. But not to absolute one hundred per cent. No, when he was pushed to his depths, when it was a matter of saving his wife from undeserved prison, he could agree to pay over, not a five-hundred rupee bribe, but one for a much greater sum and to an individual much higher in the social scale than wretched dead Shibu. That was the truth. The bitter truth.

'Considerable sums,' he snapped out, glaring at the man who had known he was not a hundred per cent honest, 'should be looked after, yes? But not, you are telling us, so well that we do not forget somehow to set down such a sum somewhere in all the crowd at the Kalighat Temple on Saturday. To be picked up by other hands. Yes?'

ACP Bhowmick smiled.

20

They hardly spoke after ACP Bhowmick
had left. Ghote had roused himself after
a little to ask Protima if, having missed
the Fairlawn's pallid mulligatawny soup and
solidly satisfying bread-and-butter pudding
while praying to Goddess Kali, she was
hungry.

'No, I am not wanting anything.'

End of communication.

He had fallen back then into his half-
savage, half-sad thoughts.

Why are there in the world such men as
Assistant Commissioner Bhowmick? Clever
men, men good at their work, who nevertheless
cannot resist climbing up by the wrong
means? Damn it, not only has the man
made himself the puppet of some high-up
at Assembly House here, corruptly paying
for promotions and postings, but now even
he is demanding money from us.

Why did we have to come up against the
man wanting money, and no little amount,
for using — what he was saying? — *such
influence as I happen to have* to allow us to
get out of this accursed city without Protima

being arrested? It is wrong. It is unfair.

What have I done to deserve this? Paid out one bribe for the best of reasons? Surely just only for that I do not deserve to be facing so much of troubles. And Protima also. She is losing now all the inheritance, all the happiness she had thought it would bring, her huge Diwali present. Because her simple, honest wishes went against the monstrous wishes of men like M. F. Tuntunwala and Assistant Commissioner Bhowmick.

Now it was Protima's turn to murmur a few battered-down words.

'What we are to do now?'

'Nothing,' he answered, finding nothing else to say.

'Nothing? You are meaning we must be just going from Calcutta? Paying him all that I was inheriting?'

'Yes.'

'But, no. No, no, no. We cannot do nothing. We cannot be just lying down under this.'

'But what else can we do? We are caught. We have come up against a force altogether too strong for us. You could say we are lucky that we are escaping so easily. You were hearing what was happening to that wretched fellow, Shibu?'

'Yes, he was saying something about him.

But I was not altogether understanding. He has died, Shibu, yes? But that is meaning the evidence against us is so much less.'

He sighed.

'It is not that the fellow has happened to die. It is that he has paid the full penalty for trying to be more cunning than Mr M. F. Tuntunwala and Mr A. K. Dutt-Dastar.'

'You mean . . . ? You are saying . . . ?'

'I must spell out same? Yes, then. Shibu was murdered, and we are lucky that someone has not been paid, been bribed, to murder us also. For being in the way when some big-big man is wanting something. We are lucky that we have just only been made to leave Calcutta and take that briefcase Mr Bhowmick was describing to put down somewhere in the Kalighat Temple for himself to pick up.'

'But that is wrong.'

'Yes. It is wrong. But it is. It is. And nothing we now can do will change it'.

★ ★ ★

Then they had gone to bed. Not, though, to sleep. Either of them. And not in the darkness of the stuffy old-style British room to encourage each other with a murmured inquiry or endearment.

In the morning it had been little different. Protima, despite having missed the meal the evening before, hardly did justice to her breakfast porridge and rejected altogether her kipper.

'You should eat,' Ghote said.

'I cannot.'

'Well, I also am not having very much of appetite.'

He heaved a long sigh.

'You know,' he added, 'your puris are much more to my liking. It will be nice no longer to have to eat stuff of this sort. To be at home once more.'

It was a foolish thing to say, though well meant.

Protima, her bhadrolok life snatched away, burst into tears and ran from the room.

He sat where he was, knowing that she would need time before she was willing to hear his apologies and explanations.

Conflicting emotions. Embarrassment at what the others in the room might be thinking. The hotel proprietress was still striding about with the ever-ready fly-swat she was accustomed to go round with at mealtimes. For a moment he thought of how he had seen himself crushed like a fly when M. F. Tuntunwala had so scathingly trounced him. The Western guests were making a heavy show of not having noticed tearful Protima. The handful of Indians in the room were frankly looking on. And, overwhelming the embarrassment, there came a twisting sadness at how this defeat was keeping Protima and himself apart when only by supporting each other could they in any measure deal with it.

He abandoned the now altogether uncrisp piece of toast on his plate and made his own way out of the room. Ringing in his ears as he went came the booming voice of the white-haired bald Englishman — must be an old Calcutta hand — whom a few minutes before he had half-heard still attempting to get Mr Deen Kogan — never now to advise on Protima's house — to visit the ruined Clive Mansion. Apparently with no success, since their talk now seemed to have become somewhat personal. 'All very well, Mr Kogan, to talk about colonialism, but, let me tell you, in our day we ran a fair administration with a proper judiciary far beyond any possibility of being bribed. And now? Now everyone's on the bloody take.'

Now everyone's on the bloody take. He felt it was a verdict. A verdict on the whole of their time in Calcutta. A verdict perhaps on all India. A verdict, if M. F. Tuntunwala was to be believed, on the whole contaminated world.

But, before he went up to do what he could to pacify Protima, it occurred to him it might help finally to convince her that they had no alternative but to obey ACP Bhowmick if he could confirm that a watch had been placed on them. A quick trip to the hotel gate provided him with his facts. On the far side of Sudder Street stood two burly men in plain clothes, so evidently detectives they might have been carrying placards labelled *CID*.

Upstairs, he found Protima, eyes dried, sitting at the faintly spotted mirror of the dressing-table.

She turned round as he entered.

'I suppose we must go soon to Dutt-Dastar.'

'Yes,' he said, seeing that there was no point now in telling her about the watch set on them. 'Some things may be got over with as soon as possible. But it is not anything I am liking to do.'

On that note of tentatively renewed togetherness they set off, Ghote unsurprised to see close behind them and making no effort to be unobtrusive one of ACP Bhowmick's watching detectives.

At A. K. Dutt-Dastar's chamber the new

peon admitted them. The clerk Haripada, inky-fingered as ever, scraped his way out of the narrow space between his table and the big old safe behind it to go and see if his master was free.

Waiting for his return, Ghote found himself recalling what Protima had told him of Tagore's poem about Haripada. How he shared his meagre room with a gecko, covered by the same rent but the lizard having the more to eat, how he saw his umbrella as being as full of holes as his pay after the fines had been deducted. And yes, he thought, when we leave a certain briefcase at the Kalighat Temple tomorrow evening a very big fine will make one giant tear in the umbrella we thought we had for our old age. Well, we must try then, like poor Haripada, to listen to the flute.

'Dutt-Dastar Babu is engaged. He would see you presently.'

A jet of rage. Engaged? No, he is not. Not when he has to obey M. F. Tuntunwala's order. Not when he has to hand us that briefcase full of money, which no doubt M. F. Tuntunwala does not know we are to pass on to ACP Bhowmick.

No, damn Dutt-Dastar is thinking that, now we are beaten down, he also can put his foot on our faces.

'Come,' he said to Protima.

And he marched straight over to the door that the clerk Haripada had just pulled closed behind him. He thrust it open and, followed by Protima, her eyes too glinting with fire, went in.

A. K. Dutt-Dastar, caught sprawling in his too big leather chair behind his too gleaming desk, sat up as if some knife-wielding goonda had suddenly touched the tip of his weapon to the back of his neck.

'What — What is — I was telling my clerk I was not ready to receive you.'

'But we are ready to be received,' Ghote shot back. 'You have a briefcase containing a certain sum for us. Let us take it and be done with it. If there is some receipt to sign, put it in front of my wife and she will sign it.'

The lawyer slowly felt across the width of his desk till he had found his wrap-around black glasses. He fumbled with them.

'No need to be wearing any specs,' Ghote said, still feeling with pleasure the rage ripping through him. 'We are well knowing you now. No need for more concealings.'

He saw the lawyer attempting to regain some dignity. And abruptly deciding it was no longer worth doing.

'All right then, all right. Here. Here is the receipt you are to sign. Let me call my clerk as witness.'

He yanked open the drawer in front of him and took from it, almost without looking he must have had it so to hand, a single sheet of paper. Then he banged on his bell for the clerk Haripada.

Protima, her anger sparking off from his own, put the five fingers of her hand down on the sheet like a kite descending, swirled it round, snatched one of the arrow-planted pens from the desk's pen-set, and raised it to sign.

'No,' Ghote barked out. 'We are not dealing with a person who can be trusted. Read all with care, and wait also for the witness to be here.'

After an instant she darted him a look of gratitude, and stood leaning over the gleamingly polished desk reading and waiting for the old clerk.

At last the door was slowly opened and the upright old man crept in.

'Signature to witness,' A. K. Dutt-Dastar said between clenched teeth.

There was little to read on the sheet, Ghote saw. No more than the bare acknowledgement of the sum paid in purchase of the house, the too-small sum. In less than two minutes

318

more Protima had finished. Once again she raised the pen. The clerk Haripada creakingly approached to a point where he could, absolutely, see the pen-point traverse the paper.

Protima signed.

'In the safe,' A. K. Dutt-Dastar said to the clerk, mouth taut with hatred, 'you will find one black leather briefcase. Be careful to show the contents to this gentleman, who is a fully suspicious inspector of police from Bombay, and when he is satisfied you may let him take the case back to where he comes from.'

So solemnly they followed the old ramrod-stiff clerk out and watched him pull away the battered bentwood chair on which he sat at his splodgy typing so that he could get to the safe. He then unlocked a small drawer underneath the table and extracted from it a large iron key. With this he opened the safe. Then, peering into its depths like a tortoise inspecting a likely leaf, he pulled out a large shiny black plastic briefcase. Ghote saw on it a seemingly accidental broad smear of white paint.

The clerk Haripada set the briefcase down beside his tall typewriter. It was evidently unlocked because he was able simply to pull it open. With a gesture of something like distaste, he invited Ghote to examine the contents.

He duly did so, if without much care.

Since every rupee inside was to be left for ACP Bhowmick to scoop up from wherever they decided to leave it in the Kalighat Temple it did not seem much to matter what sum it contained, although from the look of the banded packets of high-denomination notes inside that must be large enough.

'Very good,' he said to the clerk Haripada, somehow wishing he could tell the upright old man that he was not such a dubious character as he seemed.

But that was not to be.

21

No, Protima said.

They were once more sitting in their room at the Fairlawn. On the flowery-topped stool at the dressing-table stood the shiny black briefcase with the white paint mark. Despite the large sum inside its cheap-looking exterior, Ghote had somehow not liked to put it in the hotel safe.

'What *No it is*?'

'No, I am not willing to let that man do what he is liking.'

'Which man? If it is M. F. Tuntunwala you are talking, I am telling you, when it is someone as altogether rich, there is no good in saying No.'

'Oh, duffer. I am not talking about M. F. Tuntunwala. I am well knowing now that he can make us do whatever he is wanting. No, it is that snake of an assistant commissioner. How dare he try to take from me every rupee I was inheriting?'

'But he has. Or when tomorrow we are visiting the Kalighat Temple he will.'

He looked once more at the briefcase standing there on the stool, as if it was a work of art on a pedestal.

'No. But there must be some way we can make the flesh fall from his face like a leper's.'

Oh, here is my Bengali wife back once more, Ghote thought. All fire and explosions.

But perhaps those are better than tears and defeat.

'I would like to defeat him also,' he said. 'I can perhaps accept he should be the tool of some politician. Such things happen in Bombay. Or everywhere in India. But somehow I had thought, I had wished at some times, that in Calcutta, your Calcutta, it would not be so. And now when I am thinking he also has the powers to take our money, your money, is altogether too much.'

'Then what will you do?'

He had not till now thought of doing anything. When ACP Bhowmick had laid down his terms there had seemed to be no getting out of them. The marked briefcase, the secret exchange, the airline tickets in the envelope propped up at this moment against Protima's pot of red sindur. They had seemed so many steps on a long descent impossible not to slide down.

But need that be so?

Sitting on the other side of the bed from

Protima, he thought.

'Yes,' he said at last.

'What *yes*?'

'Yes, I think something may be done. We must leave Calcutta today itself. Instead of going tomorrow, when those air-tickets are stating, we will try to exchange them. Or even once more pay a bribe to get seats on any flight whatsoever. But, first, we would have to get rid of those two fellows standing in the street outside.'

'But how?' Protima abruptly reverted to despondency. 'How, if he has put watchers there, can we escape?'

Ghote allowed himself a small smile.

'Well, in my time I have very often been given orders to follow some badmash. Once even I was spending all day under the hot sun dressed up as a Moslem lady in a black burkha, and altogether horrible inside there it was. But you may trust one who has learnt to follow to know how not to be followed.'

With pleasure then he saw that Protima was regarding him almost with open admiration. The Bombay detective.

And are we truly on the point of going back to Bombay? he asked himself, hardly able to suppress a grin of delight. By whatever devious route may be necessary? To report for duty at Crime Branch, what a relief. Be given whatsoever difficult case I may, it will seem altogether a fine time after what Calcutta has done to me.

'So what it is we would have to do?' Protima was asking.

'Well, I have been thinking. You know you were saying that we should visit the Victoria Memorial?'

'Yes. But we were too late that day, and now . . . '

'No. Today we will go. That is a huge place, yes? Inside, there should not be too much of difficulty to give any follower a slip.'

Her eyes shone.

'Then let's go. Now. At once.'

'No, no. It would be best to wait till the afternoon. Those fellows outside will be on hundred per cent alert just now. But after a long morning when we are seeming to have no intention to leave the hotel they will not be so quick. We may even be able to get into a taxi before they can be ready to follow. Then we would not at all need to go even to the Victoria Memorial.'

'But what a pity . . . '

Her voice drained away.

Yes, he thought, you were going to say, *What a pity you should not see one more glory of Calcutta*. But then you

324

were thinking: no more need for showing off Calcutta glories, we are to be simple Bombayites once more.

And so we will be. If with more of rupees in the bank than we were once having.

He glanced again at the shiny black briefcase.

'We would have to leave all our baggages here,' he said, thinking a note of briskness was what was now needed. 'Perhaps later they will send them. Today we will take only that briefcase and its money.'

'But if the men of that good-for-nothing Bhowmick are seeing that, they will know what we are doing.'

'No, no. Quite safe. Those fellows will be just only some CID men Bhowmick is relying on. He will not have said one word about a briefcase he himself is aiming to take up in the Kalighat Temple.'

'Yes. Yes, you are right. But all the same we must not give out any sign now of what we are meaning to do. I shall even leave on the dressing-table there all my things. Then if the room-bearer has been bribed by those watchers to report on us he will suspect nothing.'

'First-class idea. So, when we have had a hearty lunch — we may not have time to eat for the rest of the day at least — we will just only walk straight out and, if a taxi is near, get into same.'

* * *

ACP Bhowmick's watchers were, however, smarter than Ghote had counted on. There was a taxi waiting almost outside the Fairlawn's gate at the moment he had chosen for their flight. But its driver was leaning out of its far window watching a party of shouting, gesticulating men erecting the bright blue draperies of a pandal — yes, he registered, Kali Puja celebration beginning, Goddess Kali will be put there — and failed for a minute or more even to notice Ghote opening the nearside door and pushing Protima and the black paint-smeared briefcase inside. The slight delay was enough for the ACP's watchers. One, a fellow in a dayglo shirt of a particularly nasty green, jumped into a cycle ricksha. His companion, Ghote saw, was struggling to tug from his belt one of the mobile phones that were the craze of Calcutta, and indeed of all metropolitan India.

So there was nothing else to be done than snap out 'Victoria Memorial' and abandon any thoughts of going directly to Dum Dum airport. And it came as no surprise, considering the density and exuberant irresponsibility of Calcutta traffic, that when they arrived at the Memorial it proved that the cycle ricksha with its burly green-shirted passenger was drawing up not twenty yards away.

'Never mind,' he said to Protima. 'Inside here we would have no difficulty to get rid of Mr Green-shirt.'

They walked past the huge seated statue of a tight-mouthed, even disapproving Queen Victoria, up towards the glaringly white, high-domed building. On either side of the wide gravelled path, on grass verdant once again after the heat of summer, families sat picnicking, little girls in frocks darting here and there like butterflies. There was a quiet calmness about the whole scene from the stately, massive white marble building down to the mellow grass of the lawns and Ghote suddenly began once more to see Calcutta in a rosy light.

Perhaps, after all, it was not such a bad place. The Bombay he was used to had its bad side, the hustle-bustle, the crimes of the Crime Capital of India, its almost absolute concentration on making money, whether legitimately or through its own particular sorts of corruption. While here, in this part of the city at least, there was a wholly different atmosphere. Not only calm, but somehow there was in the air a belief in the finer things of life, the happy play of children, the preservation of the past. Art, painting, music, poetry . . .

He thought with fond dismay that he would never now listen again to Mr Bhattacharya quietly singing alone on his rooftop. Nor would he meet Khokon Roy again, and glow happily in the light of his darting humour. And that scrupulously honest brown sahib, Gopal Deb: soon it would be all he could do to remember at times his existence. Even the clerk Haripada: he would never now learn his real name nor watch in perplexed admiration the stiff rectitude of his conduct.

For a long moment he wished that, after all, there had been no difficulties over the house, that he and Protima would actually in the end have come to live in it.

But then, perhaps because out of the corner of his eye he had seen the man in the bright green shirt looming closer, reality broke in. No, they had to get out of this city of corruption, if possible with as much of their own money as could be saved from the wreckage.

He began to think what sort of situation might arise inside the huge building ahead that would allow them to dodge out of sight of Mr Green-shirt for a few vital seconds. Just long enough to begin a headlong rush for safety.

Vaguely he was aware that Protima had fallen back into her old history-lecture, guidebook manner.

'If you are looking right up, you may see the famous statue of Victory on the very top of that magnificent dome. In old days it was able to revolve round and round. But now it has been stuck.'

Let her talk, he said to himself. This is our last few hours in her beloved Calcutta. Tomorrow, if all is going well, we would be back in down-to-earth Bombay. She will no longer be a bhadrolok lady, and I shall like her all the better.

They went up the steps to the entrance portico. On either side two bronze pictures of very historical events. Though when, as a matter of duty, he asked Protima what they were of she avoided answering.

'In any case,' he said, reading the words beneath, 'by Sir Goscombe John R. A.'

'From UK and all over the world they were coming to make this great Calcutta memorial, with funds voluntarily subscribed by the Princes and peoples of India.'

More guidebook. Must be almost the last. And *voluntarily subscribed*, that to me is saying *bribes demanded and given*.

They went in. Ghote, stooping for a moment as if to tie his shoelace, noted Green Shirt reaching into his back pocket for his wallet to pay, in his turn, the entrance fee.

And if I am having anything to do with it, he said to himself with a flick of malice, you will be losing your money.

But, inside the huge building, he saw no immediate opportunity to throw the fellow off. He became aware, too, that lugging everywhere the shiny black briefcase he was easier to keep in sight than he would like.

A black burkha, he thought, would be just the thing now. Inside tent of same it would be a child's-play to hide this damn give-away briefcase.

But, failing that, the thing to do would be to press forward as reasonably quickly as they could until there appeared one of the places he had hoped to find. Some corner to slip round, some large object to slip behind.

'Listen,' he hissed to Protima, 'be showing maximum interest in what is there to be seen. We must get that fellow behind us to believe to one hundred percent we have just only come to look at whatsoever marvels are here before we are leaving Calcutta tomorrow.'

He took then a swift survey of his surroundings. Bronze busts on pedestals of royal-looking, old-times Britishers, marble statues of the same. And, ah, yes, some sort of very old clock.

'Over here,' he whispered to Protima.

He took her with him to stand in front of the clock. *By Whitehurst of Derby*, he read. The clock was not going.

'Wonder why it is here,' he said.

'It is from old Calcutta days,' Protima answered with a touch of sharpness. 'Even then they were sending such things all the way by sail to Calcutta from UK to add to the beauties of the city.'

'Oh, yes,' he said, noting nowhere at this point to slip into momentary hiding. 'But I think now we can pretend to have seen everything in this entrance hall.'

They moved on.

'This is the Royal Gallery,' Protima announced.

He took a quick look round. Important not to be seen to be seeking any way of escape. In the middle of the big room a small piano, a writing desk and an armchair, embroidered. None of them bulky enough to hide behind from Mr Green-shirt who, he saw, had entered within a few seconds of themselves and was now standing regarding them in front of a huge painting of some white burra sahib with cheering crowds all round in what seemed to be the pink city of Jaipur.

Protima pulled him across to look more closely at the little domestic scene in the centre of the room.

'Yes,' she said, reading a notice, 'the very piano great Queen-Empress was playing as a child. Just think of that. And her desk also. And in that chair she must have been seated.'

'Nowhere to hide here, come on,' he snapped out, irritated by her not seeming fully alert to what they were meant to be doing.

Into somewhere called the Queen's Hall. Big bronze doors. Slip in behind them before Green Shirt followed? Not enough room. And in any case, here he is.

He would like to jump on the fellow and knock him senseless to the ground.

'Oh, look,' Protima exclaimed, apparently still ignoring the actual reason for their visit, 'out there on the terrace that statue must be Warren Hastings. We were almost seeing his ghost when we were at his house, remember. Come and see.'

Out on the terrace? Has she spotted a chance of making a run for it? But why then was she speaking so loudly? That damn Green Shirt must have heard. Yes, look, already he is going towards the terrace.

'Why were you saying all that?' he murmured angrily.

'Because Warren Hastings is one great Calcutta figure.'

'But — But don't you know what for we are here? Have you forgotten itself?'

'Oh, no. You are making too much of fuss. We can have some time for looking before we do what we are planning. It is my last chance to see such Calcutta sights.'

His anger, not all that fierce in any case, melted in a moment away. Yes, Protima had set her whole heart on a Calcutta life, and it had been torn from her grasp. So she was entitled to such last moments as she could snatch.

'Yes, yes. We will go and pay respects to Mr Warren Hastings. Some other things also.'

It will all add to the picture of the two of us doing no more than taking a look at what Victoria Memorial has to offer.

Solemnly they stood for two or three minutes looking at the statue. It made no impression on Ghote, and even Protima, he noticed, did not seem to be gaining any great benefit.

At last he felt he could suggest they moved on.

And perhaps after all, if they were to contrive a situation where they could suddenly double back, they could get away via this terrace.

'Now we are entering what is known by the name of the Prince's Hall,' Protima, the little guide, announced. 'And, look, here again is another statue of a famous Calcutta man of old days. It is Clive. You are remembering I was telling that famous Clive Street was re-named Netaji Subhas Road.'

He wished she had not mentioned it. The name of Calcutta's independence hero had brought vividly back to his mind, first the framed poster on the wall of *The Sentinel's* editor's desk and then Soumitra Mukerjee himself with his cultivated resemblance to the great bespectacled Bengali hero. What setbacks he had had in that bare room. To be told, when it had seemed that with the crusading newspaper's aid he might expose the huge wetlands corruption scandal, that the investigation was to go no further. And then to find that almost blackmailing Soumitra Mukerjee into revealing who had ordered him to end all inquiries had simply confronted him with M. F. Tuntunwala. M. F. Tuntunwala at whose cold command they were to be expelled from Calcutta like a pair of anti-socials being externed from Bombay.

But then, swept up by Protima to the statue of Clive — 'Clive of India. A true world figure from Calcutta' — he found his spirits abruptly restored. The representation of the man, seemingly weighed down by care, put into his mind once more Calcutta as city of corruption. Here was the white sahib who by bribing the arch-traitor, Mir Jafar, had won the Battle of Plassey and secured Calcutta, and its wealth, for the British. And at any moment now they would be quitting the place, and with safe inside the briefcase he was clutching all those bundles of banknotes.

He glanced behind.

Yes, Green Shirt must have left that terrace almost as soon as ourselves. There he is, pretending to be peering at those old-time guns but keeping us altogether under his watch.

They went on into the Durbar Hall. Once more for him to be reminded of the traitor Mir Jafar. Massively present at the far end of the room was a circular block of black stone some six feet across and perhaps eighteen inches high. Drawn almost magnetically to it, they saw the notice at its foot recording that this was the Musnud of the Nawabs of

Bengal carved from a single piece of stone on which after the Battle of Plassey Clive had installed Mir Jafar and saluted him in his turn as Nawab.

'Let's go,' Protima jabbed out, suddenly abandoning history-book reminiscences.

They hurried off.

It was only when they were going, at the same fast pace they had unconsciously adopted, through yet another gallery of paintings — Sir Elijah Impey, Ghote glimpsed, another corrupt Britisher and Rudyard Kipling, pipe in mouth, reminding him of incorruptible Gopal Deb — that he realized their sudden haste had done for them what no amount of manoeuvring had achieved before. Green Shirt had somehow got left behind.

'Quick,' he said. 'Run. Run through into there.'

Protima immediately grasped what had happened. Gathering up her sari — it was one of her new plain-colour, intricately-bordered Calcutta ones, and worn Bengali style — she set off. With one quick look behind to make sure they were still unobserved, he pelted after her, the big shiny briefcase banging and thumping against his thigh.

Through one more gallery. Sharp turn at the end. Through another. No time now to take in what was in them — glass cases with collections of stamps? Stamps? — on they ran. There were few people about and most of those made way for them, perhaps thinking Protima was ill.

And then, almost missing it, Ghote saw a narrow blank door marked in faded red paint *No Exit*. No exit, he thought, mind racing. Must mean exit, but not for public use.

He caught Protima, half a yard ahead, by the elbow.

'Here,' he panted. 'Through here we would be safe.'

The door was fastened by a movable bar. He wrenched it up, pushed the door open.

Daylight. Daylight and safety.

Then into the rectangle of bright light in front of them there stepped a man. Tall, broad-chested, in uniform. An attendant. Or . . . ? Or something else?'

Beneath his big bushy moustache he was very slightly smiling.

'No way out,' he said.

22

A museum attendant? Or had that been a police uniform? Another of ACP Bhowmick's men, glimpsed before he had banged the door shut? It was plain, whichever it was, that their escape had been prevented.

On the whole, Ghote thought, it is most likely Mr Bhowmick has taken more trouble than I was counting on to make sure we cannot leave Calcutta until this briefcase has been put down somewhere in the Kalighat Temple. If he has set up such a net as we have been caught in here, he is not going to let us get away wheresoever we may go.

Sadly he trailed with Protima through to an official exit, noting that once more Green Shirt was only a few paces behind.

Nowhere else to go now but the Fairlawn Hotel.

Even there they felt, in unspoken agreement, they should stay in their room rather than attempt to sit outside where they would come under the eyes of Green Shirt and another watcher who had established themselves opposite as soon as they had once more entered the gate. They did go

338

down to the dining room when, at eight o'clock precisely, the imperious imperial gong summoned them. But neither of them did much justice to the very English fare.

All next day they felt themselves equally imprisoned, allowed out of their cell as it were only for breakfast porridge and kipper, lunchtime solid curry. At last, with the onset of evening, the time for departure came. Time to go, on ACP Bhowmick's orders, with their luggage in hand first to the Kalighat Temple then, leaving behind one paint-smeared briefcase, on to Dum Dum Airport and liberty. If that truly was what they were going to be allowed.

As the hotel bearer put their cases into a taxi, under the eyes of Green Shirt, now in fact dayglo Blue Shirt, already in an autoricksha with his fellow watcher speaking into his mobile phone, Ghote realized that Calcutta was already well caught up in celebrations for Kali Puja. The moonless night had come, exactly two weeks after the full-moon of Laxmi Puja under which they had arrived. The atmosphere all round was already electric with joyousness.

But it was not so in the taxi.

There, as their driver slowly ploughed through the laughing, dancing, shouting, waving, exuberant crowds, Protima abruptly burst into tears. For an instant Ghote was enraged.

I have troubles enough, isn't it? What for does she —

And then he thought. Protima is not one of those women who weep at everything, weep at anything, weep at nothing. Far from it. Tears do not often come to her eyes, let alone pour from them. And now, today, at this moment at the start of our journey away from Calcutta, her beloved Calcutta, if ever she has a right to weep, she has it now.

He put his arm round her shoulders.

'No,' he said. 'No, do not cry. Yes, it is bad. End of all our hopes. But not end of world itself. Holy Ganga has not yet dried up.'

And she recovered. Sniffed. Dug inside her sari — and at that moment he realized she was not wearing one of her new Calcutta ones, and nor had she put it on Bengali fashion — found a handkerchief and blew her nose. With vigour.

From a band of musicians in their bright yet battered uniforms at the entrance of a side street there came a brassy echo to her small nasal trumpeting rising up from cornets, trombones, tubas over the hectic sea of noise all round.

'Yes. I am sorry. It was just only . . . '

'Never mind, never mind. We have to go through with this, so let us just only go through with it.'

'Yes'.

Outside the swift darkness of night descended. Doubly dark without the moon. Now and again Ghote saw a rocket streaking up into the sky, much as he had done when Protima had kept him out of bed to look on at the Laxmi Puja celebrations. He remembered seeing then in the lane below the outline of the immense garbage heap he had later watched being attacked by animal specimens of what old Mr Bhattacharya had described as the corrupters of his city.

Well, he thought, at least no more will Protima and myself be among those eating away at this place.

Whether, when they got back to Bombay they would be in a similar fashion corrupters of that city, was something he felt unable to decide.

But will we get back? he asked himself in a sudden access of something like fear. Does ACP Bhowmick intend to take the big bribe we have been forced to offer him, and still to use his power to put myself behind the bars? Or — worse, worse, worse — Protima behind bars? It is something he could do. We have committed the crime of offering an illegal inducement, true enough.

The taxi was forced to a halt by a cluster of revellers escorting a ricksha toweringly loaded with a statue of Goddess Kali on her way to be set up at a pandal, ten feet or more high. In the light of the flares all round, her tall body glinted blackly, her red protruding tongue easy to make out in the middle of her garland of human heads. The body of her husband Siva, in a bright shade of pink, was just visible under her feet as she danced on him where he had lain in her path to halt her too terrible triumph after killing the giant demon oppressing even the gods.

'Just like the statue we had in the house each and every Kali Puja,' Protima said, in sudden excitement. 'I am remembering so well. Until almost our last year here I was in very much fear of her. Promising and promising I would be good when she was brought inside. But that year my father was taking me first to Kumartuli by the river in North Calcutta, where they are making the idols of all the gods for each and every festival. And when I saw Ma Kali just as the men had made her out of thick grey clay — it is coming from the mouth of the Hooghly, you know, many miles away — then I was able to feel just only joy when, painted, she came to us.'

Back to her old Calcutta praising self, Ghote registered. Well, if she is feeling that much better, we may get to the end of this day in something of a good state. Sadness for her, yes. But for me? To be going back to Bombay where I am belonging? Not altogether sadness.

Unless ACP Bhowmick has decided we will not in the end reach Bombay.

Tall Goddess Kali on her frail ricksha moved away, swaying and wobbling. Slowly the taxi progressed. Ghote began to wonder if they would arrive at the Kalighat Temple in time to leave the briefcase before getting to Dum Dum for the flight. If they were to be allowed to board it.

He glanced once more out of the taxi's back window. And, yes, there not even separated from them by a single other vehicle was Blue Shirt — that garish colour catching the light — insolently following. Clearly, ACP Bhowmick did not mean them to do anything but go straight to the temple. And, clearly, he meant that to be known.

Well, nothing else to be expected.

As they got nearer, the pandals at street corners became more numerous. Rising up twenty or thirty feet, their cloth-covered bamboo structures painted — as often as not with added commercial advertisements — and lit by green, red and yellow tubes of light. In each a Goddess Kali was installed, grim with blood, the destroyer.

Destroyer, please, of just only the wicked, Ghote found himself thinking, almost praying. And we two, we are not wicked. Surely, surely. Or not very wicked. We have bribed, but we have not corrupted.

Then, silent beside his silent wife, he began questioning whether there truly was a line dividing those states. A line, hard-drawn, between bribery that kept things going in the world, and corruption, that ate away at the whole fabric? Did it exist, that line, as he had always somehow believed, if without thinking too much about it? Or did bribery slip into corruption, the muddy but holy Ganges water of the Hooghly River merging unnoticeably into the thick foul solid mud of its banks?

He had not come to any decision when they arrived at the temple.

In the darkness — even if it was sporadically illuminated by flares, rockets and firecrackers — it was difficult to make out more than the vague outline of the building as they stood beside the taxi, guarding their two large suitcases with the wretched, heavy black briefcase of cash hard-clutched. All that was to be seen was the tall dome,

344

just visible against the sky, and, even less to be made out, a balustrade looking curiously like one of Calcutta's British-style buildings. From somewhere ahead, above the din and music of the crowd, there could be heard the bleating of hundreds of goats ready for sacrifice.

Then something made him turn to look behind him.

And there he saw Blue Shirt, not many yards away, ordering his cycle ricksha driver to turn. He set off then, leaving them apparently unwatched.

But, oh yes, Ghote thought, he has had his orders. ACP Bhowmick is not at all wanting any detective in the force to see him going away with the black briefcase I am this moment holding. And that must be meaning . . .

'Look,' Protima said at that moment. 'There by that lamp-post.'

He looked where she had indicated. ACP Bhowmick, hovering, waiting for the briefcase to be set down for him.

He began to glance about for a suitable spot.

But suddenly Protima plucked him by the sleeve.

'Give me the briefcase,' she said, 'and you come with the suitcases.'

'But why? Where to?'

He felt a dart of bewilderment.

'This way, this way.'

Puzzled, he followed her at as quick a pace as he could lugging both their heavy cases. Puffing and panting he pushed after her through the denser crowd nearer the temple itself, jabbering, singing bhajans, shouting out *Jai, Ma Kali*.

What on earth . . . ?

He caught up with her as she stopped outside the shed-like structure from which the noise of goats' bleating had been emerging more and more loudly. She was slipping the chappals off her feet. Rapidly he tugged off his shoes and left them amid the flotilla of footwear already removed by other pilgrims. Protima turned to him.

'Give me some money.'

'But what for? How much? What money?'

'For buying a goat, of course.'

'What goat? These are here for sacrifices, isn't it?'

'Of course. That is why I am wanting. You make a wish, and if it is a goat that has cost enough, Ma Kali is sure to grant same.'

'But — '

He had just sense enough not to say that this was nonsense.

'But what wish are you wanting to make?'

'Mustn't say. Duffer. Don't you know that?'

Damn it, now at the last minute she was becoming even more of a hothead Bengali than before. Never in Bombay had she called him a duffer, and not very often had she told him there was something he ought to know and did not.

But this was her last hour as a Bengali in Calcutta, and he remembered how much two weeks ago coming here had meant to her.

He pulled out the new wallet he had to buy.

She plunged her fingers in and extracted some notes. Many more than he liked.

He stood, holding the wretched briefcase she had thrust at him, the two big cases between his legs, while Protima hurried away to buy her goat and gain whatever wish it was that had come into her head.

Is she wishing, he thought, that somehow ACP Bhowmick will be unable to take the money? Can she still be hoping, wishing, praying to Goddess Kali, that somehow she will be able to leave Calcutta with the whole sum the forced sale of the house has brought in?

Or, worse, can she possibly be hoping, now when it is far, far too late, to get the house back, to stay here in Calcutta?

At this, a great grey cloud descended. Dust thicker than any floating in the air of Calcutta. Not to go back to Bombay. No longer to be a police officer.

'Let me have another hundred.'

She had come back from where, in among all the frantic bleatings, she had been trying to buy a kid.

'A hundred? Another — '

Then he caved in, pulled two notes from the wallet, thrust them at her.

As if they were two daggers.

He felt rage. Pure searing rage. Not only was she now planning not to go back permanently to Bombay, but she was spending a huge sum to get, no doubt, one of the very fattest kids, one most acceptable to the destroyer Goddess Kali.

No, what it is, she is bribing the goddess. Even corrupting her with such a costly sacrifice. It is intolerable. Intolerable.

But he had made no attempt to stop her, and he knew that it was really right not to have done so. Losing the house, losing Calcutta, losing her bhadrolok life, they meant so much to her that it would have been cruel beyond anything to have deprived her of this one ridiculous, and expensive, chance to change everything round.

He saw that she had concluded her

bargaining. A kid, as fat as any there, was being washed before the sacrifice.

So what must I do? Wait, I suppose, until Goddess Kali has had her chance to produce a miracle, and only then set down this briefcase, with all our wealth in it, somewhere where ACP Bhowmick can quickly pick it up.

No sign of the ACP in here. But he has only to wait where he can see the entrance. And then, when we come out, he would be able to see if we still are having the briefcase with us.

Or, when we are coming out, will he no longer be there? Will he himself somehow be under arrest even? And Protima's prayer to Kali answered?

Now was the moment. Protima came back with a brahman carrying by its tied legs her kid, a garland of bright red hibiscus flowers round its neck, bleating frantically. She took the briefcase from him.

'Now we must go to the bolo where the sacrifice will take place,' she said.

He hefted up the suitcases and followed, feeling the laid-down flower offerings of the pilgrims squashing under his shoeless feet.

The sacrifice, when it happened, was the very briefest of ceremonies. The kid was placed in a wooden trough. A wooden pin was passed through two holes at its top to keep the fat little bleating creature in place. The big, bare-chested executioner raised his sword, flashed it down. Blood jetted from the headless corpse. It was released from the trough and carried back further into the temple. Ghote, still weighed down by the cases, followed. Protima, with the briefcase full of its banded banknotes, went up to the brahmans there.

Is she going to give them, as her offering, the whole briefcase? Ghote asked himself in something like horror. If she does and ACP Bhowmick sees us come out of here without it, will he guess what she has done, have us arrested after all? Years in jail? Unending misery? No help from Mother Kali then.

But Protima did no more than give the priests a handful of crushed banknotes. A tilak in goat's blood was smeared on her forehead. She turned away. He followed her out. In the noise and hurlyburly under the rocket-lined sky they slipped chappals and shoes back on.

ACP Bhowmick had not disappeared. He stood, just illuminated by the same lamp, looking and looking.

'We must put the briefcase down now,' Ghote said.

'Yes.'

Dry-eyed, Protima simply deposited the whitesmeared case against the wall nearby, and, head up, walked off. Ghote, feeling the weight of the two suitcases dragging at his arm muscles, followed. After heaving and pushing through the crowd for some ten or fifteen yards he turned to look back. He had just one glimpse of the tall form of the ACP striding away in the other direction. The briefcase swung from his right hand.

23

High above the Ganges Valley the plane sped smoothly through the night. Ghote and Protima sat, once again, in silence. There was nothing to say. There had been no difficulty over their departure. The tickets ACP Bhowmick had left for them in their white envelope in the heavily furnished bedroom at the Fairlawn had been honoured without so much as a raised eyebrow. The plane had left Dum Dum Airport not any later than almost all flights do.

But the tension Ghote had felt in all the time since they had walked out of the Kalighat Temple and found a taxi had been so strong that at times he had thought he would not be able to take one step more forwards. But take those steps he had, gone through the complexities of boarding he had. And now, sitting beside Protima, he at last began to unwind.

Abruptly he felt able to speak after all.

He leant towards her so that what he said would be inaudible under the thrumming of the engines.

'Corruption is there,' he said.

It was the culmination of a long train of thought that he had hardly been aware had taken place in his head.

'What you are talking?'

'It is what I have been thinking, thinking, I believe, for a long time. There is corruption. It exists. It exists, I know now, in Calcutta as much as in Bombay. Very well, when a bad case comes in front of us and there is a possibility to do something to stop same, then we must do it. But that will not put an end to corruption. To bribery, corruption also. It is something that is part of life, and we must be ready to admit'.

Protima sat pondering the words he had poured so suddenly into her jewel-decorated ear.

Then she spoke.

'Yes. You are right. We must endure same'.

Once more they lapsed into silence.

'Bribery also?' she asked eventually.

'Yes. Yes, I am thinking so. You know, you cannot draw any line between. Yes, some oiling of wheels is sometimes all right. Some speed money also. But too much is bad, yes, not at all a good thing. So one must try always not to do it. Howsoevermuch it is there. Yes'.

Through the night the plane droned on.

On towards distant Bombay.

Ghote began to wonder whether he ought to say anything about their arrival, about what they would do when they reached home.

Home. Home where it had always been. In Bombay. A city with its burden of corruption, different perhaps from Calcutta's but in sum no more and no less. Bombay where to ease the difficulties of daily life they each would have, yes, from time to time to pay out some bribe or other. Bombay, where doubtless at this moment huge corrupt deals were being negotiated, every bit as bad as the one M. F. Tuntunwala and his collaborator in the Ministry were contriving in Calcutta. The deal which, though for a few hours it had looked as if he might be able to put a jamming woodblock under the wheels of that juggernaut, he knew really he had never had a hope of halting.

He sighed.

And then into his mind there came a question he would like to hear the answer to.

He turned to his wife once more.

'Your wish to Ma Kali,' he said, 'was it answered?'

She smiled.

'Tell me, what did you think I had wished?'

Should I tell her? Did she really wish, back then, that ACP Bhowmick might, for no reason, for some reason, be arrested? Or magically swept out of the world?

'I was thinking you were wishing that somehow we could defeat that man ACP Bhowmick,' he admitted, almost shyly.

Again she smiled.

'Well, it was not that. But what I was wishing has come true, so I may tell you what it was.'

'Yes? Yes? What?'

'Just this only: that we could go home to Bombay and be as we have always been. That and no more.'

THE END

We do hope that you have enjoyed reading this large print book.

Did you know that all of our titles are available for purchase?

We publish a wide range of high quality large print books including:
Romances, Mysteries, Classics, General Fiction, Non Fiction and Westerns.

Special interest titles available in large print are:
**The Little Oxford Dictionary
Music Book
Song Book
Hymn Book
Service Book**

Also available from us courtesy of Oxford University Press:
**Young Readers' Dictionary
(large print edition)
Young Readers' Thesaurus
(large print edition)**

For further information or a free brochure, please contact us at:
**Ulverscroft Large Print Books Ltd.,
The Green, Bradgate Road, Anstey,
Leicester, LE7 7FU, England.
Tel:** (00 44) **0116 236 4325
Fax:** (00 44) **0116 234 0205**

THE WORLD AT NIGHT

Alan Furst

Jean Casson, a well-dressed, well-bred Parisian film producer, spends his days in the finest cafes and bistros, his evenings at elegant dinner parties and nights in the apartments of numerous women friends — until his agreeable lifestyle is changed for ever by the German invasion. As he struggles to put his world back together and to come to terms with the uncomfortable realities of life under German occupation, he becomes caught up — reluctantly — in the early activities of what was to become the French Resistance, and is faced with the first of many impossible choices.

BLOOD PROOF

Bill Knox

Colin Thane of the elite Scottish Crime Squad is sent north from Glasgow to the Scottish Highlands after a vicious arson attack at Broch Distillery has left three men dead and eight million pounds worth of prime stock destroyed. Finn Rankin, who runs the distillery with the aid of his three daughters, is at first unhelpful, then events take a dramatic turn for the worse. To uncover the truth, Thane must head back to Glasgow and its underworld, with one more race back to the mountains needed before the terror can finally be ended.

ISLAND OF FLOWERS

Jean M. Long

'Swallowfield' had belonged to Bethany Tyler's family for generations, but now Aunt Sophie, who lived on Jersey, was claiming her share of the property. It seemed that the only way of raising the capital was to sell the house, but then, unexpectedly, Justin Rochel arrived in Sussex and things took on a new dimension. Bethany accompanied her father and sister to Jersey, where there were shocks in store for her. She was attracted to Justin, but could she trust him?

BIRD

Jane Adams

Marcie has come to the bedside of her dying grandfather to make her peace. For Jack Whitney was the man who raised her, who loved her as if she was his own daughter, and from whom she ran away when she was just sixteen . . . But Jack is haunted by the terrible vision of a body hanging from a tree and the ghostly image of 'Rebekkah', a woman he insists is standing beside him, a noose around her neck. Marcie vows to uncover the true story behind this woman — even if it points to her grandfather being a murderer . . .